Flash Memory

Also by Anna Castle

The Francis Bacon Mystery Series
Murder by Misrule
Death by Disputation
The Widow's Guild

The Lost Hat, Texas Mystery Series
Black & White & Dead All Over
Flash Memory

A Lost Hat, Texas Mystery — #2

Flash Memory

Anna Castle

To Gary —
I hope you enjoy it!
Anna Castle

Flash Memory
A Lost Hat, Texas Mystery — #2

Print Edition | March 2016
Discover more works by Anna Castle at www.annacastle.com

Copyright © 2016 by Anna Castle
Cover design by Renée Barratt at The Cover Counts.
Editorial services by Quiethouse Copy-Editing.

All rights reserved. No parts of this book may be used or reproduced in any manner whatsoever, including Internet usage, without written permission from the author, except in the case of brief quotations embodied in critical articles and reviews.

This is a work of fiction. Characters, places, and events are the product of the author's imagination or are used fictitiously and are not to be construed as real. Any resemblance to events, locales, organizations, or persons, living or dead, is entirely coincidental.

ISBN-10: 0986413062
ISBN-13: 978-0-9864130-6-3
Produced in the United States of America

Acknowledgements

I want to thank my critique group, the Capitol Crime Writers: Russell Ashworth, Will Chandler, K.P. Gresham, Connie Newton, and Dan Roessler. Lucky for this city girl, most of them grew up in small towns. This book was further improved by the attentions of the beta readers and editors at Quiethouse Copy-Editing.

Chapter 1

I shot the sheriff just after ten. It wasn't easy; he kept squirming around and cracking jokes. I was booked to shoot the chief deputy at eleven and hoped he would be more cooperative.

It might not be art, but it was a living.

The Penelope Trigg Photography Studio in Lost Hat brought in enough to cover property taxes and utilities, thanks to the low rates out here in west central Texas, plus my assistant's wages—so far. I had enough savings to keep me in canned soup and coffee for one year. After that, I would have to get creative.

"One down, one to go." I slid the check for a hundred and fifty dollars into the deposit bag and handed it to Tillie across the reception counter. Not bad for an hour's work. I still had the editing and the printing, but my time didn't count as an expense. What else did I have to do?

"There'll be more when we get the campaign posters made." Tillie's twisted smile managed to convey optimism and anxiety in one tangled expression. She was wearing way too much makeup and had dyed a garish pink streak down the length of her blue-black hair. Possibly a lingering influence of the graduating seniors we'd done portraits for all last month. Such extreme adversity does have strange after-effects.

Deputy Dare Thompson pulled his county vehicle into a space in front of the studio at 11:00 sharp. He had driven over from the Long County Law Enforcement Center, a whole two blocks away on the other side of the courthouse square.

Wasteful? Well, yes. But if the gods had intended Texans to walk, they wouldn't have given us trucks.

Dare hopped up the curb and strode smartly through the door. He was trim as a cadet, his black hair neatly barbered and his brown eyes bright as agates. I'd pegged him for an ex-Army sergeant the first time I laid eyes on him. I'd seen enough of them, growing up.

"Howdy, Dare." I stepped forward to shake hands. He had a nice firm grip, not too soft and not too hard.

"Penny. What's the procedure?"

We were on first-name terms because he was dating Diana Hawkins, who was the sister of my boyfriend and most important client, Tyler. When you bump heads over the coffeepot in your jammies on Sunday morning, formal titles fall by the wayside.

I led him back to the screened area I use for portraits, leaving Tillie at the front desk behind the counter. My studio was a limestone classic, built in 1928. It was about seventy by thirty feet with fifteen-foot ceilings, oak trim, and heart pine floors. I loved it with a helpless passion. The light could be extraordinary, streaming through the big front windows, reflecting off the mellow stone walls, and setting the wood aglow. The second floor was stuffed to the rafters with the antiques I'd inherited from my Great-Aunt Sophia along with the building. I'd also gotten her three-bedroom bungalow and a three-quarter ton GMC truck that I called "The Hulk" on account of its being large, ugly, and green.

I'd hung a drape down the wall at the back of the studio and rigged a set of white canvas screens on casters that I could move around to control the light and provide privacy for my portrait clients. I settled the deputy in a chair inside the screens and adjusted the lights and reflector umbrellas.

Dare didn't squirm and he didn't crack wise. He also never smiled. He sat there with a straight back and a solemn face, watching me like he was observing a crime in progress.

His gaze was intimidating and made me feel vaguely guilty—definitely not the best look for a campaign poster. If he wanted to give Sheriff Hopper a run for his money, he needed to loosen up. I knew he could smile; I'd seen him do it at the Hawkins' house. Diana had promised to come help me with him, but she'd flaked out. I did my best to bring out his lighter side, cracking lame Army jokes and pretending to trip over extension cords. No joy. I even tried some of Diana's flirty nonsense, like, "Come on along, Dare-a-ling-dong," but that turned his jaw to granite and his glare to ice.

I needed fresh inspiration. Then the bell over the front door jangled.

"Tillie, what on earth have you done with your hair?" My cousin Marion Albrecht's clarion tones rang against the rock walls. When I moved to Lost Hat, Marion appointed herself my surrogate aunt, with full rights to meddle in my business. She was the Long County Extension Agent for Family and Consumer Sciences and had an office in the courthouse across the street. She knew everything about everything and never hesitated to share her bounty.

Tillie mumbled something.

"It won't do you one bit of good to imitate that flibbertigibbet Diana, you know," Marion scolded.

I backed up a step and poked my head around the screen. "Language, Marion, please! I've got a deputy sheriff in here."

I looked back at Dare and repeated the word *flibbertigibbet* in my best Donald Duck voice. That got an honest-to-gosh, full-on smile out of him. I managed to get three shots off before it faded. Thank you, Donald! Who knew the deadpan deputy liked cartoons?

Our eyes met. I licked my finger and drew a point in the air. Game over; the photographer wins again. We were finished, so we walked on up to the front.

"Marion." Dare tilted his head in a short nod.

"Dare." She turned to face him, one hand planted on her hip, the other balanced on the reception counter. "When is that silly girl coming back? I'm at the end of my rope over there."

The silly girl was Diana. She was the administrative assistant at the Extension Office and she'd been AWOL for over a week. According to Tillie, this was the sort of thing Diana used to do all the time: haring off with her wild friends for a weeks-long toot in Dallas. She had settled down considerably after taking up with Dare last fall, staying sober and getting a steady job with Marion, the Czarina of Stability.

"Don't give up on her, Marion," Dare said. "People don't change overnight. She's come a long way in the last year. We have to be patient with her." His voice was calm, but worry shaded the fine lines at the corners of his eyes. I wondered if their relationship had hit a bump that knocked her off the wagon.

Then he added his spin. "I think she wanted a little time-out. Time alone. Ty's been pressuring her pretty hard about that project of his." He shot a look at me. Ty was restoring the ranch he and Diana had inherited and I was doing a photo-documentary of the process.

"You could be right," I said. Ty was hands down my favorite boyfriend so far. He might even be the One. But he was more than a little competitive and could be a shade on the bossy side. Diana, in my observation, did not like to be pushed.

"She might have consulted *me*," Marion said. "When the Extension Office falls into total chaos, I suppose the whole county will have to be patient too." Marion sounded severely miffed, but then that was one of her favorite moods. She wore it like a perfume: *Eau de Huffy*.

"That's why I'm here." She looked at me. "I want Tillie to take Diana's job, at least temporarily. Graduation season is long over. You can't afford an assistant anymore."

Tillie looked half stricken at the idea of working for Marion and half pleased to be wanted. She shrank into her chair at the desk behind the counter. I didn't like the implication that I didn't have enough work to keep an employee, even if it might be true. Ty's project was enough to keep me going, barely, but I didn't need Tillie for that. Spending the profits from the graduation portraits to keep her around for company was sheer extravagance.

But it was my call, not Marion's. I didn't want to lose Tillie. The Espinoza clan formed a major pillar of the Lost Hat community. Tillie's mother and grandfather owned a popular Mexican restaurant, one of her aunts owned a popular beauty salon, and one of her uncles was a desk sergeant in the sheriff's department. I got all the hottest gossip, straight off the griddle. That was important, and not just for the entertainment value. I had only moved to Lost Hat last December and was still getting oriented, people-wise.

Tillie would earn her keep eventually by bringing in more business. Besides, we'd been through some tough times last February and taken each other's measure, as my father put it. We were pals.

"Get your own Tillie." I leaned in to wrap my arms around her plump shoulders. "This one's mine."

Tillie giggled. Marion scowled. I smirked.

Dare said, "Diana will be back before you know it, Marion. You can survive another week without her." A bleakness in the back of his eyes contradicted his optimistic words. Maybe she'd broken up with him and left to give them both a time-out?

He wrote me a check and we set a date for him to come back to look at the campaign poster layouts. He held the door for Marion, who gave Tillie a stern parting look. "Think about my offer, young lady. County benefits. *Secure* employment."

We stood by the desk, watching her walk across the hot street into the shade of the magnificent old pecan trees around the courthouse.

"You probably should think about it," I said. "County benefits are nothing to sneeze at." I'd given up sneezing myself, since I couldn't afford health insurance. "If Diana doesn't sober up and come home pretty soon, her job is going to be a hot commodity."

"Work for Marion? All the whole week?" Tillie shuddered. "Besides, there isn't going to be any job. Diana will come breezing back in like the Queen of Siam and everyone will forgive her, as per usual."

I caught a visual of Diana riding into the courthouse square on an elephant and had to blink hard to clear it.

Tillie sat behind the desk and entered Dare's check into the accounting thingy she'd set up for me. Another reason I needed her: I wasn't much good at the number-crunching. They'd carelessly neglected to give us courses in small business management at art school.

"Who's up next?"

Tillie glanced at her desk calendar. "There's the commissioner tomorrow—Carson Caine. More campaign posters." She flipped to the next week and the one following. "After that, um…"

After that, nothing, I already knew. "Something'll come up. Maybe Caine's opponent will be so impressed he'll want us to do his posters too."

"But they won't want makeup. The deputies didn't." Tillie was the makeup expert as well as the chief accounting officer.

"Maybe somebody will get married. Then they'll all need makeup, groom included."

Tillie's round face brightened. "Like Diana and Dare, maybe. Mom said that Sheriff Hopper's sister said that Dare was like this close to popping the question." She measured a millimeter with her fingers.

"More like this close." I held out my hands like I was bragging about a fish. "Since she's hiding out in Dallas."

"I'm not so sure about that," Tillie said. Her black eyes glittered, a sign of gossip simmering up. "At least not the Dallas part."

"What have you heard?"

"Not heard, exactly. But you know that developer guy, Roger Bainbridge?"

"Don't we all?" Roger "Call me the Dodger" Bainbridge had been making the rounds of Long County landowners lately, trying to hustle up some bargain acreage. He had somehow persuaded himself that we were next in line for a boom in the Hill Country outdoor recreation market. He wanted a piece of Ty's spa project so badly it made him drool, and I mean that literally. He kept licking his lips and clearing his throat, wearing the same hungry expression when he looked at the landscape as when he looked at Diana.

"He took me and Ben out for drinks the other night," Tillie said, "to see if we might be interested in buying a house, or so he said. We're nowhere near ready, but Ben said, 'Why turn down a free beer?'"

I shrugged. "Can't imagine that guy giving anything away without a *looong* string attached."

"Yeah. He spent like two seconds on that topic and then asked a bunch of questions about Ben's father's pasture lease at Ty's ranch. How long had he had it, how many cattle, how hard would it be to move them somewhere else…"

"As if it was any of his business! Ty can't stand the guy. I mean he really, seriously, growling-in-the-back-of-the-throat despises him. And the way he looks at Diana—"

"Yeah," Tillie said, with heat this time. "Turns out that's what he really wanted. Ben was telling him about how the lease works, being polite, you know. Answering the guy's questions. But Roger just blatantly stopped listening, looking around at the waitresses like he was totally bored. Then, before Ben even finished, he interrupted him, like, 'Uh-huh. That's great. So, have y'all known Diana a long time? How serious is her thing with that cop?'"

I clucked my tongue.

"That's what I thought," Tillie said. "What he really wanted was some dirt on Dare. Like we had any! It was horrible. And you know how twitchy Ben gets whenever anybody mentions the almighty *Lady Di*."

I had not known that interesting fact, but I did now. The snark in her tone was unmistakable. That pink hair stripe made more sense too. I shook my head. "Roger's hot for her, that's obvious. He looks at her like—"

"Like she was a three-scoop banana split with extra fudge sauce. It's disgusting."

I was going to say a juicy steak with extra mushrooms, but to each her own. "So let him look. Diana might like to flirt, but she's not stupid. What could she possibly see in that bozo? He's bogus from top to bottom. He's bogosity times ten."

"I don't know." Tillie sounded doubtful. "He is kind of good-looking. And he's got a really cool car. A brand new red Cadillac Escalade. The seats are genuine leather and they have these little heaters inside to warm them up. Ben said it was worth the bullshit just for the ride."

"A cow has a real leather seat." I'd meant that to be sassy, but it occurred to me that cattle also produced a lot of bullshit and you didn't ride them, so not actually all that funny. Ah, well. You can't score every time. "What you're saying is, we might not be shooting the Dare-Diana wedding anytime soon."

"Probably not. But lots of people get married after graduation. Or maybe there'll be a reunion or something. Can we do reunions?"

"We can do anything. Worst comes to worst, we can even do pornography."

Tillie's eyes popped. "Um, I don't think my husband…"

"Just kidding." I was saving pornography for a really, really rainy day. I slapped my hands together. "Well, old partner, old pal. We'll just to have to get out there and dig up some more business."

Chapter 2

My alarm went off five a.m. on Friday morning, getting me up to go out and shoot the sunrise from Mt. Keno on Ty's ranch. This morning I also planned to identify some anchor points—recognizable features of the landscape to be photographed at different times of day and in different seasons.

Tyler Hawkins was a man with a plan: turning the run-down, over-grazed ranch he and Diana had inherited from their father into an ecologically sensitive dude ranch and spa. He intended to restore the rangeland to its natural glory and had hired me to document the transformation, making the process part of the attraction. We planned to do a nice lobby exhibit and offer lectures and demonstrations about Hill Country ecology. Guests could learn about nature between yoga classes, mountain bike tours, and massages.

It was a dream job for a nature photographer like me and a sound investment for a venture capitalist like Ty. Tourism was booming in the Hill Country, thanks to the explosive growth of the big Texas cities. People would pay real money for a glimpse of a golden-cheeked warbler. Why wouldn't they pay to watch prairie grasses grow?

I put on a pot of coffee and then stood in front of the bathroom mirror for the two excruciating minutes it takes to French-braid my long blonde hair. I dressed for a day outdoors: khaki pants with big pockets, a camo cami with a sun shirt over it, and my snake-proof hiking boots. I'd packed my camera bag at the studio. Now I filled a day pack with water bottles, energy bars, and sunscreen. When the coffee was done, I filled up my mega-mug and was good to go.

Two minutes later, I was out on Ranch Road 1625, cruising into the hills. In Austin, it would have taken me forty weary minutes to get past the ever-expanding suburbs, even at this hour. I rolled my window all the way down to savor the cool of the June morning and the smell of dew-dappled greenery.

The entrance to Ty's ranch wasn't easy to spot. Rusting scaffolds supporting a weathered sign marked the gate. You could barely read the words *Lazy H - Hawkins* carved across the top. Weeds and brush crowded the posts. It looked like the gateway to a ghost ranch, not an upscale resort.

Bumping over the cattle guard, I picked my way along the rutted caliche road. As I passed the house, I saw Ty's silver BMW SUV gleaming in the yard. He was back already. He must've gotten in pretty late last night or surely he would have called.

I stopped, motor idling while I dithered. Should I park and go in? He was probably asleep and might not like being woken up at the crack of dawn. Plus if I stopped, I'd miss the sunrise and then I'd have to get up at 5:00 tomorrow.

Work first; play later.

I drove on up to Mt. Keno. This wasn't a mountain like you'd find in the Rockies, the Alps, or even the Appalachians. But at seven-hundred-eighty feet, it boasted the highest elevation in this area, so it got the grand title. *Keno* means *hill* in Comanche, thus proving the original inhabitants had a better sense of proportion. Also that the newcomers didn't trouble themselves to learn any words in the old-comers' language.

I parked the Hulk under some Ashe junipers below the crest of the hill on the west side and hoofed it the rest of the way up. I didn't want a rackety green truck in my serene landscape photographs.

Flash Memory

The top of the hill is broad and fairly flat, mostly covered with prickly pear cactus and straggling grasses. Native buffalo and blue grama battled invasive king ranch bluestem and johnson grass in the thin soil. An old windmill, twenty or thirty feet tall, made of rusting metal and splintery gray wood, stood near the center. A cluster of wind-twisted live oaks with bee brush at their feet shaded the remains of an old rock wall surrounding a hollow. The rocks were still stacked in rows here and there, but most had tumbled into the grass.

Nobody knew what the wall had been for: maybe a tiny house or a herder's shelter. I liked to think of it as the bones of a fort, built up here where you could see danger coming a long way off. The windmill would have pumped water for soldiers or goats, depending on your theory.

The view was awesome, all three hundred and sixty degrees. On a clear day, like after a norther blew through, you could see halfway to Austin. In this gray pre-dawn light, I felt like the only living creature standing at the pinnacle of the world beside the remains of a long-forgotten civilization. Now, if only I could capture that feeling...

I put my bags down by a section of wall, took out my tripod, and set it up facing the band of lighter sky in the east. Then I got out my new Canon Eos 7D, which I had paid for by selling my gently-used Ford Escape when I left Austin. That deal had stuck me with the Hulk for transportation, but I loved the camera a million times more than I hated the truck.

I decided to start with a standard 50mm lens for the pre-sunrise show. My first target was an old stone house with a tall chimney almost due east of where I stood. It sat at the top of a hill on the neighboring ranch, just across the boundary of the Lazy H. It had a ridgy tin roof and a forlorn quality, out by itself in the lonesome country. An array of cloud puffs streamed south, starting to turn pink and gold across the bottom. A minute later, the horizon lit up: hot pink, blaze orange, and heavenly gold shading into lavender, peach, and delicate blue. I took a dozen shots in quick succession, adjusting speed and aperture for different effects.

This is what it was all about, the fine arts degree and the crappy studio jobs that got me so used to having a camera in my hand I could almost adjust the settings with my eyes closed. All so I could get out here at the crack of dawn, half asleep, with the breeze chapping my cheeks, and fire away like a hopped-up mobster, knowing that the shots would be sixty percent keepers with a few real beauties.

When the sunrise was over, I detached my camera from the tripod and put it around my neck to walk around a little and see what I could see. There was a thin trail like a deer track zig-zagging down the east side of Mt. Keno. The terrain between the two hills was rocky and uneven. Yucca, greenthread, and Indian blanket dotted stretches of calf-high grass. I took a few general shots and started looking for some focal points. Stone House Hill crumbled into a jumble of boulders with one sheer rock face. The road bordering the boundary fence took a sharp curve under the cliff, winding intriguingly out of sight around the hill. Its rough caliche surface shone white in contrast to the scrub oaks and cedars inside the curve.

I looked through the viewfinder, focusing on the curve, when a big antelope kind of animal stepped onto the road. My whole body flinched. Then I remembered he wasn't close enough to get me. He didn't even notice me, over here on my side of the divide hiding behind my camera.

My heart rate slowed to normal. He was beautiful, regal, with tall spiraling horns. I held my breath and shot him. Twice.

That was exciting! Time for a snack. I climbed back up the hill, collecting my tripod on the way. Unfortunately, I had left my coffee in the Hulk, so I had to settle for water to wash down my Clif Bar. I tucked the wrapper in my pack and set the tripod up inside the stone enclosure. I was focusing on a sun-streaked patch of yucca against the silver-gray wall when I heard the growl of a small motor coming up the hill. I smiled into the back of the camera, feeling a warm glow of sensory anticipation. Could this be a tall, green-eyed man coming up to offer me encouragement and possibly fresh coffee? I got my shot and turned around.

Sure enough, here came my very own Tyler Hawkins with his trusty sidekick, Jake, the big brown dog. Jake bounded out of the Gator—the ranch utility vehicle—and I flexed my knees, assuming the position for an incoming Labrador. He plowed into me at full force, nearly knocking me over. His idea of a cheery greeting. I ruffled his ears and bent to let him lick my chin, then he took himself off on a sniffing tour of the hilltop.

Ty swung his long legs out of the Gator and headed toward me. He wore faded jeans, a grey T-shirt, and a pair of well-worn boots. On him, it looked totally GQ. I arrowed into his arms and tilted my head up for a long good-morning-and-gosh-I-missed-you kiss.

"Hey, baby." He feathered a few extra kisses into my hair.

"You're home early." I closed my eyes and burrowed my nose in his chest, savoring the aroma of sandalwood and man.

"Got in around midnight. I drove past your house, but the lights were out, so I didn't stop."

"How'd you know I was up here?"

"Jake wakes up at the crack of dawn. Then I saw headlights and figured it was you. Who else would be out here at this hour?"

I tilted my head back again and gave him a sassyfrass grin. "Nobody but us hard-working photographers."

He kissed me on the chin. "Don't let me interrupt you. I thought you might like some coffee."

"Indeed, I might." I broke away from him and homed in on one of the mugs balanced on the passenger seat. "I left mine in the Hulk." I leaned against the Gator's flatbed and took a sip of the life-giving beverage.

Ty held out his empty arms and spoke to the air. "That's all she wants from me. Access to the ranch twenty-four/seven and coffee on demand."

"That's not *all* I want." I waggled my eyebrows at him suggestively.

Two long strides and his arm wrapped around my waist. He nuzzled my neck as he reached behind me for his own coffee mug. I landed a smooch on his chin, getting a grin in reward. We stood side by side in silence for a few minutes, leaning against the Gator, surveying the view and enjoying the brew.

After a few moments of silent bliss, I asked, "How'd your meetings go?"

Ty grunted. "Not great. People are generally positive about the project, but nobody can commit actual resources until I get the corporation set up. And I can't do that without Diana's signature. Half the land is hers. She could waltz in and put a stop to the whole process at any minute. Then my investors would lose whatever they'd put up at that point."

"That's frustrating."

"I'd wring her pretty little neck, if she were here. That girl needs to learn to make up her mind." He shot me a sidelong look. "I know it's my fault, partly. It's possible that I've been a bit of an asshole about the timetable."

"You have been a little on the dictatorial side. 'Diana, sign this and then this and now sit down and shut up.'"

"Hey! I'm not that bad. Am I?" He saw my raised eyebrows and frowned. "Humph. Anyway, I have apologized, you may be impressed to learn. I sent her an email saying I was sorry for being a jerk and if she would kindly please come home and sign the goddamn papers, I promise to take her ideas more seriously and give her a more integral role in the planning process."

"That sounds fair."

"I'm a fair man."

"You're a dark man. Tall, dark, and dictatorial."

"Hey. I resemble that remark."

We giggled at each other. Nonsensical conversations are an essential part of courtship.

"So, what did she say?"

"She wrote back pretty quick, which is something. But she said she wasn't ready to come home. She has other issues besides me and needs time to think about everything."

"Dare."

"Yep." Ty nodded. "That guy really needs to back off. If she says she's not ready, she's not ready. And I'll tell you, if he keeps pushing, he's going to find me pushing back."

"I'm sure she can handle Dare on her own."

"I'm not."

I let that drop. Poor Diana! No wonder she needed a time-out. Ty and Dare were great guys—honest, loving, decent men. They were also strong-minded men who both wanted to be Diana's chief protector. She had barely gotten her feet under her after years of floundering; now she was getting pressure from two directions to make complicated decisions with lasting consequences.

Dallas wouldn't be far enough for me, in her shoes. Los Angeles, maybe—or China.

Ty, as usual, stayed on his original track. "She did say I could fax her the papers and she would get a friend to look at them. Then she said she would most likely sign them and fax them back."

"That's great! Isn't it? Is a fax good enough?"

"Oh, heck yeah. As long as the friend isn't that scum-sucking Roger Bainbridge. But once I get her signature, I can get some investors signed up—some real ones—and shut him out once and for all. Then I'll get some contractors out here and get this show on the road. I want to clear the cedars out of that southeast pasture and start burning brush."

"Uh-oh." I pushed off from the Gator. "I'd better get busy."

"Damn straight." He shook his finger at me sternly. Like a dictator, one might say, if dictators had love lights in their eyes while they did their dictating. "Am I paying you to lounge around drinking coffee?"

"No, sir!" I snapped a salute, clocking myself on the head with my coffee mug. Luckily, it was plastic and empty.

"Do you mind if I hang out while you work?"

"Oh, I don't know." I frowned at him, pretending to object. "Do you mean 'hang out' as in 'stand behind me looking over my shoulder and asking a lot of stupid questions?'"

Ty shrugged reluctantly. "Well, okay, if that's what you want. But I'd rather sit here in the Gator and get some work done." He held up a legal pad. He liked to make lists on legal pads: things to do, people to call, costs to budget for. He had stacks of them in his dining room and at least one in each vehicle. He smirked at me. "I know how to manage talent, darlin'. Pay 'em well and stay the hell out of their way."

We grinned at each other. Then I sashayed back to my tripod and Ty settled himself comfortably with his pad.

The sunlight had grown brighter, but long, interesting shadows still stretched westward. A stream of thin clouds had appeared in the east, as bright as bleached cotton, banding the sky behind the old stone house on the next hill. I loved the lines and the clarity, except for a messy fuzz of scrub oaks across the bottom. If I could get up ten feet,

I could get a pure shot with nothing but the dark line of the horizon, the uplift of the old house, and the lines of bright clouds across the sky.

Light changed from moment to moment, especially at this time of day. Hesitation would lose me the shot.

To think is to do. The windmill had a ladder and most of the rungs looked okay. I started climbing, paying more attention to the view than the structure beneath me, until I realized I wasn't the only thing moving. I got about halfway up when I heard a sharp crack over my head. The ladder tilted abruptly, settled for a moment, then shifted again. A thin, scraping creak told me it was coming down.

I wrapped my arms around the long vertical support and slid a few feet to the first crossbar. That felt sturdy for about two seconds. Then something went *crack* and the bar swung free. I had to wrap my arms and legs around the rusty post and cling for dear life.

I slipped a few inches, scraping the insides of my arms. I couldn't see how far down the next crossbar was and had no idea if it would hold me any better than the last one had.

I slipped another bunch of inches and let dignity fly. "Help! Help!"

Both man and dog came running to my rescue. Jake jumped up and down, helpfully shouting, "Look, she's up there!" in Labradorian.

Ty put his hands on his hips and looked up at me, shaking his head. "Penny, what the hell do you think you're doing?"

"Grab my camera!" I clutched the support as hard as I could with my legs and one arm while I carefully pulled the camera strap over my head. I dangled the precious object down into Ty's upstretched hands.

He put it around his neck and then reached up for me. "I'm not sure how to—"

"I'm okay. I think I can get down myself." I had spotted the crossbar and extended one foot toward it, but

I lost my grip on the vertical and somehow missed the damn thing.

"Aaaa!" I fell about six feet onto the leaf-covered ground. I managed to roll as I landed, ending up more dirty than hurt. I lay flat for a moment, contemplating my condition.

Ty came over to peer down at me. "Are you okay?" His strangled tone betrayed his suppressed laughter.

"I'm fine, thank you very much." I held out a hand and he helped me onto my feet. "This ground isn't as hard-packed as I would've expected. It's actually kind of fluffy. Have y'all ever planted anything up here?"

"Not that I know of." Ty returned my camera, which I looped around my neck. His gaze was turned up, not down, studying the windmill as if assessing the damage.

Jake, on the other hand, shared my interest in the state of the earth. He snuffled his flaring nose through a rill of leaves and then started pawing at the ground, throwing up clumps of loose dirt. One of them struck me on the shin.

"Hey!"

Ty whistled sharply. "Jako! Cut that out!"

The dog ignored him, digging furiously, churning up a stream of rocks and clods. "Enough of that, Mister!" I grabbed him by the collar, peering past him to see what he was digging at. He tugged an arm out of the dirt with the ragged ruin of a hand flopping at the end. A silver chain dangling silver charms glinted around the wrist.

I shrieked. "No, Jake, no!"

Ty loomed behind me. "Lord God Almighty!" He grabbed the collar and dragged the dog away.

I backed up, patting myself on the chest. "Oh my God, oh my God, oh my God!"

Neither of us could take our eyes off of that arm. We kept backing up until our legs met the low rock wall. I sat down with a bump and shook my head, trying to shake away that foul image. Then I looked at Ty.

He stood staring unblinking at the arm, his face drawn into lines of horror. His body was taut and he gripped Jake's collar so hard the dog's feet came off the ground. "That bracelet," he said, his voice thick. "It's Diana's. I gave it to her."

He let go of the dog and staggered like a zombie back toward the arm. I lunged for Jake and caught his collar, swinging around to block Ty's path. I couldn't bear the thought of him touching that thing and didn't want to think about what—or who—was under there. "Ty, don't. Come away. We gotta call the cops!"

I gripped the struggling dog and herded the dazed man back toward the Gator. "Call the sheriff." I snagged Jake's leash off the seat and snapped it onto his collar. Then I hooked the leash around the tow bar under the flat bed and turned back to Ty.

He was standing there with his cell phone in his hand like he couldn't remember what it was or how to use it. I took it from him and dialed 911. When the dispatcher answered, I said, "Come quick. The Hawkins ranch—the Lazy H. The dog dug up—we found a body. It might be— it's wearing Diana's bracelet. Hurry!"

I hung up and slid the phone into Ty's pocket. "Sit down, honey." I gently pushed him onto the passenger seat and stood in front of him, holding both his hands. And so we waited.

Chapter 3

Ten minutes later, sirens wailed on the highway below. Another five minutes and a county car growled onto the hilltop. Deputy Dare Thompson got out and strode toward us, his eyes landing on the dog, the Gator, Ty, and me as he walked. "Where is she?"

I pointed toward the stone enclosure and he started in that direction, but Ty jumped up, pushing past me, getting in front of Dare and blocking his path.

"You're not going in there, Thompson. That's a crime scene."

"I'm the senior deputy in this county. Stand aside and let me do my job."

"No way in hell am I going to let *you* in there."

"What are you hiding, Hawkins? What have done to her?"

"*Me!*" Ty's face flushed with anger. "Are you insane?" He leaned forward with his fists clenched.

"I'm ordering you to stand aside. This is a crime scene and I'm taking control." Dare grasped Ty by the shoulder to turn him away.

Bad move. Ty jerked himself free and pushed back. Dare grabbed his arm and gave it a yank. Ty pulled his other arm back and swung his fist smack into Dare's jaw. Dare staggered, almost falling, then recovered his balance and came at Ty with his head down and grappled him around the waist.

Jake lunged to the end of his leash, rocking the Gator and barking furiously. Never attack a man in front of his dog.

"Hush!" I went around the Gator to calm him down, but he was as out of his head as the two angry men.

When I turned back, they'd somehow knocked each other down and were rolling around on the stony ground whacking each other, cursing and grunting. I danced around them, flapping my arms like an idiot, shouting, "Stop it! Stop it! Stop it!" to no avail.

Then the sheriff's gold and white vehicle pulled up onto the hilltop, followed closely by another black and white. Doors flew open. Lawmen leapt out and ran toward the brawling men. Two deputies took hold of Dare and bodily hauled him up and over to the cars. The sheriff got his hands under Ty's shoulders and raised him to his feet, standing behind him with one meaty hand gripping his arm.

Ty, a busy executive who burned stress playing racquetball and pickup hoops, pivoted sharply on one toe, shouting, "Get your goddamn hands off me!" He shoved unseeing at the man behind him, hard. The sheriff went down with a grunt, flat on his butt in the dirt.

Everyone stopped. Silence wrapped the hilltop for three, four, five seconds, broken at last by the *click-click* of handcuffs snapping around Ty's wrists and Deputy Penateka's dry twang. "Tyler Hawkins, you are under arrest for assaulting an officer of the law."

The sheriff lumbered onto his feet and planted his hands on his hips. "Everybody just calm down," he said in a bullhorn voice. Sheriff Willard "Hap" Hopper was a big man, as tall as Ty and twice as wide, more beef than fat. When he wanted volume, he had the system to produce it.

The crisis had passed, but the sheriff's words leached the last of the aggression from Ty's posture and wiped the smirk off Dare's face. He nodded at them, satisfied, and turned to me. "Where's the body?"

I pointed into the enclosure.

He walked over and stood outside the tumbled rock wall, studying the ground in that intent way cops have. Then he turned around and walked slowly back to the group. He cocked his head at Dare and Ty, each still guarded by a deputy. "I don't know what you boys think you were fighting about. Whoever that is under there, it sure ain't Diana. That arm belongs to a man."

"What!" Dare glared at me. "You told the dispatcher it was Diana."

"No, I didn't. I said it was Diana's bracelet."

"It doesn't make sense, Sheriff," Ty said. "Why would a man be wearing Di's charm bracelet?"

"No point in speculating," the sheriff said. "But there are black hairs on the back of that hand and the shirt's a man's blue oxford, as far as I can see. That's not your sister, son."

"Thank God." Ty hung his head, but not before I caught the flash of tears in his eyes. I felt the sting of salt water in mine as well. A knot of dread held tight by all the tumult loosened in my chest. A dead body in the ground was still plenty bad, but the authorities were here to deal with it and we knew it wasn't Diana.

We could breathe again.

The sheriff started handing out orders. "Deputy Freshwater, take Mr. Hawkins downtown to enjoy a night at county expense."

I thought Ty would protest, but apparently he knew better. He seemed resigned, now that his worst fears had been allayed. He caught my eyes and said, "Take care of my dog."

Jake had stopped barking when the fighting stopped. Now he watched his master be led to the county vehicle and tucked into the back seat. When the car drove down off the hill, he whined a little and lay down in the shade behind the Gator with his nose pointing after the car.

"Thompson," the sheriff said, "I want you to get on the horn to the Rangers. We need a crime scene team out here pronto. I want the rest of my people to seal off this ranch. Then you go back down to the station and coordinate."

"Sheriff, I can—"

"No, Deputy, you cannot. I don't want you anywhere near this ranch until I know exactly what's been going on out here."

Dare's eyes narrowed and his jaw tightened, but he said, "Yes, sir," and got into his vehicle. He had his phone out of his pocket and was punching buttons before the car began to roll. We watched until he disappeared down the road.

That left me and Deputy Penateka. The sheriff chewed on his lip while he considered me and the camera hanging around my neck. "Well, we can't wait for the Rangers. Could be hours before they get here. News'll be all over the county by now. Half the folks'll be calling the other half and flying into a panic if anyone fails to pick up on the first ring. I don't have the manpower to keep them off this ranch."

He nodded to himself, thinking it through. "The Rangers won't like it, but we need to know who that is. We'll do it by the book. Penateka, you do the digging—crumb by crumb, slow and careful. Let's not miss one scrap of evidence. Penny, I want you to photograph every spadeful. You're the best I've got right now. Think you can handle it?"

I gulped. I'd expected him to send me home; in fact, I'd been hoping for it. I wanted to holler, *No way!* but my mouth opened and out came the words, "Yes, sir." Sometimes I have more courage than sense.

Deputy Penateka went to the sheriff's car and got a shovel, a whisk broom, and a stack of numbered cards out of the trunk. We marked out a ten-by-ten perimeter with loose rocks. The ground inside the enclosure had been thoroughly disturbed by me falling on it and Jake digging in it. Small rocks, clods of clay, and loose dirt were scattered in a wide area around the arm. Oak leaves were mixed in there too, even though the closest tree was several yards away outside the low wall. Someone might have scattered those leaves over the dirt on purpose.

The sheriff stood outside the enclosure and took out his phone, keeping an eye on us while he made a series of calls. Penateka and I got to work, settling into a rhythm. He removed a thin layer of dirt, turned it over outside our designated area, and set down a numbered card. Then I moved in and snapped a couple of shots.

Weirdly, I can look at anything through the lens of a camera, however horrible. It's a Zen thing, or maybe an art school thing. Balance, proportion, rhythm, unity: everything becomes a pure composition of form and light, even when the goal was absolute realism.

"This dirt sure is easy to move," Penateka said. "Loose pretty far down and not as many rocks as you'd expect."

Yes, let's focus on the soil.

"Ty said his old gang thought it used to be an Indian graveyard." I winced, remembering that he was half Comanche. "No offense."

He shrugged one shoulder to say, *None taken.*

We made good progress, if anything about this could be called good. We avoided the head at first, working around the perimeter of the torso and then exposing each limb. The limbs moved too loosely—the joints were decomposing—but the clothes were still in good shape and kept things together. The legs were clad in dark denim with nothing but a pair of black socks covering the feet.

"Somebody must've taken his shoes," I said. "Does that make sense?"

"Some boots can be pricey," Penateka said.

He carefully uncovered the rest of the torso. The body lay curled, knees to chest. The blue oxford shirt was buttoned to the neck. Both sleeves were neatly rolled up, revealing bloated skin turning greenish-black under a fine coat of black hair. I snapped my pictures with my brain set to professional mode. I'd acquired that trick during a senior seminar on documenting humanitarian crises, during which we'd looked at hundreds of photographs of truly appalling things.

I focused on anything that might help explain what happened. Diana's feminine bracelet looked incongruous on the now obviously masculine arm. The silver charms winked in the bright sunlight: a big heart, a little horsey, a capital D, a Texas.

I took a deep breath and regretted it instantly. A foul odor emanated from the hole. I gagged and Penateka handed me a tube of camphor to smear under my nose. That was better, in the sense of giving me a different intense odor to contend with.

The sheriff slid his phone into his pocket and came over to stand at the edge of our perimeter with his hands on his hips. "All right, now. Y'all need to stop pussy-footing around and uncover his head."

Penateka and I traded glances. He said, "Yes, sir." I took a shallow sniff of the camphor on my upper lip and promised myself a long, fragrant bubble bath later.

Another deputy came into the enclosure. I hadn't heard him drive up. A state trooper appeared too. The second deputy knelt to help Penateka carefully remove the dirt from around the head, both using only their gloved hands. All the men now gathered in a circle to watch as the face was exposed.

"Well, I'll be switched," the sheriff said. "It's that real estate guy. Roger Bainbridge. What the dickens is he doing up here?"

Chapter 4

The sheriff told me to make prints of the photographs—three copies—and two CDs of the digital files, and bring them over as soon as possible along with an invoice. Then he sent me home. As I was unhooking Jake from the Gator, I heard him say, "We'd better impound that vehicle. Penateka, you and Freshwater go get started on the house."

Search Ty's house and impound his vehicle? For one hot-tempered shove?

I fretted about it all the way home, with Jake panting by my side. I rubbed the camphor off my lip and opened the windows wide. We both needed the air. When we walked in the door, my house seemed as unfamiliar as if I'd been away for a month. It felt hollow and cool, like the inside of an abandoned cave.

I took Jake straight to the back yard and let him off the leash, sitting on the back steps to watch him. I twisted a stem off the big rosemary bush by the steps and pinched the fragrant needles off one by one, crumbling them under my nose while I pondered the weirdness of my day so far.

Ty would be spending the night in jail, not with me. This was sad, but not entirely bad. I'd been shocked by the wildness of his anger at Dare and was not altogether unhappy to have him held to account for it. Give him time to contemplate the downside of a loose temper.

Then there was the body on the hilltop, Roger Bainbridge, murdered, one supposed, and buried on Ty's ranch. I happily had acquired no knowledge about decomposing corpses thus far in my short life, but that body had seemed fairly intact and the clothes were fine, apart from being dirty. It hadn't been underground for long. It had probably been buried sometime during this past week, while Ty was in Austin.

The authorities would be able to pin that down, though I had learned it could take a couple of months for the Austin lab to get around to examining a body from the boonies. Hopefully, the need to catch a murderer would move us closer to the front of the queue.

I couldn't muster up much grief for Roger. I'd only met him once and his oily manner had put my back up. Still, he had been wrongfully killed and would never now have a chance to become a better man. That part made me sad, for sure.

But the part that tied a knot in my gut whenever I came back to it was Diana's charm bracelet fastened around Roger's wrist. It seemed contemptuous, like it wasn't enough to murder the guy and bury him in the middle of nowhere, you had to ridicule him on top of it. Or was it meant to connect him to Diana? A way to say, "This is why I killed him?" That thought had disturbing implications.

Jake came over and thrust his head between my knees to be petted. I obliged him. Then we went into the kitchen where I found a big plastic bowl to serve as a water dish and filled it up for him. I poured myself a glass of iced tea and drank it leaning against the counter.

What would I feed this big brown dog? Did I even have a dog-food compatible dish? I started opening cupboards, staring at the motley collection of stuff my great-aunt had left me, as if somehow one of the three mixers or the Fiesta ware pitchers would turn into a box of Milk Bones. I gave a Jake a Clif Bar to tide him over and ate another one myself.

I needed to get over to the studio to print the photographs, but I felt drained, like I'd put in a long day building trails. The Kit-Kat clock over the door said 10:15. I'd only been up for five hours, but I desperately needed a nap. After that, I could run to the market for a couple of cans of dog food.

"Come on, Jako." I led my guest to the back bedroom, where we sprawled face down on top of the covers.

I must have fallen sound asleep. When my cellphone rang, Jake barked and I practically levitated straight into the air. I fished my phone out of my thigh pocket and looked at the screen. Tillie.

"What's up?"

"Penny! Are you okay?"

"Of course," I said, but then I blinked and woke all the way up. Mt. Keno, Ty, the sheriff. The body. "I'm fine. Really. Don't worry."

"Okay, I won't. But, um—did you forget about Mr. Caine this morning?"

"Mr. Caine!" Another politician wanting a billboard-quality portrait. This one was running for county commissioner. "What time is it?"

"Almost eleven."

"Yikes! We'll be right over."

"We?"

"Me and Jake. Ty's dog. I'll tell you about it when I get there."

I took a fast shower and changed clothes, with Jake dogging me every step of the way. I thought about leaving him in the yard, but he acted so clingy, he might howl and drive the neighbors crazy. Plus it was already too hot and my yard didn't have much shade. I decided to bring him with me. Tillie could look after him while I worked with the client.

She met me at the back door, wrapping me in a giant bear hug. "Oh, Penny! I can't believe it! It's so horrible!"

I disengaged myself and she bent to wrap her arms around Jake. He soaked it up, being basically a petting sponge. At least Ty wouldn't have to worry about his dog. Jake had two women eager to attend to his every need.

Tillie found a water bowl and filled it, then gave him some oatmeal cookies. Then she turned her large, sympathetic, black eyes to me. "Are you sure you're all right?"

"I'm okay, really. I had a long nap." Sleep worked wonders. The images of the morning had receded from my visual memory considerably.

The bell rang over the front door and we both went out to greet the new client, closing the kitchen door behind us.

Carson Cameron Caine IV was something of a big shot hereabouts. The Caine Ranch, which bordered Ty's on two sides, was the largest in Long County. His family had been among the founders of Lost Hat; hence the Caine Savings and Loan, the Cameron Public Library, and the Caine Municipal Park, three well-groomed acres along the Mariposa River.

I knew a couple of Camerons, both blond as sunshine. We Triggs are in the summer wheat division, hairwise. The Caines—at least this one—ran several shades darker, pushing into the toasted French bread end of the spectrum. He had blue eyes, a tennis tan, and an expensive aura, like rich people on TV.

I held out a hand for shaking. "You must be Mr. Caine."

"Please, call me Carson." He smiled affably. "Mr. Caine sounds like my grandfather."

"Carson, then. I'm Penny Trigg."

Tillie said, "Hi, Mr. Caine," and he beamed at her. She slipped behind the front counter to sit at her desk.

Carson turned the beam back to me. "I know all about *you*, Penny, thanks to the small town grapevine. You're Marion Albrecht's second cousin and Sophia Ernst's great grand-niece, right?"

That kind of trick had impressed me more when I first moved to town. Since then, I'd gained firsthand experience of the famous grapevine. News travelled fast and far, true, but often picked up a lot of glitches along the way.

Carson made an expansive gesture toward the walls. "I can't believe how different this place looks. It's like a New York gallery."

"Oh, hardly," I said, flattered. I'd busted a gut and burned most of my savings turning my great-aunt's shabby antique store into a functional, yet attractive, photography studio.

"What happened to all the stuff?" Carson asked. "I remember this place being crammed to the rafters. It's lighter too, isn't it? I remember it being sort of gloomy and mysterious."

"You remember right. I hired Marion's son and one of his friends to help me haul everything upstairs and paint the ceilings. I sanded the floors myself."

"You must be Superwoman." Carson gave me an admiring look.

He assumed the Museum Pose, hands linked behind his back, and strolled around to look at the framed photographs I had hung to show off my work. Most of them bore discrete price tags, because you never knew. Somebody might buy one someday.

I don't like to hover, so I let him stroll alone. He lingered on some of the more difficult pieces, like the ones about the degradation of the native prairie, which impressed me. Most people grimace and slide on by. He lingered longest at a study of the fall foliage at Lost Maples State Park. Very pretty and a limited edition at three hundred and fifty dollars each. I crossed my fingers. If he bought one, I could pay Tillie for another week.

"These are good, Penny. Really good." He shot a discreet glance at the price tag.

"Thanks."

He made the full circuit, ending up back at the front counter. Then his genial smile faded into a more somber expression. "I appreciate your taking me today, Penny, after all that's happened."

"You've heard already."

"My secretary's sister works in central booking at the county jail. And of course we heard the commotion when all the county cars went screaming out of the lot across the street from my bank." Carson shook his head. "It's a bad business. Ty's arrest has shocked everyone."

Tillie nodded, her dark eyes still liquid with sympathy. "No one knows what to think."

"It's nothing," I said, waving the subject off with a flap of my hand. "We thought it might be Diana at first and Ty got a little crazed. Then Dare came up, a little crazed himself, and they got into it. When the other guys got there and started breaking them up, Ty accidentally gave the sheriff a little shove. The big man got a little dirt on his backside, that's all."

"It's quite enough," Carson said. "The sheriff can't allow such affronts to his dignity."

"Oh, please! Is he that touchy?"

"It isn't a matter of his personal pride," Carson said. "Hap Hopper's an easy-going guy, off duty. But the sheriff relies on the authority of his office to keep the peace, especially in a rural county. He doesn't have an army behind him, only a handful of deputies, who might well be twenty miles away when trouble arises. He might have to walk into a situation full of drunken, angry men and settle everybody down by the sheer force of his presence. If he's an ordinary man who can be pushed into the dirt, his ability to do his job is seriously impaired."

"Huh." I chewed on that for a minute. "Okay, I get it. But Dare was just as much to blame. He started in with the attitude the minute he got out of his car."

"Deputy Thompson threw the first punch?" Carson asked.

"Now that you ask, I'm not sure who started it." But I did know: Ty.

"Then Ty assaulted *two* officers this morning."

"Okay, probably. I guess a night in jail won't hurt him."

Tillie caught her bottom lip with her teeth, an expression that meant she had more bad news. She shot a glance at Carson, who frowned and nodded.

"Y'all obviously know something else," I said. "Tell me."

Tillie said, "Aunt Dolly called to say Uncle Flip said they had a second charge against Ty before they even got through booking him on the first one."

Her uncle, Felipe "Flip" Garza, was the desk sergeant at the sheriff's department. His wife, Dolorcitas Espinoza Garza, owned Dolly's Doll House of Beauty. Between the two of them, they knew everything that happened in Lost Hat almost before the people it was happening to.

I thought about Diana's bracelet strung around Roger's wrist and a cold dread clenched my heart. "What charge?"

"Uncle Flip said it was manslaughter?" Tillie's round face crumpled with distress.

"What!" I glared at Carson, the closest thing to a public official that I had. "That's outrageous!"

He shrugged. "They seem to have some pretty good evidence."

"What evidence?"

Tillie answered. "First, they found traces of blood in Ty's Gator. Human blood, they said. They have these little tester thingies. And one of the deputies heard that Ty and Mr. Bainbridge had a big fight at the barbecue place on 331 last week, loud enough for everyone to hear. Someone said they were fighting about Diana."

"Someone named Dare Thompson?" I asked.

"I don't know," Tillie said. "Also, they found a legal pad in Ty's house where he wrote something like, 'If Roger tries to get at me through my sister again, I'll kill the son of a—.'" She had been too properly brought up to finish that sentence.

"That's ridiculous," I said, a righteous wrath raising my tone. "People say stuff like that all the time. It doesn't mean anything."

Carson shrugged one slim shoulder. "Until the person in question turns up dead."

"I'll tell you what I think." I tapped a finger on the counter, hard. "I think they arrested Ty because he's handy. They already have him for assaulting the sheriff's almighty dignity. Why bother to look any further?"

"Now, Penny," Carson said. "I'm sure they'll get it all sorted out in short order."

"Not short enough. It's an election year, must I remind you? The sheriff can't leave a crime this big unsolved, not even for a minute. So they charge the first guy they get their hands on."

"If he's innocent, he has nothing to worry about. I'm sure Ty will obtain the very best legal counsel," Carson said. "He's probably got a top-notch defender on the way here already."

"That's true," I said. "That's very true." I drummed my fingers on the counter, cooling down. Ty could afford the best lawyer in Texas. Some hot-shot from Austin or Houston, high powered, sophisticated, big city. He wouldn't know diddly about Long County. Some uptown guy in a designer suit that nobody local would talk to…

I thought about Diana's bracelet again. I wanted to bring it up, but it didn't seem to be part of Uncle Flip's news flash, so maybe the sheriff was keeping it under his hat. I couldn't imagine why, but it was a distinctive detail. It must be important. Somehow, it dragged Diana into the center of the situation.

"Has anyone heard from Diana?" Carson asked.

I blinked at him for a minute. Had he read my mind? "Ty's gotten some emails from her in the past couple of days, I think."

"Well, that's a relief. My secretary said she'd gone missing. Some people were worried about her too." Carson smiled. "I'm sure she'll come straight home, as soon as she hears that her brother's in trouble."

Who would deliver that news to her? Deputy Dare? Had he heard from her recently? He had more motive to hate Roger Bainbridge than Ty. I glanced at Tillie's furrowed brow and pink-streaked hair. What lay behind her simmering jealousy?

My Spidey sense told me Diana was at the heart of this crime. I wished I knew more about her past—her old boyfriends, her rivals, if she ever had any. I'd had dinner with Ty at the Hawkins house most weekends over the past six months. Diana and Dare had been there as often as not. But we talked about the future more than the past, full of plans and blue-sky ideas for the resort. I should talk to people who had known Ty and Diana for years.

I turned a bright smile toward my client.

Carson was about Ty's age and had grown up on the ranch next door. He probably knew all sorts of things about the Hawkins family. And he was evidently plugged into the main line of county gossip. You're supposed to ask people questions while you do their portraits, get them talking about themselves, to keep them from thinking about the camera. This was a prime opportunity to do a little investigating of my own.

"Shall we get started?" I ushered him around the screen and got him seated in the chair. I smiled my bland professional smile as I shifted the tripod into position. "Did you grow up in Long County?"

Carson chuckled. "From about sixth grade on. My parents believed the country lifestyle was better for children than the city with all the crime and pollution, and now that I have kids of my own, I have to agree."

A well-crafted answer that he probably handed it out at every fund-raiser. "Were you friends with Ty?" I shifted left to get his profile.

"Oh, sure. We're almost exactly the same age. We were best friends until we went to college. We lost touch then, even though we both went to UT."

"It's a big school."

"Didn't somebody mention you went there too?"

"I did." I motioned for him to turn his head back and level his chin. "Were you part of Ty's old—"

"Did you major in art?"

"Yes. Well, photography."

"When did you graduate?"

"In 2007. Did Diana hang out—"

"That would make you, let's see, about thirty?"

"Birthday next week."

"Congratulations!" He flashed a smile of genuine pleasure. I took three shots in quick succession. They were great. We'd use one of them for sure.

Carson was a cooperative subject and happy to chat, but I wasn't getting any answers. It would help if I had the slightest clue what to ask. "Do you remember anything about Diana's—"

"How did you and Ty meet, anyway? That must be a good story."

"Diana introduced us at the courthouse Christmas party, a couple of weeks after I moved out here. Ty had heard about me from a mutual acquaintance at the Ladybird Johnson Wildflower Center. I've done some work for them, photographing some of their restoration projects. We had that in common right off the bat."

"What good luck for Ty, finding you in the old home town when he finally decided to come back."

"Lucky for me too. Did you know the Hawkins kids when—"

"Shall we try a few standing up?" Carson hopped to his feet. He composed himself while I raised the tripod and adjusted the reflectors. "You're not from Texas originally, are you, Penny? Your accent isn't quite native."

"We moved around a lot. My dad's a doctor in the Army. I finished high school in Killeen, though, and my mother's family is from the Hill Country."

"Aunt Sophia and Cousin Marion, that's right. So it's something of homecoming for you too, isn't it? Discovering your roots and all that?"

"That's part of it." I'd completely lost track of what I wanted to ask him.

"Well, we're glad to have you." He glanced at his watch. "Oh, my goodness, look at the time. We'd better wrap this up."

As portrait sessions go, it had been a success. Carson was one of the most photogenic clients I'd ever had. As interrogation sessions go, it was a total bust. Like a blind date with a lawyer, he'd asked all the questions. He got my life history and I got zip.

We made an appointment to review the proofs in a few days. He also ordered a print of that Lost Maples photo. Tillie took his credit card and sat at the desk to do the receipt.

While we were waiting, he said, "Penny, I know it's not my place, but I heard about your, ah, adventures last January. I get the impression that you're the proactive type. Which is great, don't get me wrong. But if you'll allow me, I might suggest that you be careful about getting too involved in this business with Ty. I'd hate to see you to get hurt."

"I appreciate the advice, Carson, but I can look out for myself."

Carson glanced at Tillie, trading pressed lips for her doubtful frown. "I don't mean physical danger; I'm sure you'll be sensible in that regard. But you've only known Ty a few months. There are some dark pages in the Hawkins' family history. I'm as sure as you are that he's innocent, but stories might get stirred up, not all of them pleasant ones. Just try to keep an open mind."

Chapter 5

Tillie left on Carson's heels. She did the books at her aunt's beauty salon Friday afternoons. She promised to find out everything she could while proclaiming Ty's perfect innocence to one and all, but I wasn't optimistic about either part. I kept thinking about those dark pages in the Hawkins' family history, a book everyone in town but me had probably read. Had Carson been hinting at something specific?

I let Jake out of the kitchen and he set off on a sniffing tour of the studio. It occurred to me that some Nosey Nellie might pop in looking for a first-hand report, so I turned the sign on the front door to *Closed* and shut the blinds on the front windows.

Time to take a look at the crime scene photos. I powered up my Mac and connected the camera, then remembered neither Jake nor I had eaten anything but a Clif Bar all day. I also realized that if I wanted to eat, I'd better do it before reviewing those photographs.

I saved the new files to one folder, turned off the camera, and headed back to the kitchen with Jake at my heels. Tillie and I keep an assortment of lunch items on hand, as well as late-night snack food for me when I'm on a darkroom binge. I made canned soup for both of us, adding frozen vegetables to mine and Lazy Woman Croutons—broken pretzel pieces—to both.

We took a short stroll up and down the alley and then Jake was ready to do what Labradors do best. He curled up in a corner and soon began to snore.

Thus refreshed, I was finally ready to face those pictures. First, I sorted my sunrise shots from the ones for the sheriff's department, putting them under the folder for Ty's project and updating the notes in the project log. Some of the sunrise pictures were pretty good, if I said so myself. I also liked the one of the beautiful spiral-horned animal posing in front of the tumbled boulders. Ty would enjoy looking at these when he got out of jail.

Which would be soon. I believed it right down to my Birkenstocks. I had to believe it. It would be unbearable to find out that the man I'd been sleeping with for the past six months—a man I might be seriously in love with—had committed murder.

True, Ty had that competitive streak. He'd made a fortune in the high tech industry, after all, and he was not a man who liked to sit around and let nature take her course. He made plans and took steps and expected others to fall in line.

He hadn't mentioned the argument he'd allegedly had at the barbecue place with Roger Bainbridge, but we hadn't had time to talk before the trouble started. It didn't have to be much to get people gossiping about it. A few loud words, a fist on the table, and it would have made the evening news, if we had a local TV station.

But say the fight was huge. Say they nearly came to blows. I could easily guess the central conflict: Diana, and Roger's pursuit of same. Ty had a paternal attitude toward his kid sister—overly protective, in my opinion—but even so, he wouldn't murder a man to keep him away from her.

I moved the sheriff's photos into a separate folder and started browsing through the thumbnails. Looking at photos of that isolated hilltop, it occurred to me that Ty was also an intelligent man and a long-term strategizer. I'd spent hours talking with him about how to mesh the rangeland restoration project with the resort development process. He planned years into the future, visualizing how some cedar-infested acreage would look as a meadow with knee-high grass ruffling in the breeze or how run-off from improved roads could be captured in rain gardens within sight of the cabins.

If he had buried a body on Mt. Keno, would he have let me and the dog roam around up there? Of course not. Furthermore, he was planning to build a yoga pavilion on that hill. There would be backhoes chugging away, digging everything up. Ty knew the whole plan; in fact, he was the only person who knew the whole plan. He could have chosen some remote spot where nothing would ever get built.

I sorted the thumbnails into batches for the proof sheets, careful to maintain the sequence. I've gotten to where I can sort photographs with only minimal attention to their contents, so I got past the gross ones easily enough. I did slow down a little, wondering about how Roger had been killed. His shirt front seemed intact—no bright red bullet hole over the heart, anyway. The head was a mess, but I didn't know if that was from injury or natural processes. The medical examiner would figure out the cause of death soon, one hoped.

I lingered on the pictures that showed Diana's bracelet most clearly. That and the missing footwear were the only clues that I could see. Okay, they'd found blood in the Gator, which must mean that Roger had been killed somewhere else and transported up to Mt. Keno. I guessed that also made the location itself a clue.

I studied the silver charms again: a heart, a capital D, a horse, and an outline of the state of Texas. We do love the shape of our state. The horse was no mystery; Diana loved horses. She wanted a big stable for the resort, with trail rides as a major feature. Ty thought mountain bikes would be more practical, since they didn't have to be fed. They also weren't beautiful when galloping across a meadow in the morning light, I might have pointed out, if I was dumb enough to stick my nose into that debate.

The D was for Diana, of course. Or perhaps for Dare? The heart was interesting. It looked handmade and a bit tarnished. The others were as shiny as polished steel. I'd bet the heart was real silver and I'd further bet it had been bought in Mexico. It looked like one of the *milagros* people pin to altar cloths to pray for something desirable, like corn or a car. Ty and I had seen them in the market in Cancun last February.

Had Diana and Dare ever been to Mexico? I could find that out easily enough. If not, who gave it to her? Good old Roger Dodger, perhaps.

I wasn't a jewelry-oriented woman, but surely wearing a man's charm indicated something serious going on. If I were the official boyfriend and saw another guy's heart on my girlfriend's wrist, I might be inclined to lose my temper next time I caught up with that other guy.

Not only that, I might then be pissed off enough to snick the offending bracelet around the dead guy's wrist so he could take it to hell with him. Serve him right!

Yes. Yes, indeedy. I twisted my computer chair from side to side, fired by the energy of that idea. My brilliant theory explained the most puzzling elements in this situation. It didn't necessarily point straight at Deputy Dare Thompson, though.

Men were drawn to Diana's Hollywood looks and megawatt charm and she drew energy from their attention. She tossed a dash of flirtation into most interactions. It didn't mean anything; it was just her style. Most people enjoyed the little boost to the ego, but maybe someone had taken it personally. Maybe whoever she'd been seeing before she hooked up with Dare hadn't accepted the old, "It's not you, it's me." Maybe Roger had been one beau too many and someone decided to shorten the queue.

Would the sheriff bother to seek out Diana's old flames? Or would he be content with the suspect he already had in custody? Why squander department funds on a theory?

I didn't think Sheriff Hopper was lazy, but he might consider money a more important motive than love. Many people did. He would undoubtedly find out everything he could about Roger Bainbridge's business dealings. Good. I couldn't do anything about any of that. He could get people looking for Roger's car too, which must be around somewhere. I couldn't do that either.

What I could do was find out more about Diana's past and present admirers. I could also find out who Roger had been hustling in Long County. Ty hadn't been the only local landowner getting the hard sell. You wouldn't murder a man to keep him from buying your property, but maybe Roger had been romancing other women with an eye on their acreage. Thanks to Tillie, I had a better source of local gossip than the cops.

And I would be double-dog damned if I was going sit on my lily-white butt while my boyfriend sat in jail, wrongfully accused of a horrible crime. At the very least, I could come up with a good alternative suspect for Ty's lawyer to wave at the judge.

I sent the proof sheets to the printer and got up to rummage in the storage closet for a spiral memo book. I wrote *Things to Find Out* on the top of the first page and started listing everything I could think of, leaving blank spaces for the answers.

First and foremost: why there? That hilltop had the best view in Long County, but otherwise, it was not exactly convenient. And why go to the trouble of burying the guy? Why not toss him into the scrub oaks alongside any highway you chose? We were in the western half of Texas, after all. Open country everywhere.

And what happened to Roger's car? I vaguely remembered it being big and red and expensive looking. It would stick out like a—like a big, red car. Where were his shoes, or his pricey boots? Where the heck was Diana and how did she fit into this?

I wanted to keep an open mind, like Carson had said, but one person stood out a mile already: Deputy Dare. He loved Diana more than she loved him; you could see it in the way they walked, the way they set the table, the way they loaded the dishwasher after supper. She moved, he followed. She laughed and talked with everyone around; he kept his somber agate eyes on her.

Dare had spent a lot of time on the ranch. He'd been given the full tour by Ty himself. He knew about Roger's efforts to horn in on the project and about the tug-of-war Ty and Diana were having over the contract. He must have known Roger was making a major play for Diana's affections. Worse—much worse—he was in a position to see that no real investigation took place.

I didn't know what I could do if the answer turned out to be Dare. But I couldn't be certain anyone else would even bother to ask the question. The least I could do was poke around, see if anything squeaked.

Chapter 6

The next morning, I woke to find myself clinging to the edge of the bed with Jake sprawled full length down the middle. He twisted his head around and gave me a big slurp up the side of the head.

Slimed. What a lovely way to start the day.

I let him out in the back yard while I put the coffee on and drank a cup to get the motor running. Then I suited up for my morning run. I might not have proper dog food, but I could provide dog-appropriate entertainment. We took the three-mile loop around the center of town, circling the jail twice. I couldn't see anything through the wire-meshed windows, but maybe Ty could see us and know we were thinking about him.

Jake seemed content to hang out with me, though he padded up to the front windows now and then to look out onto the street. I understood. I kept picking up my phone to check the screen, hoping to find a call from Ty that I'd somehow managed to miss.

I fixed cereal for breakfast for both of us, using the last of the milk. How long could a dog get by on people food? He must be missing crucial nutrients. I'd hit the grocery store first thing and then go over to the sheriff's department to deliver the prints. Then perhaps, if I was a good girl and said, "Pretty please," they'd let me visit Ty.

The parking lot at DeGroot's Groceries was empty except for an enormous black pickup truck with red flames painted along the sides in the center front row. I found a patch of shade under a hackberry tree at the back of the gravel lot and pulled into it.

Flash Memory

As I walked across the lot to the store, a guy came out dressed in redneck Goth from head to toe: black hat, black jeans, black leather belt with silver studs, and black boots with silver-tipped toes. His black T-shirt had red flames on the front—to match the truck, one presumed. Very stylish. He had a pack of smokes rolled up in one sleeve, displaying a tattoo of a skull and crossbones with a cowboy hat, and carried a carton of beer under one arm. He was as thin as a length of twisted steel cable, wiry muscles stretched over long bones. He had sandy blond hair pulled back in a ponytail and a full General Custer moustache. His eyes were too close together, which I noticed because he glared at me like I was the reincarnation of Sitting Bull.

If he was trying to scare me, it worked. The short hairs on the back of my neck rose and I shivered in spite of the June sunshine.

I glanced reflexively at my chest, wondering if I'd accidentally put on one of my radical environmentalist T-shirts. Nope. It said, "Pedernales State Park," surely as inoffensive as a shirt could be.

The fiery redneck stomped past me, trailing a wake of stale cigarette smoke, and swung into his truck, gunning the engine and peeling out in a cloud of gravel dust.

I let out a *boo* as I entered the air-conditioned store. One of the girls I'd done a portrait of stood behind the check-out stand. A long-legged gal with yellow hair, she wore cut-offs, a camisole, and an apron. She stood on one foot with the other crooked onto her thigh like a stork, glaring out the window at the dust cloud and snapping her gum in disgust.

"Hi, Alexis," I said, fishing her name out of my memory.

"Ms. Trigg!" She lowered her foot and slid it back into her flip-flop. "My family *adores* that portrait you did of me. I'm trying to talk my mom into getting one. It's way better than a selfie!"

"Anytime." Faint praise, but I'd take it. "Hey, who was that guy who just left? The guy in the black pick-up?"

"Hank Roeder?" She shuddered. "He gives me the creeps."

"What's his deal? He seemed pissed off about something."

"He's always pissed off about something. He thinks he's this big super bad-ass—oops! Pardon me!"

I smiled weakly. She'd assigned me to the fuddy-duddy generation. "I've heard worse."

"Ignore him. That's what I do, except for ringing up his morning brewskis."

"Isn't it a little early for beer?"

"Not for Hank."

I got a cart and toured the aisles. I kept hoping that one day a natural foods section would magically appear, but so far, no luck. When Ty's spa opened, maybe the owner would stock a few items to appeal to the tourists.

Unless Ty went to prison, of course.

DeGroot's is not a big store, but the rows are tall and there are no signs hanging above them to tell you what's where. Like everything else in a small town, you're supposed to already know. I had never bought dog food before and I wasn't finding it.

I rounded the back of an aisle and came upon the little group that hung out at the market. On nice days, meaning not in the summer, they'd sit outside on the front porch. When temperatures rose too high or fell too low, they'd move inside to sit on metal folding chairs set up in a wide spot in front of the office, drinking coffee out of Styrofoam cups.

Two old farts—a fat one and a skinny one—and an old fartess. One of them was the owner, Willie DeGroot, but since I didn't know if Willie was male or female, I'd never dared to hazard a greeting.

There was one younger guy, Peter Schmidzinsky, the new owner of Mariposa Internet Services. He'd bought the business cheap from the former owner's estate and moved it closer to downtown. Like every other IT guy on planet Earth, he was pasty and pudgy with ill-cut hair and dark-rimmed glasses. They must clone these guys in a laboratory somewhere. He'd gotten in the habit of spending his coffee breaks at DeGroot's, sliding into the gang of old farts like an apprentice learning the trade.

Usually, I'd smile politely and roll on by, but today they stared at me with such expectant looks, I felt compelled to stop. "Could y'all point me toward the dog food section?"

"Got yourself a dog?" the old fartess asked.

"He's not mine. I'm taking care of him for a friend."

"Would that friend be Tyler Hawkins?" This was from the old fart with the super-sized belly bulging under green suspenders.

"You were there, weren't you," the cubicle guy said. "Yesterday, when they found the body."

I'd been dreading this. I had no idea how to handle the gossip factor. I'd been the topic of the month last January, during the outbreak of internet blackmail and random murders, and had finally managed to shrink back down to normal. This would start it all up again, the endless speculations about my character, my history, my habits.

If I'd been in Austin, I could have said something evasive and taken my business elsewhere for the rest of my life. But in Lost Hat, if I wanted to eat, DeGroot's was pretty much it. The only way out of this was through.

I took a deep breath. "I was there."

"It must have been horrible." The old woman leaned forward in her chair, eyes shining and lips parted.

"I heard it was the dog that found him," the skinny old fart said. He looked to be somewhere in his seventies. "I heard he dug him up and practically chewed his arm off."

"No," I said, too loudly. I lowered my voice. "The dog found him, and yes, it was horrible, but no, there was no chewing of any kind, nor did any parts come off."

The old woman said, "I wouldn't have that dog in my house. Now he's got a taste for it."

That repulsive idea left me speechless.

"If you ask me, it was that crazy will," the skinny guy said. He reached for a donut from the box on an extra chair. He took a bite, dribbling powdered sugar on his stubbled chin.

"That's right," the fat guy said. "Old Carl Hawkins must have been clean out of his mind to split up his land that way. Begging for trouble, you ask me."

Ty's father had left the ranch divided between his two children. Divided geographically, that is; split down the middle, not half shares in the whole property. The trolls had leapt right over Roger's body to the probable cause of contention. I couldn't decide if that showed they were less stupid or more excitable than I'd thought.

"Alcoholic dementia," the cubicle guy said. "From what y'all told me." They all nodded.

"Carl Hawkins drank himself to death," the skinny guy informed me. His lips were shaped in a pious purse, but gossipy malice glittered in his eyes. The rest of them nodded in unison.

"That boy should never have left," the fat guy said. "Should've stayed home and took care of the ranch, like a good son. Instead, he left his old man to become a drunkard and his sister to become a—"

He broke off and they exchanged a round of knowing looks. What a lovely portrait they were painting of the Hawkins family!

"You can't think Ty killed that guy," I said. "Because he didn't. Nobody knows what happened yet. They haven't even had time to do an autopsy. They don't know when he died or even exactly how."

"Oh, they know," the old woman said. "They brought the body straight to Doc Ladsworth. They'll find whatever they need to find to convict that boy."

I didn't like the sound of that. What was this, *The Night the Lights Went Out in Lost Hat?* "They won't find any evidence against Ty, because he didn't do it."

"They wouldn't have arrested him if he hadn't done it," the fat guy said.

"Where there's smoke, there's fire," the skinny guy said.

I hated that expression. How did they know it wasn't fog? Or dry ice? Or even dust? "There's no smoke! Ty had no real conflict with Roger Bainbridge."

"Yes, he did," the cubicle guy said. "Everybody knows Bainbridge was sniffing after Diana with an eye on her share of that ranch. He'd get to control her half against Ty. That's a heck of a motive. What is that place, about five hundred acres?"

"More like a couple of thousand," the skinny guy said. "Hawkins have held that land for five generations." He nodded sagely at the others. "Follow the money and it'll lead you straight to the killer. That's how it works."

"That's a capital crime too," the woman said. "Murder for profit."

"*What?* That's ridiculous!" They were making things up as they went along.

"Death penalty," the cubicle guy said.

"That's right," the fat guy said.

Another round of knowing nods. Case solved. Execute the prisoner. Be sure to bring plenty of popcorn. I hoped none of these bloodthirsty trolls would be on the jury, if it came to a trial.

"Ty and Diana were partners," I said, trying not to sound pitiful. "They both benefited from working together and they both knew that. Sure, they had some arguments.

Siblings argue. If Ty really wanted sole control, he would have bought Diana out."

"Couldn't afford it, is my guess," the fat guy said. "Land ain't cash, little lady. Far from it."

"That's right," the old woman said. "He may drive a fancy car, but that don't mean he's as rich as he says. Nobody knows one small thing about what Tyler Hawkins has been up to, off in Austin all these years with never a visit home until the day his poor father was buried."

Now demented alcoholic Carl Hawkins was the wrongfully neglected father. If one shoe didn't fit, grab another one and shove it on.

"He was in the computer business," the cubicle guy told the others, as if they didn't know. "He probably lost his shirt in the tech bust and was forced to come back."

The others nodded, humming, "Um-hmm," like a circle of financial sorcerers intoning fundamental truths.

"The bust was years ago," I said. "Now he's building a full-featured resort. That takes money, investors. He knows what he's doing, don't worry about that." But as I said the words, I realized I didn't really know anything about Ty's financial standing. He could be rock-bottom broke and putting on a good front. Maybe he was in deep water. Maybe Roger had known it and had been applying pressure somehow.

Then why bother to go through the charade of hiring me? It wouldn't impress anyone and my services did not come cheap.

"Appearances can be deceiving," the old woman said.

"That's right," said the fat guy. "Ty was always high-and-mighty as a young feller. Acting like he was too good for this county, when everybody knew he was just a Hawkins and never going to be nothing else."

"Never was much good in that family," the skinny guy said.

"Not a lick," the woman agreed. "But Ty was a sly one. How'd he get the money for college, I'd like to know?"

"He won a scholarship," I said.

She smiled at me pityingly. "Tyler wasn't much of an athlete. He just did the 4-H and you don't get scholarships for that."

Evidently she had never heard of academic scholarships.

"He lit out of here the day after graduation," the skinny guy said. "Took his diploma and walked straight to the bus station."

I didn't blame him. These evil-minded trolls almost made me reconsider staying in Lost Hat and I mostly loved it here.

The cubicle guy dusted sugar from his thin red moustache. "I'll tell you what." The others looked at him attentively. He pointed at me. "I'll bet Diana did it."

"*What?* That's ridiculous!" I realized I was repeating myself. I also realized the idea might not be totally off base.

The old woman nodded, her wrinkled eyes shrewd. "Where is she? Hm?"

"Ty's gotten a couple of emails from her in the last week," I said. "He thinks she's in Dallas."

"But he doesn't know for sure," the skinny guy said.

"Besides, you can fake all that stuff," the cubicle guy said with authority.

"All what stuff?" I knew better than to respond, but I couldn't help myself.

"She's probably sitting on a beach in Mexico," the fat guy said. "Drinking margaritas and laughing her socks off."

"That's right," the skinny guy said. "Escaping the law."

The old woman started snapping her fingers, palm down. "I'll tell you what," she said, excitement thrumming in her voice. "Those two Hawkinses are in it together. Like that *Law & Order* show with the twins. Remember that one? Nobody could tell which one of 'em did it, so both of them wicked kids got off."

"That's right," the fat guy and the skinny guy said together.

"They're not twins!" I cried, my exasperation echoing from the metal rafters. I grabbed my cart and rolled away as fast as the crooked front wheel would let me, snatching at a bag of dog food as I went.

Cackling laughter pursued me all the way to the front.

Chapter 7

I pondered the idea of Diana as Suspect Number One on the way over to the Law Enforcement Center, which wasn't far enough to reach any conclusions. The center had been built in the early nineties with more thought to efficiency than aesthetics. Three stories tall, it took up a block southeast of the courthouse square, not including the parking lot, which reflected the summer sun off an additional half block. It seemed like overkill for a county with only 5,000 inhabitants, but law enforcement was a growth industry in Texas. Rural counties could earn significant extra revenues by renting out beds to overflowing jails in the urban counties.

The reception desk stood in the middle of the ground floor, with the jail administration offices to the left and the sheriff's offices to the right. I asked the woman at the desk about visiting hours for prisoners and she gave me a brochure. I would be able to see Ty in about an hour, enough time to talk to the sheriff first.

I walked down a short corridor past the restrooms and entered a big open area with four desks in the middle and four glass-fronted offices around the perimeter.

A lone officer sat at one of the central desks, talking on the phone. The other desks were empty. Two of the small offices were occupied, one by Dare and one by Deputy Penateka. Sheriff Hopper stood next to a printer, waiting for something colorful to emerge. When it came out, he held it up and grinned. He spotted me and came out to the bullpen. He'd made himself a flyer with a round space for a picture in the middle and the caption *You'll be Happy if you vote for Hap Hopper* at the top.

"What do you think of this, Penny?"

It took me a couple of seconds to respond. I'd expected everyone to be hard at work on the Hawkins case, not fiddling around with campaign slogans.

But this fiddler was the sheriff, so I gave him a thumbs-up. "Catchy. Why don't you email that doc to Tillie, so she can use it on your posters?"

"Good idea."

He'd been the sheriff for umpteen years and had a few more terms left in him. A *bona fide* people-pleaser, he was the odds-on favorite, according to Marion. He loved his job and was always ready to lend a hand around the county: drive a senior citizen home from the grocery store, speak to a classroom, or lead a cemetery clean-up. He excelled at breaking up bar fights and pacifying battling spouses.

I let him savor his flyer for another half minute and then said, "I've got the crime scene photographs."

"Good girl! Let's go have us a little look-see." He beckoned me follow him back to his office.

I peeked into Dare's window as I passed. He sat hunched over his computer, working on a flyer that read *A vote for Thompson is a vote for Security.* I wasn't sure how persuasive that would be in a county where three goats loose in the neighbor's peach orchard constituted a major crime spree.

Sheriff Hopper sat behind his polished and nearly empty oak desk. He waved at a chair on the other side. I took the manila envelope with photos, CDs, and invoice out of my backpack and handed it to him. Then I sat down, folded my hands in my lap, and asked, "Has there been any progress on the investigation?"

The sheriff opened the envelope and slid the contents onto his desk, spreading them out and studying each of the proof sheets before answering. "It's not like on TV, Penny. These things take time. We sent the body to Austin for the autopsy, and we're waiting for results to come back from the DPS lab. Soil samples and such. Until we get the facts on the table, there isn't a whole lot we can do."

That didn't sound good. Last January I'd learned that it could take months for the over-worked state labs to produce results. I scooted forward on my chair and clasped my hands together on his desk in a supplication pose. "I know I don't have any official standing here, Sheriff, but I'm really worried about Tyler. I'd like to be kept informed about the investigation, if that's possible."

Sheriff Hopper gave me a measuring look, then nodded shortly. "Deputy Penateka is in charge of the Hawkins investigation. You can talk to him about it from time to time, as long as you don't get in his way."

"No, sir. I would never do that." I might get in his hair, up his nose, and on his back, but definitely not in his way. "Uh—will Deputy Thompson be working on this case?"

"He will not. That'd be a conflict of interest, Penny. We don't work that way here. But I don't have enough men to send him home for the duration. We have other cases. He'll focus on those."

Conflict of interest—a mild way of saying Dare might have done the deed himself. In other circumstances, though, I would want him on the case. He was the senior deputy and took every extra training course he could find, always building his skills. The man liked to learn. I respected that.

Deputy Penateka had just graduated from the Law Enforcement Academy at Sul Ross, according to the photos lining the hall. I didn't know much about him, other than that he took himself seriously, looked good in the tan uniform, and was a couple of years younger than Tillie.

Had he ever worked a homicide case before? I doubted it.

The sheriff shuffled the photographs and CDs together and stuffed them back into the manila envelope. "Penateka'll want to see these." He held out the envelope.

I took it and walked back across the bullpen to the deputy's small office. I displayed the envelope and he flicked his fingers to wave me in. I sat in the small armless chair in front of his desk and handed him the package. "These are the photos from the scene."

"Let's have a look." He gave the whole set a quick scan and then went back to the first page to scrutinize each picture. "These are good. Sharp and clear. Better than I would have done."

I politely resisted the urge to say, *Well, duh!*

He pulled out a yellow legal pad and a ballpoint pen and handed them to me. "I'll need a signed statement from you, Ms. Trigg. Write down what you did and what you yourself personally observed, starting from your arrival at the ranch that morning."

"Now?" I hadn't been expecting an essay exam. I would have prepared. They probably sprung it on you on purpose, so you wouldn't have time to cook up a lie.

"No time like the present. You can use an interrogation room, if you like."

"This is fine." I settled back in my chair and wrote, starting from leaving my house in the dark early morning and ending with Ty being driven off in handcuffs. It didn't take long. I wrote quickly, not trying to be clever. *Just the facts, ma'am.* I signed the bottom of the last page with a flourish and handed the pad back to him.

Penateka flipped through the pages, raising one dark eyebrow near the end where I gave my version of Ty's arrest. I thought they'd jumped the gun, handcuffing a man who had obviously made a simple mistake in judgement and posed no threat to anyone. A little dust on the sheriff's butt, which, yes, meant an affront to the dignity of the office—thank you, Carson Caine—but still did not constitute a threat to society.

I was diplomatic about it, though. I managed not to use words like "brain-damaged" or "outrageous."

The deputy was diplomatic too and kept his comments to himself. "We've got your prints on file already, Ms. Trigg. I just have a couple other questions." He put my statement in a folder and turned to a fresh sheet of the legal pad. "Have either you or Tyler cut yourselves or gotten a bad scrape while you've been out in that Gator recently?"

"No."

"Are you sure?"

"I think I'd remember cutting myself. I can't swear to Ty's condition, but I doubt it. Why?"

"We found smears of blood on the mat in the flatbed. We won't get the DNA analysis back from the lab for weeks, but I thought I'd try to rule out it's being one of y'all's."

"You think it's Roger Bainbridge's."

"Seems likely. The perpetrator would've had to get the body up there somehow. It's quite a distance from the house."

"Was he killed at the Hawkins' house?"

"That hasn't been determined."

"Have you even looked?"

Penateka's black eyes narrowed. "I spent a good hour turning that house inside out, Ms. Trigg."

And it still hadn't been determined? Good news, maybe, depending on how the deed had been done. There might be ways to kill somebody that didn't make a mess, like poisoning. The thought of Ty or Diana cold-bloodedly poisoning a man sent a chill down my spine. Or maybe it was the air-conditioning—this building was freezing cold.

Then I remembered the trolls at the supermarket saying Dr. Ladsworth had examined the body. "How did he die? Has that been determined?"

"The preliminary examination indicates blunt force trauma to the back of the head."

I tried for a mental image of Ty sneaking up behind Roger with a baseball bat, but couldn't get there. "Ty's not the kind of guy who would hit a person from behind."

Penateka held up a long finger. "First place, nobody seems like that kind of guy until they do it. Second place, that's probably not what happened. He had bruises on his face too."

"Like somebody hit him?"

He nodded. "The working theory is that the perpetrator struck him with sufficient force to throw him against something hard enough to crack his skull. The nature of the wound suggests a stone surface."

"Sounds like he got into a fight."

Penateka tilted his head, but didn't answer.

I closed my eyes and did a mental walkabout of the house, reviewing the surfaces. "There aren't any stone walls or floors in Ty's house, except around the fireplace."

"I did manage to notice that, Ms. Trigg."

"Hey, but there's that wall up on Mt. Keno! Maybe he was killed up there." Then my brain caught up with my mouth. "Oh, but then why would there be blood in the Gator?"

The deputy crooked a half smile. "We went back up there after the moon set and sprayed the whole wall with Luminol, but no luck."

"Well, there's a limestone cliff around the spring, if you count natural walls." I didn't know how this could help Ty, but I couldn't stop trying. "And that old house on the ranch across the dirt road looks like it's made of limestone."

Penateka granted me a thin smile. "The whole state of Texas is made of limestone. There isn't enough Luminol in the world to test every location. We'll have to find another way to narrow it down."

"Sounds like pretty much everybody in Texas had access to the murder weapon."

"You could put it that way."

"So could you. Did the doctor determine the time of death?"

"It's not that easy."

"Give me a ballpark, Deputy. More than a week, less than a week…I did help you dig the guy up, remember."

Penateka conceded that point with a quirk of the lips. "Don't quote me, because this is not official, but Doc Ladsworth guessed it had to be at least a week. And so far, we haven't found anyone who saw Mr. Bainbridge after he was involved in a public altercation with Mr. Hawkins."

"The thing at the barbecue place." I scowled at the carpet. Where had Roger gone after that? Not straight over to Ty's place to be killed. Ty and Diana had had their argument later that same evening.

Penateka regarded me for a moment, a touch of sympathy in his dark eyes. He looked so young. I sure hoped he'd aced all his classes. "I understand you don't want to believe your boyfriend could do such a thing."

"I don't want to and I don't. There's too many parts that don't make sense."

"Name some." He sat back in his chair, ready to listen. He might be a kid, but he seemed willing to do things right. That was all the encouragement I needed.

"All right." I got out my memo book and flipped it open. "First and foremost, why would Ty let me wander around up there and let the dog run loose, if he had buried a body inside the one interesting feature in that field?"

"Could have been arrogance. Some perpetrators enjoy the risk. Or he could have wanted the body to be found by someone else. That's how most killers get caught, you know—arrogance plus stupidity. They get carried away with their own cleverness."

He had a point. I didn't like it, but he had a point. I still thought my point was stronger. Or sharper, rather, being a point.

"All right, then," I said. "What about the motive? Y'all think he murdered Roger because he was manipulating Diana in order to get control of the ranch." And here we walked straight into a Louis L'Amour novel. "But why bother? I mean, sure, Ty and Diana had their conflicts, but they were working them out. Roger didn't stand a chance of getting between them, not in the long run."

"First place," Penateka said, "so far, we're not calling it murder. Hawkins has been charged with manslaughter, which fits our theory of a violent altercation."

I shook my head. "No way. Okay, yes, Ty has a temper, and yes, I'm sure he would hold his own in a fight. But with words, not fists. He likes to shake facts in your face. I've never seen him do so much as kick a table leg."

"You don't see a man's temper until he shows it to you. Everybody's got that trigger, however deep it's set."

That sounded more like personal experience than a quote from a textbook. My estimation of the young deputy rose a notch. I frowned at him, struggling for a fresh argument that didn't involve Dare or Diana. I wasn't ready to voice either of those suspicions out loud, not here. I looked at my list of *Things to Find Out* and asked, "What about those stocking feet? Any clues about the shoes?"

"The victim had a prior encounter with one of our deputies, having to do with real estate. Deputy Freshwater remembered that Bainbridge was wearing a pair of genuine alligator boots. That's a very expensive item."

"How expensive?" My neighbor sported python boots that had set him back five hundred bucks.

"Upwards of ten thousand, from what I've learned."

"For *boots?*" More than I would pay Tillie in a whole year.

Penateka's dark eyes sparkled, the first sign of humor I'd seen. "Some men do admire a fine pair of boots. Item like that won't stay hidden for long. I put the word out and we'll keep our eyes peeled. They'll turn up for sale somewhere sooner or later." He eyed my memo book. "Are you working my investigation for me?"

"What investigation?" I closed the book and slipped it into my backpack. Time to go visit Ty. "As far as I can see, y'all think you've got your perp all wrapped up and ready to railroad."

A dark blush flared on Penateka's brown cheeks. "I resent that, Ms. Trigg. I'm not going to railroad anybody. There's not much we can do until the results come back from the labs. Meantime, we've got Hawkins on means, motive, and opportunity, with no other suspects in view."

"You're not even looking. You said yourself everybody in the state had the means—a stone surface. Opportunity—that's whoever could have buried him on that hill, right?"

He nodded, or at least, he lowered his chin briefly.

"Well, that gate was hardly ever locked. And Ty was in Austin most of last week."

"So he says."

"Can't that be checked?"

"It's being checked. I put in a call to the Travis County sheriff yesterday."

"All right, then. But the opportunity part could apply to lots of people. There must've been half a dozen people out there in the past month. Surveyors, the rangeland restoration guy. And Roger Bainbridge had his nose in everywhere."

"We're aware of that. I got a list of visitors from Hawkins and we're checking them out, one by one."

"Okay, then. That's good." I drew in a breath. "Any word from Diana?"

"Not yet."

The clipped tones and compressed lips sent a clear signal to let it drop. I chose to ignore it. "Hasn't Dare called her?"

"Deputy Thompson is not a part of this investigation, owing to a conflict of interest."

Not an answer, but definitely a closed door. Maybe Ty had called her; somebody must have. The next question ought to be less controversial. "What about Roger's car? Have you found that? Wouldn't it tell you something, like where he was actually killed?"

"It might tell us a lot. Me and Deputy Freshwater spent the better part of Friday afternoon going over the Lazy H with a fine-tooth comb, with no luck. We've got a BOLO out, though; it'll turn up."

"Tillie said he drove a Cadillac, a big, red SUV. Sounds like it'd be hard to hide."

"Not as hard as you think. There's a lot of empty country out here. You could push it off a cliff into a canyon and it could lie there for years with nobody the wiser."

Sad, but true. The Lazy H was a thousand-acre ranch, about one and a half square miles of jumbled up, scrub-covered, creek-riddled country. The ranch next door was six times as large, and there was a ten-thousand acre wilderness protection area not many miles away. A fit man like Ty could hike five miles down a deserted country highway by the light of the moon in an hour and a half, easy.

Opportunity gave me nothing. "Looks like it pretty much boils down to motive."

"And Hawkins has a good one." Penateka leveled his gaze at me. "From what we understand, he needed his sister's full cooperation or his big project would collapse. A lot of time and money down the drain. According to our source, Diana was frustrated with his treatment and had been talking about selling her half to someone else or bringing in her own partner. Our source said that partner would likely have been Roger Bainbridge, the victim. Hawkins has made no secret of his animosity toward Bainbridge."

Could that be true? Diana had been frustrated, for sure; I'd seen it myself, last time we'd all had dinner together. But would she really get into business—or bed—with Roger Bainbridge to spite Ty?

And who might be this famous source, one might ask if one didn't already know the answer. Deputy Dare, perhaps? The one with the conflict of interest that was supposed to be keeping him off the case? Not far enough off, apparently.

Penateka had been watching me assimilate that information. He gave me a tight smile that looked almost like sympathy. "Nobody's going to railroad Tyler Hawkins, Ms. Trigg, I can promise you that. But we can't let him go. He's a wealthy man with powerful connections. He could easily flee the country."

"He wouldn't do that."

"I'll tell you what. You come by and chat with me whenever you like. We have an open door policy here in the Long County Sheriff's Department. I'll keep you apprised of our progress and you return the favor by clueing me in on whatever you find out. People might tell you something they wouldn't share with the authorities." He gave me a stern look. "Have faith, Ms. Trigg. Justice will prevail."

Back to Louis L'Amour country. But I didn't see a white hat on his head and I couldn't stop worrying about the black hat sitting in the office across the bullpen. Dare could drop a hint here and an innuendo there, under the cover of guiding his greenhorn colleague through his first big case. Where would that leave Ty?

Chapter 8

The officer at the visitation center checked my identification, made me walk through a metal detector, and took my backpack away. Then he pointed me at an empty waiting area where they left me alone for a full half hour. I sat and stewed about my conversation with Deputy Penateka, doubts and worries bubbling up.

Dare or Ty? Ty or Dare? Both men had pretty much the same means and opportunity and both had good reason to hate Roger Bainbridge.

I remembered how quickly the two of them had come to blows yesterday morning and could imagine either of them getting into a fight with the obnoxious developer. But both Ty and Dare would have called 911 as soon as things went south. They were stand-up guys who took responsibility for their actions. I couldn't see either one hoisting Roger's body onto the Gator and burying him on Mt. Keno.

That part foxed me. What was the point of carrying him up there?

The guard came to lead me into the visiting area, which had two long rows of faux-wood tables with low plastic dividers down the middle and between each pair of seats. I sat in one of the yellow plastic chairs and waited some more, watching through the glass wall on the cell side. In a few minutes, Ty came striding down the corridor, his head held high, wearing a hot pink jumpsuit with his ankles showing above a pair of black slip-on sneakers.

He took the seat opposite me and gave me a grateful smile. "Thanks for coming." He looked terrible, with dark hollows under his eyes and dark stubble on his chin. His thick brown hair looked like he'd combed it with a fork. The pink of the jumpsuit electrified the green of eyes, making them seem manic.

My heart went out to him. "How are you?"

"I'm okay, all things considered."

"Can I bring you anything?"

He shrugged. "I don't know what I'm allowed to have. Books would be nice. A couple of legal pads."

"I'll ask." Books were the least I could do. I'd bring him half the library, if they'd let me.

"How's my dog?"

"Jake's fine. He has both me and Tillie waiting on him hand and, er, paw. Don't worry about him."

"I won't. Thanks. How are you?"

"Oh, Ty!" I wasn't the one in the pink jumpsuit. "You look terrible."

He rubbed the stubble on his chin. "I wasn't expecting company so soon. I'll shave for you next time."

I liked the stubble; that wasn't the worrisome part. "What's up with the pink?"

"The Sheriff of Mason County believes pink uniforms decrease recidivism. The results support him and the trend is spreading." He glanced down at himself and shook his head. "It certainly convinces *me* to give up my life of crime."

We chuckled a bit. It helped. I caught his eyes. "I talked to Deputy Penateka."

"I didn't do it, Penny."

"I believe you." I tried to keep my voice level and not betray the tiny doubts sprouting in the depths of my mind.

He held my gaze for a long time. I blinked first.

He let it go. "I'm not sure they're looking very hard for the real killer, since they've got me to blame."

"Penateka said they were waiting for the autopsy and lab results. The theory is that you lost your temper in an argument and things got out of hand."

"Never happened." Ty gave me a look that was half rue and half resistance. "But it's not beyond the realm of the reasonable, as theories go. I did get into a few fights in high school and small towns have long memories." He shrugged again. "What can I say? I was a kid with a chip on his shoulder. I have better methods of conflict resolution now."

"You fought with Dare yesterday."

"Yes, and I take full responsibility." He held up a hand like a scout taking a pledge. "But remember, at that moment I thought it was my sister under there. My brain wasn't working right."

"Dare's wasn't either. He thought it was Diana too, remember? In which case, he had no business even answering that call."

"I can't blame him for that," Ty said. "He must have been half-crazy with fear, same as me. When it comes to Diana, I guess we both have short fuses."

He sounded fair-minded and reasonable, the Ty I knew and loved. No way in hell did he get into a violent altercation, kill a man, and then try to conceal what he'd done. Seeing his calm face, dark circles notwithstanding, and listening to his warm voice, made me feel better than I had all day. I reached a hand across the plastic divider and he gripped it. The contact fortified both of us.

The guard cleared his throat. "Hands behind the barrier, please."

I almost growled at the guy. Couldn't he give us one measly minute? I sighed and folded my hands on the table. "We need to talk anyway. I'm trying to get a handle on all this so I can help you. At least help manage the rumor mill." I did a mental run-through of the questions in my backpack. "Penateka said Diana had talked about bringing in her own investor."

Ty blew out a lip fart. "She talked, sure. She likes to see how far she can push me."

"What would happen to your plans if she did?"

"It won't come to that. But okay, if that's the motive they're pushing, let's say it does. Say she takes out a loan and brings in her own partner, or even sells her half of the ranch to someone else."

"I can't believe she'd go that far."

"She won't. But say she does. Then I negotiate with the new guy, even if he's a sleaze-machine like Roger Bainbridge." He grimaced at that idea, but shook it off. "Deals are what I do, darlin'. If Diana has to bring in her own white knight to feel like a player, I can live with it. A thing like this is a big deal. A lot of people will get involved over the course of the project."

"Bottom line, then. It wouldn't wipe you out, financially? Scuttle the whole deal?"

"It would not." He chuckled. "I'm good at money, darlin'. I may not be great at relationships, but money and me, we get along fine. I went through the tech boom in Austin at warp speed and came out on top after the crash. I'm not going to lose my shirt building a resort on my own property."

His confidence rang true. If that flimsy motive was all they had, he'd be out in no time.

I felt cheered, but Ty's expression grew somber again. "I'm worried about Diana. I don't know if anyone's talked to her. Did Penateka…"

I shook my head. "He wouldn't tell me. I kind of don't think so."

"I tried to call her yesterday, but her voice mail was full."

"That could mean anything. Or nothing." I hesitated, wishing for a smooth way to ask the next question, but knowing there wasn't one. "Do you think she could possibly have had anything to do with Roger's death?"

"No way!" Ty's shout rang against the bare walls, jolting the guard into alert mode. Ty held up both hands in the universal sign for *No trouble here, Boss*. He gave himself a minute, then said, "I keep seeing that bracelet in my mind's eye and it scares me, Penny. I'm afraid she might be under there somewhere too."

"Oh, my God, Ty! Don't even think that!" I rejected the horrible idea while simultaneously wondering why I hadn't already thought of it. Then I remembered why not and the shock leached out of my system. "You've heard from her in the past couple of days, remember? She sent you those emails. She's fine, honey. Her phone's in her purse with the battery run down and she's out lounging by some pool somewhere."

Hopefully, not in Mexico under an assumed name.

Ty didn't seem much reassured, but he said, "You're right. I hope you're right. It's a morbid fantasy." He tried for a lopsided grin and almost made it. "It's probably the prison food."

"Or the disturbing pink jumpsuit."

That got me a small chuckle. "I wish they'd let me have another look at those emails. I might be able to narrow down where they came from. Or my guys at the office could."

Ty specialized in security systems and had an office full of reformed hackers at his beck and call. They could make mincemeat out of those messages in no time flat.

"When was the last time you saw her?" I asked.

"A week ago Wednesday. We had a big argument." He gave me a wry look. "Do you want the whole statement, Detective Trigg?"

"Actually, I kind of do." I gave him a sheepish grin. "You wouldn't believe the rumors flying around out there, and Penateka only lets loose one tidbit at a time. It would help a lot if I could hear the true story in one fell swoop."

"One swoop, coming right up." Ty rubbed his palms together, gazing blankly at the wall, organizing his thoughts. Then he leaned forward on both elbows with his fingers steepled and angled toward me. "This starts last week, Wednesday evening, with me being a hard-ass, twice. First time was with Bainbridge. Diana had insisted I listen to him one last time, so I met him at 331 BBQ around six. He started babbling the usual real estate drivel. Then he implied that he had Diana in some kind of compromising situation and would get what he wanted one way or another."

"How is that possible? She's an adult, single, independent. How could she be compromised?"

"I don't know. He might have meant she could be embarrassed, which could mean drugs, drinking, cheating on Dare… Not a disaster, but it would hurt her and others. If he was responsible for anything like that happening, I'd beat the son of a bitch into a—"

I drew in a sharp breath. "You might want to watch those words."

Ty shook his head with a frustrated growl. "You're right, you're right. Of course I don't mean it literally. That guy was pushing me hard, though, and I got mad. I banged my fist on the table and spoke loudly, telling him to stay the hell away from my sister. That's strike one in the case against me."

"Then you went home and argued with Diana."

"Not immediately, but yes. She came home an hour or so later. Marion made her work late, catching up on paperwork. I'd been preparing for my meeting in Austin and stupidly insisted on discussing the contract right then and there. I was high-handed, treating her like a kid. It put her back up and she refused to sign. She screamed, 'Screw you and your contract too!' and stormed into her room. Five minutes later, she stalked out the front door with a big bag over her shoulder. I heard her drive off and that was that."

"Where do you think she went?"

"That's the question, isn't it? I would've expected her to go to Dare's. Otherwise, honestly? I don't know. She had a wild crowd in Dallas she used to hang with. A year ago, that's where she'd go. But those days are behind her, or so I thought." Worry drew lines down his face. "If I pushed her off the wagon, I'll never forgive myself."

"No, no, no, and no again." I shook my finger at him. I had experience in this area. My brother Nick had a history with drugs and alcohol and my parents had been in and out of sobriety all my life. The Trigg family had a few dark pages of its own. "You can't push someone off the wagon who isn't ready to jump. You're allowed to argue with your family, Ty. It doesn't make you responsible for everything that happens afterward."

He smiled sadly, rejecting my wise counsel. "I've always been responsible for Diana. She's my baby sister."

I wouldn't even try to argue with that. "Okay. She leaves, you go to bed, you get up and you drive to Austin. When did you get the first email from her?"

"I shot her a text before I went to bed, apologizing for being such an asshole. She texted me back sometime during the night. I don't remember exactly when." He shot a dark look at the guard. "Prisoners can't have phones."

"That makes sense for most prisoners. You know, drug dealers, people like that."

"I know, I know. Anyway, she texted me back something like, 'Okay. Luv ya.' I also found an email in my inbox saying she was sorry too, but we needed to work on my temper and she needed time to think. She said she'd be back in a couple of weeks and we'd sort things out then."

"That makes sense to me."

"Yeah." He sighed. "Me too. It's no more than I deserve. But there's another message from her, sent not long after the first one, I think. She turned around a hundred and eighty degrees. She ragged on me about my temper and said if I didn't stop bossing her, she'd find her own ally. She said Roger was ready and willing."

I clucked that away. "Flip-flopping is Diana's specialty. You can't let it mess with your head."

"I know. Believe me, I know that better than anybody. I waited until I got to my office to answer her. Plenty cool. I told her to take all the time she needs, but to please trust my judgement about people a little bit and not get any further involved with Bainbridge. He does not—did not— have her best interests at heart."

I thought about how I would react to a note like that from my brother. As crazy as Nick had gotten sometimes in the bad days, I still trusted him more than most people. "That would work for me. I mean, I'd for sure at least consider it."

Ty gave me the smile that turns my heart inside out. "Thank you, darlin.' Your faith means more to me than anything else in this whole mess."

"Was that it, then? I thought you got something from her a few days ago."

"I did. And this is where things get weird, because I think there was a message from Bainbridge in the mix, dated after they tell me he must have been killed."

"That's not possible."

"Hence the weirdness. I got another message on Sunday, I'm pretty sure, warning me that if I didn't give Bainbridge a piece of my pie, he might go in with Carson Caine on an airstrip that would be accessed via the road running alongside my property."

"An airstrip? Can they even do that?"

"Sure. It's expensive, but lots of large ranches have airstrips. That was the first I'd heard of any such idea, though, and I thought I'd done my homework on all this."

"Is it a bad thing? Couldn't your guests use it to fly straight here?"

"Probably, but it would do more harm than good, Penny. Planes are noisy. Some days you'd be able to smell the exhaust fumes. The strips and the roads serving them scar the landscape and spoil that sense of escape from the modern world I'm aiming for. Depending on where Caine wanted to put it, it could significantly alter my plans."

I flapped it away with one hand. "It sounds bogus to me. Roger probably made it up to yank your chain."

Ty caught my eyes, his face dead serious. "While lying two feet underground?"

I blinked, backing up mentally. "You got that message Sunday?"

"I think so. And it gets worse. I got another one Wednesday, I think, supposedly forwarding a message from Bainbridge, asking for a meeting at my earliest convenience. He wanted to take me up to Mt. Keno and show me exactly where the road and the airstrip would go."

"Wait a minute. This past Wednesday? You mean two days before we uncovered his week-old body?"

We stared at each other while the clock ticked loudly over the door and the guard gazed blankly at the wall. Seconds passed, many of them. Finally, I said, "Somebody's messing with your head."

"And we know it isn't Roger Bainbridge."

"Would Diana—"

Ty held up his hands, surrendering. "Yesterday, I would have said, 'No way.' Today? I don't know what to think."

"Maybe your lawyer can get access to Diana's email account and have a look."

"She can get into mine," Ty said. "We can start with that."

"You've remembered it wrong. That's all. We don't need to get all buggity-buggity until we have some actual facts."

My inimitable prose stylings had their usual effect. Ty chuckled, mustering something like a smile. "Sound advice, Penelope. But you know how I hate to wait."

"I know." I shared that attitude. My brain was already sniffing out ways to get my nose into Ty's inbox.

He detected my intention. "Don't even think about it, Penny. You'll get in trouble and you might contaminate the evidence."

I grumbled at him, but had to concede the main point.

The guard walked over and clapped Ty on the shoulder. "Time to go, Hawkins."

Ty stood up and pointed at me. "You keep working on my project, Ms. Trigg. Get started on that southeast pasture. I'll be out on bail before you know it and I expect to see some photographs."

"I will." I didn't mention that I would also be searching for alternative suspects, but once again, he read my mind.

He shook the pointing finger. "Don't do anything reckless. And share whatever you find out with my lawyer. I'll send her over to your studio when she's done here on Monday."

She? "Shouldn't you have a local lawyer? Someone who knows everybody?"

"I don't know any of the locals well enough to trust them with this."

"Are you sure you can trust this one?"

"Absolutely." He grinned. "She's my ex."

Chapter 9

I left the Law Enforcement Center feeling wrung out and hungry, with too many contradictory ideas tumbling around in my brain. I decided to go to the cafe on the square for a late lunch. Perline, the proprietress, was Ty's cousin. I might get some family history as a side dish. She and I were on friendly terms. We'd bartered fifty meals for a spiffy website, so I ate there every other day.

The Pearl Inn was your basic small town diner in terms of hours, location, and menu. The interior decor, on the other hand, was unique. Graham "Cracker" McCrocklin, a former Navy cook, had always dreamed of retiring to Tahiti. So when he married Perline and settled in Lost Hat—a good three hundred and fifty miles from the coast—she'd done up the cafe as a Tahitian fantasy.

The walls were painted aquamarine with nets, sea shells, plastic fish, and nautical instruments hanging everywhere, even from the sky-blue ceiling. A mural of a ship sailing into a tropical harbor covered one whole wall. A sailor who resembled Cracker stood in the prow grinning at a native girl in a hula skirt who looked a lot like Perline.

The lunch rush had come and gone, apart from a couple of men lingering over coffee at a table by the front window. Good. I didn't want a re-run of my grocery store experience.

I slid into my favorite booth at the back and studied the two-page menu. Perline came swinging out of the kitchen doors with a bus tub in her arms and started clearing tables. A petite woman with a plush figure, she colored her brown hair with too much red, balancing it out with blue shadow over her light brown eyes.

She saw me and started to say something, but one of the guys waved his cup at her and she detoured to the coffee station. She refilled their cups and brought me a glass of iced tea, my regular drink. Then she slid into the booth across from me and took both my hands in hers.

"Honey. We heard about you and Ty and your horrible ordeal. We're both just worried sick about it."

"It's not fair for him to be in jail." The warmth in her eyes made tears well up in mine. I retrieved my hand and busied myself with the sweetener.

She nodded, watching me. "It must have been a terrible shock for you."

"For Ty too." I took a sip of cold tea. "For everybody."

Perline stood up, dabbing the corner of her eyes with her apron. "Let's get you some food and then we'll have a talk. The special is meatloaf, how does that sound?"

It sounded fine. She went back to the kitchen, taking a tub full of dishes with her, and came out again in a few minutes. "Do you know anything about what's going on?"

I nodded. "I've just been to see Ty and I talked to Deputy Penateka before that."

"How's my favorite cousin holding up? I'm meaning to get over there this afternoon. I want to bring him some food, if they'll let me."

"He's okay, all things considered. I don't know if they let you bring him stuff. He's got a lawyer coming on Monday."

"Not 'til Monday? Can't they do anything sooner?"

"I guess not. It's his ex-wife, he said."

"He's hiring his ex for his lawyer?"

I shrugged. "Do you know her?"

Perline shook her head. "Ty hasn't been around much in the past fifteen years. He walked straight to the bus station after his high school graduation and didn't come back once until their father died. He didn't even come to my wedding, though he did send us a nice present. I don't think anybody went to his, except Diana and Uncle Carl. We got all our news about Ty from Diana."

Rats. I'd been hoping for details about this ex-wife lawyer. Like, was she prettier than me? She was probably smarter in the important ways and we could safely assume she was richer.

Perline got up and started wiping tables. "I don't believe for one minute that Ty would do such a terrible thing." She shook the rag at me for emphasis. "It's sneaky, for one thing, and Ty Hawkins might have a temper, but he always owned up to his mistakes."

"I agree. And thank you. I hadn't thought of that particular point."

She set a hand on her hip, looking thoughtful. "He is awful protective about Diana, though. He practically raised her, you know, after their mother left."

"What happened to their mother, anyway? Ty mentioned once that she left, but in that tone of voice that says, 'Don't go there.'"

Perline sighed, raising both shoulders and letting them fall. "They never talk about it. It pretty much knocked the stuffing out of Uncle Carl. Aunt Daisy was a lot like Diana in some ways, I guess. A beautiful woman who loved to have fun. Things got too hard for her out on that ranch—too much work and not enough play. Or money. She went to the store one day and never came back. Turned out she ran off with some siding salesman she'd met at the Trick."

The Hat Trick Saloon was Lost Hat's pool and dance hall.

"Poor children! That must've been awful. How old were they?"

"Ty was about ten, so Diana would've been six-ish." She shook her head sadly. "Uncle Carl fell right to pieces. We all tried to help out. My folks would've taken those kids in, gladly. What's a couple more? But Ty refused to budge. He was such a serious boy. He took charge of things, getting Diana ready for school, getting supper on the table in the evening."

"Poor baby." That explained so much about him. When we had dinner at his house, Ty cooked, set the table, and dished up the food, while Diana entertained us with her lively stories. I'd thought it was for me, to show off, or because he was a shade controlling and liked things done his way. Now I understood where the control came from—the need to keep his little family together as best he could. I loved him more in that moment than I had ever loved anyone outside my own family.

"So, there wasn't any—you know." I hated to say it, but it had to be asked. "Family violence. Their father didn't hit them?"

"Uncle Carl? Never! That man wouldn't swat a fly. He shrank into himself, getting smaller and quieter. He was the sad kind of drunk, not the mad kind." She wagged her finger at me. "And we'd've known. We were in and out of that house all the time, bringing casseroles and whatnot. Nobody ever hit anybody."

She glared at me as if I'd been spreading ugly rumors.

"Who never hit who?" Cracker came out of the kitchen with a Shiner Bock in his hand and my lunch in the other. He was a large man all the way around, tall and barrel-chested, with a square head and a nose that looked like it'd been broken. A ruckus of wiry red hair covered most of his head. He pulled a chair over and sat down at the end of my booth.

"We're talking about Tyler," Perline said.

"I can't imagine Ty in a brawl." He winked at me. "Might scuff those fancy boots."

"They're saying Ty and Roger Bainbridge got into a big fight a week ago Wednesday and Ty hit Roger so hard it cracked his skull on something."

Cracker tucked his chin. "If that's their story, they're way off base."

"That's their story, all right." My spirits were rising. I had allies. I also had meatloaf, moist and oniony with a tart ketchup glaze. I liked to mince it up and mix it with my mashed potatoes.

Cracker sipped his beer and watched me eat for a while. Perline finished wiping down the tables and gave the guys by the window their check. They paid and she came back to sit across from me again.

"I don't believe it and I never will," she said.

"I don't know Ty that well," Cracker said. "I only met him for the first time a month ago, when he came in and told us about that spa thing he wants to build out there. I've been looking forward to having a new class of clientele."

The word 'clientele' sounded exotic in Cracker's Georgia drawl.

"This meatloaf is great." I tried not to sound too skeptical. "But it's not exactly spa cuisine."

Cracker puffed out his chest. "I can cook anything from sushi to souvlaki. I make a vegetable curry that'll put hair on your chest."

A new spa treatment! How well would that sell? "All right, all right." I raised my tea glass to him. "Here's hoping you get your chance."

Perline said, "Sheriff Hopper must have gone plain crazy. He can't have anything to back up these ridiculous charges against Ty."

"The main thing seems to be the argument at the barbecue place," I said.

Cracker blew a disdainful raspberry. "Well, if that's all they've got, we're home free. That guy Bainbridge got up a lot of people's noses. He tried to hustle us one afternoon, talking about turning the old title company down there—" He jerked his chin toward the corner of the square across from my studio. "Into a four-star restaurant. 'Collaborate or compete, it's your choice.' That's what he said, word for word, right to our faces."

"Like a threat, I took it." Perline's eyes sparked with the challenge.

"An empty one." I pointed my fork at the vanishing meatloaf. "I'd give this five stars right here and it's not even my favorite thing on y'all's menu."

They beamed at me, the model diner. I polished off my excellent lunch under their approving gazes, thinking about how Roger-Dodger had tried to play the same game with these folks as he had with Ty. Collaborate or compete, eh? That would piss off pretty much anybody.

I laid my utensils on the empty plate and wiped my lips with the napkin. Cracker took the plate and set it on the table behind him. "How about a slice of lemon pie?"

"In a bit." I dug into my backpack and pulled out my memo book. "First, we have to help Ty."

"Help Ty, then pie," Cracker said with a broad grin.

Perline gave him a light swat on the shoulder and eyed my notebook with interest. "What've you got there?"

"A list of questions I think the sheriff should be asking."

"Who's in charge of the case?" Cracker asked. "Please tell me it's Dare Thompson."

"No," I said. "He's got a conflict of interest. The sheriff put Penateka on it."

Perline and Cracker frowned in unison. She said, "He's a nice young man, but he's as green as spring grass. Fresh out of the academy, according to Marion, and he can't be a day over twenty-two."

"Green or not, he's what we've got."

"Another rhyme," Cracker said. "What's the conflict of interest? Dare doesn't even own that scrap of land his trailer sits on."

"There's an idea that this might all have something to do with Diana." I flipped open the book and looked expectantly into their puzzled faces. "We need alternative suspects for Ty's lawyer. We have to think of people other than Ty who could've gotten mad enough at Roger Bainbridge to knock him into a stone wall. Especially people who might at some time or another have been involved in some way or another with Diana. Any ideas?"

Perline rolled her eyes. "You're gonna need a bigger notebook." She went over to the cash register counter and rummaged underneath it. She found a stack of shrink-wrapped legal pads, slit it open with a lacquered thumbnail, and brought me one, dropping it on the table in front of me with a flourish.

I stared at her. "What, does this run in the family?" I started copying my *Things to Find Out* onto the spacious pages.

Cracker chuckled, then caught himself. "None of this is really funny, I know. But those two questions let in half the county."

"You're thinking Diana had something going with Roger, aren't you?" Perline nodded, answering for me. "They had lunch in here last week. It looked like business—they had papers out and were looking at some kind of map—but I thought I detected a little undercurrent."

"She's keen on undercurrents." Cracker waved a meaty hand at the mural.

Perline gave him a wifely look. "Don't you have veggies to prep or something?"

He chuckled. "I hear girl talk coming. Time to make myself scarce." He levered himself up and went back the kitchen, taking my plate with him.

Perline slid into the seat across from me. She leaned in and lowered her voice, even though we had the place to ourselves. "I got the feeling they were working on something behind Ty's back. You know what I mean? Making some kind of secret plan about that spa." She tapped a finger on my legal pad. "You should write that down."

"I don't have to. That's the main motive they have for Ty, that he killed Roger to keep him away from Diana. We need somebody else."

"Like Dare, you mean. Do you think she was cheating on him?"

"Maybe," I said. "What do you think?"

She gazed at a glittery starfish slowly turning in the breeze from the air vent, her lipsticked mouth twisted with the effort of calculation. "No. At least, not yet. But there were smiles, you know. Private kinds of smiles. A touch of the hand, a giggle or two." She shrugged. "She might've been playing him, you know. Using him to get some leverage with Ty. She's a lovely woman, don't get me wrong, but men do things for beautiful women and they kind of get used to the service. The next step is getting used to kind of encouraging them, not necessarily exactly on purpose."

"I get it. Not so much poor Diana being manipulated by the dastardly salesman as two old pros trying to con each other."

Perline hummed at that. "*Con* might be a shade too strong. But Diana wasn't above flirting her way out of trouble or into something good. I love that girl like a sister, but they spoiled her rotten. Ty was only a kid himself when their mother left. He figured the way to take care of Diana was to give her whatever she wanted. She had those two men of hers wrapped around her little finger—and every other man who crossed her path from then on."

"Who, specifically?" I turned to a blank sheet and wrote *Old flames* across the top. "Old boyfriends? Any grudges, torches still being carried?"

"Old boyfriends in a line from here to Dallas..." She cocked her head to think about it. "She dated Ben Jernigan back in high school. They were Homecoming King and Queen, as a matter of fact."

"Tillie's husband?"

"Uh-huh. Talk about carrying a torch! He could've won the Olympics. He must've asked her to marry him a hundred times. I'm sorry to say she kept him dangling for a good while."

"Why did Ben marry Tillie, then? If he was so hot for Diana." I felt a pang of sympathy for my best friend.

"I guess he finally wised up. Tillie is such a sweet girl. They got together round about the last time Diana went up to Dallas."

"Did she spend a lot of time there?" This had all happened before I'd moved to Lost Hat. I knew Diana intimately, in the sense that we'd chatted while brushing our teeth, but not well in terms of historical details. The Hawkins kids left the past in the past.

"She used to go back and forth," Perline said. "Up there for a while, here for a while, working at the Hat Trick Saloon. Then last year, I guess she'd had enough. She might've gotten a DUI in Dallas or something that shook her up. She went into rehab for most of April, which didn't quite take. She tried again in August and started dating Dare right after that. She's been as good as gold ever since, as far as I know."

My opinion of Diana rose several notches. It takes courage to keep picking yourself up and going back to ask for more help. I sincerely hoped that wherever she was right now, she was sober, for her own sake. Sober, alive, and not guilty of manslaughter.

In the meantime, my boyfriend was still in jail. "So that's Ben Jernigan," I said, writing it down. "Who else?"

"She and Wade Pankey—the guy who owns the Hat Trick—had a thing going for a while. But he's been in a wheelchair for the past five years. He wrecked his car on 88 one night after work."

"Oh. That lets him out." I drew a line through the name I'd just written down. "We need people who could've hauled a body up to Mt. Keno and dug a grave. Which reminds me of one of my main questions: why there?"

"It does seem like a lot of trouble, now that you mention it." Perline thought for a moment. "Although it is a lovely spot. I wouldn't mind being buried up there myself."

She had a point; an excellent point. But how did it fit in? Was the killer remorseful or did he—or she, or they—choose that spot in a deliberate attempt to implicate Ty? "Ty told me once they used to play up there when he was a kid. Do you know who all was in his old gang?"

"Of course! Me and my sisters played up there too, sometimes. Not often. The boys were into rougher games, like Rangers and Indians."

"That's right. They thought that stone enclosure might have once been some kind of Indian graveyard."

"That was mostly Hank. He thinks he's part Apache." She gave a mock shudder. "Creepiest thing on earth, having that boy stalk you through the woods. That's mainly why I didn't like their games."

"Wait—you don't mean Hank Roeder? The one with the skull tattoo? He was friends with Ty?"

"Oh, yes." Perline laughed. "He wasn't quite the ultimate Redneck Devil back then. Just a skinny kid with a bad attitude. The Roeders work for the Caines and live on the 3C. Then there's the Matslars right across the road. The four boys—Ty, Carson, Hank, and Sid—were all about the same age, in the same class at school, so naturally they ran around together." She smiled fondly. "It's a lot of fun, growing up on a ranch. Being a townie, I always envied them that."

I finished writing down the three names. "This is good, Perline. Any of these guys would know the roads on the

Lazy H and have a soft spot for Mt. Keno. They'd probably have a pretty good idea of when Ty was out of town too."

Perline frowned at my notes. "I don't know, Penny. I don't want to get those guys in trouble. Hank's a bit of wildcat, but I've got nothing against him. And Sid and Carson are both solid citizens. Married, kids, responsible positions in the community. They both work at Caine Bank, you know. Carson's running for county commissioner come fall."

"We're not getting anyone in trouble," I said. "We're just expanding the realm of the possible to where Ty's not the only one. The goal is to force the sheriff to look harder for the real murderer."

"Hm. Well, all right. But if it has to have a connection to Diana, then I don't see one. She wouldn't touch Hank with a long-handled barbecue fork."

"What about Sid Matslar?"

"No. He's not her type." Perline wrinkled her nose. "She likes 'em good-looking and ready for fun. Sid's kind of a Sad Sack, although in fairness, they're going through a nasty divorce. His wife is taking him to the cleaners, by all accounts, even though she's the one that had the affair."

"Oh." I wrote "nasty divorce" next to Sid's name. "That can make people crazy. Did he have anything to do with Roger Bainbridge?"

"His family owns land in Long County, so that would be a yes. But I don't know of anything in particular."

"Okay. How about Carson Caine?" I waited with pen uplifted. "He's definitely good-looking."

"And married, must I add? Diana wouldn't stoop that low. Although she did have a powerful crush on Carson back when they were kids. But he was older, you know, and four years is a huge difference at that age. She tagged after him and he tried not to notice. By the time she got to high school, the boys had gone off to college. She started dating

Ben and that was that. Besides—" She wagged her finger and shook her head.

"Besides what?"

"A Caine and a Hawkins?" She put a finger to the tip of her nose and tilted it toward the ceiling. "Never happen, honey. Carson married a rich society gal from Dallas. They have two little boys. He's stepping right into his grandfather's shoes, turning himself into a pillar of the community."

Pillars could be toppled by a scandal and there was that business about the airstrip. Although that gave Ty a better motive than anybody else. I leaned back in the booth, tapping my pen on the paper.

Perline leaned back on her side, watching the pen go up and down with her arms crossed over her chest. After a minute, she caught my gaze and held it. "Are you thinking what I'm thinking?"

What were the odds? "I don't know."

"I'm thinking about Thelma and Louise."

"Oh, my God!" I sat up straight and pointed the pen at her. "That is *exactly* what I was thinking, except I didn't realize I was thinking exactly that!"

She cocked her head at me and I backed up a bit. "I mean, I've been thinking of the possibility that Diana killed Roger—by accident, like maybe he came on too strong or something. But I hadn't thought of the movie connection."

"It fits, don't you think?" She nodded to answer for me. "I wouldn't put date rape past old Roger Dodger. He was not a man who liked to hear the word, 'No.'"

"Yeah. And Diana's no shrinking violet. She'd fight back. The thing I'm wondering though is if she's strong enough. Could she hoist a guy onto the bed of the Gator?"

"Oh, sure!" Perline flapped her hand at me. "She grew up on a ranch. And she's a horse lover. She was in lots of events in high school and for a few years after. I've seen her toss a bale of hay onto a truck. Roger would've weighed more than a small bale, but if she had the need, she could get it done."

We nodded at each other for a moment, working along the same track. Then Perline said, "She'd more likely get help. That would be her style."

"Enter Louise. But which of the old flames would she call? If she were in serious trouble, don't you think she'd go to Dare?"

"She'd go to Ty first."

"She'd just had a big fight with Ty."

Perline tsked. "Besides, he'd make her call the cops. He's always been a stickler."

"He'd make a lousy Louise," I agreed. "On the other hand, Dare *is* the cops."

"But he loves her so much. He'd do almost anything for her…" Perline frowned and started shaking her head. "I don't know, Penny. I can't quite see Dare as Louise. Ben would be better. Dare is too cool."

"Louise was cool, right up to the end. Desperate, but totally cool. That's how she kept it together for so long. Let's hope nobody drives anybody off any cliffs."

Chapter 10

Jake woke me at sunrise on Sunday morning, wanting to go out. I stood on the concrete back steps in my bare feet and shorty pajamas, looking at the sky and savoring the morning breeze. It was as close to cool as it gets in the summer and my neighbor's old-fashioned honeysuckle sweetened the faint breeze. I had planned to spend the day at the studio slaving away at a hot computer, but that could wait until afternoon. Right now I wanted to get out for a ramble.

I also had an urge to go back to Ty's ranch, to try to figure out what could have happened. The hilltop might be officially off-limits, but on Sunday morning, bright and early? Nobody else would be out there. I could do a little reconnoitering and then Jake and I could have a long run on the ranch roads.

We were suited up and out the door in fifteen minutes flat. I stopped by the studio to grab my camera bag. One more stop at the gas station on 88 for coffee and breakfast tacos and we were on the road.

A word to the wise: don't feed dogs tacos inside the car. They don't understand the tortilla component and the results are not attractive.

The gate at the entrance to the Lazy H hung open. The cops should've locked it, but then I remembered that Mr. Jernigan Sr. had to get in there to look after his cows. Yellow crime scene tape made the sagging front porch seem almost festive. Ty's BMW stood next to his beat-up ranch truck in the otherwise empty yard.

Jake stuck his head out the window as we drove past the turn to the house and whined. I felt like whining myself. "Not today, buddy."

The vehicles that had come and gone over the last two days had driven ruts into the field on top of Mt. Keno. More crime scene tape wrapped all the way around the stone enclosure. They must buy the stuff by the trainload.

I stood on the highest part of the hill under the windmill, turning slowly in a circle, trying to imagine what had happened. The official theory played pretty well.

Ty and Di had had their fight and she left. Then Roger Bainbridge turned up, maybe after a few more drinks, wanting to press his case. Ty wouldn't let him in the house, so they argued outside. Things got hot, fists flew, and Roger ended up on the ground with a cracked skull. Ty panicked and decided to hide the body. The Gator was handy and burying him on the ranch would've seemed obvious.

That's where the theory fell apart. Ty knew this ranch better than anyone. He knew where he planned to build cabins and trails. Surely he would have chosen someplace better than the site of the future yoga pavilion and sunset observation lounge.

Why here? The view was spectacular. I wouldn't mind being buried up here, after dying a natural death at a ripe old age. But its attractions made it a bad choice for hiding a body, especially given the abundant alternatives.

Miles of empty countryside stretched to the north and west, where only a couple of narrow ranch roads wound away into the hillscape. To the south across 1625, I could see the half-finished house on the Matslar property. Somebody was home. A car sat in the driveway.

Maybe Roger had gone to visit Sid. Maybe he'd met Diana somewhere and they'd gone together. She could've called Roger or Sid on her way out, looking for a sympathetic ear. Maybe Roger, still angry himself, tried to rape her. She and/or Sid struck back and then they decided to hide the body, etcetera, etcetera, as before.

The whole facade of that house was limestone. Sid could've sent Diana out of harm's way and waited until Ty left for Austin the next morning. Then he'd've had acres of time to do as he pleased on the Lazy H.

Penateka should be looking at Sid Matslar on grounds of pure proximity.

Once proximity entered the frame, they should also take a long look at the old stone house on the 3C to the east. Carson Caine's ranch. That place sang to me in its splendid isolation. Ty told me they used to hang out there back in the day, to smoke pot and cigarettes.

Maybe Diana had gone there to think and mope—or even better, to drink and dope. She'd been sober for about a year. I knew from my parents' experience that sobriety anniversaries were tough. Maybe the stress of the argument had driven her off the wagon and she'd gone up there to console herself with a bottle of tequila. She could've called her secret lover and told him to meet her there. Maybe Roger had been with the secret lover and had tagged along.

My maybes were radically out-running my facts. I decided to sneak over and take a peek at that house. If it was filled to the rafters with bags of deer corn, I could shake it out of my head and move on. On the other hand, if there were empty bottles strewn around a big feather bed, I might have myself another clue.

I could at least walk as far as the fence and check out the Gatorability of the terrain. A girl could look at a fence, couldn't she?

I let Jake off the leash and headed down the deer track on the east side of Mt. Keno. My running shoes got soaked in the dew as I waded through the ankle-high grass at the bottom. I stood at the juncture of the two fences, hesitating about crossing onto the 3C. What would I say if someone caught me?

I fiddled with my lens cap. I could say I was taking pictures for Ty and I wanted to get a comprehensive shot of Mt. Keno. The only way to do that was from the top of Stone House Hill.

Trespassing was illegal. A good girl would never do such a thing. I generally thought of myself as a good girl, but I was also a curious girl. A curious girl with a camera, all alone out here in the perfect morning light.

As I dithered, I saw a flash of tawny tail disappearing into the scrub oaks on the other side of the road. Jake, having no conflict between curiosity and the law, wriggled under the fence and took off after the leaping animal at full speed.

Well, now I had to go after my dog, didn't I?

I clambered over the fence at the T-junction where it was the sturdiest and walked around the bend. I wasn't really worried about Jake. He knew his way around this country better than I did. The 3C was loaded with exotic game animals for whom barbed wire fences were no obstacle. They roamed at will. This must be a regular sport for him.

I strode along the road, enjoying the peace of the morning, wishing I had a jolly photography song to hum. Somebody should write one. Bird-watching and nature photography were rapidly catching up to hunting and fishing as major recreational activities in Texas. *Texas Parks and Wildlife Magazine* ran a monthly article about digital photography, right in there with the reviews of fishing rods and the hunting forecasts.

All we needed were some tall tales and a ballad and us tree-hugging, nature-loving, pantywaists could be Number One.

The road forked on the other side of the hill. The main branch ran north, probably toward the main house. The narrower track took me right up to the stone house, as I'd expected. This side had an oak door set in a weathered gray frame. I didn't see any signs of occupation, apart from an old truck with no license plates parked under a couple of skinny live oaks. The hood still shimmered with morning dew.

I didn't see a padlock on the door. I'd take one little peek and be on my way.

My boots crunched lightly on the caliche gravel as I walked toward the house. I caught a glint of silver in the dust and bent to look. It was a charm, the figure of a man with a bow and arrow.

"I knew it," I whispered. Diana had come up here, sometime recently enough for that charm not to be buried by wind and rain.

I almost picked it up, but stopped myself. Once I moved it, it lost its value as evidence. Penateka had to see it in place. But what were the odds of my getting him up here?

I couldn't take it and I couldn't bring him here, so I did the next best thing. I took a picture of it. It isn't easy to get establishing context for a charm the size of a dime lying in a road, but I did the best I could. I flopped on my belly in the dust to try to get the base of the house in the background behind the charm.

It would have to do.

I stood up and slapped the dirt off my clothes. Then I heard a chair scrape on the floor inside the house and a raspy voice say, "Something something varmint."

The road behind me held zero cover, so I sprinted into the woods behind the truck. I ducked into a thicket of sumacs as a guy came out of the house carrying an enormous rifle with a telephoto lens. He wore black from hat to boots with a flame-circled skull on his T-shirt.

Hank Roeder.

He shouldered the rifle, sighted through the lens, and turned in a slow circle, singing "Here, piggy, piggy," in a low croon.

I backed up as quietly as I could into the thicker brush behind me. I heard something rustle and turned to look. Not a good time for Jake to show his furry face. But the eyes that met mine were not the melting brown ones of a Labrador retriever. They were small and black and set too close to a long bristly snout.

"Oh, shit."

Caught between a redneck with a rifle and a feral hog. Bring on a hailstorm and my rural Texas nightmare would be complete.

The hog went, "Snort!"

I went, "Eek!"

The great big rifle went, "Boom!"

I took off running as fast as I could, zigzagging through the short trees like they do in the movies. I could hear Hank laughing. "Run, piggy, run!"

The rifle boomed again and a branch cracked off a tree in front of me.

I veered away, scrambling over rocks and around clumps of prickly pear, hoping I wouldn't step on a snake or turn an ankle. I made it down the west side of the hill and climbed over the fence, scratching my hand on a barb in my frenzy to get back onto the Lazy H. I raced up the deer track, too scared to look behind me to see if Hank was tracking me with his scope.

I made it back to my truck and found Jake lying in the shade, panting. He jumped up when he saw me and danced around my knees. I opened the door and pushed him up onto the seat, fishing my keys out of my pocket and leaping in after him. I hauled out of there, down the hill, past the house, and onto the county road.

"That was a little too exciting for a Sunday morning," I said to Jake. He licked my ear.

At least I had another suspect: a twitchy, antisocial redneck with a big gun and a short fuse.

Chapter 11

On Monday morning, I studied my list while Jake and I ate breakfast. I had two excellent alternative suspects—Dare Thompson and Hank Roeder—although I had no motive for Hank yet. I couldn't imagine Diana going to him for help with real estate matters or to cover up a crime. He was the least likely Louise in the bunch.

Dare, on the other hand, had Louise written all over him. He loved Diana enough to do anything for her. Instinct and training would motivate him to defend and protect. He knew the territory, he knew Ty's schedule, he probably knew Diana's password and could thus have sent the bogus messages from her account.

He had motive, assuming the *Thelma and Louise* scenario. He had means, because he was a resident of the state of Texas and thus had access to an infinite supply of limestone rocks. He had opportunity, as far as I knew. Where had he been on the night in question? And which night was that, anyway?

I didn't like suspecting Dare. I wanted to trust the guys with the badges. But he had all the points. Sooner or later, I'd have to bring it up with Penateka and not long after that, I'd have to face Dare with my suspicions. Worrying about that confrontation tied knots in my tummy. If it had to happen, I'd just as soon get to it.

Ty's arraignment would take place this morning, so I passed on my usual khakis and camo in favor of a pair of eggplant linen pants and a lilac T-shirt with nothing written on it. I slid my feet into my dress-up Birkenstocks and grabbed the crocheted top that my mother made me as a defense against the air-conditioning. That would have to do. My wardrobe didn't extend to business wear.

I left Jake with Tillie at the studio and walked over to the law enforcement center. So peculiar, all this walking, but they say Texans love their eccentrics. Maybe being out on my feet in the hot sun would endear me to the townsfolk.

A couple of patrol officers occupied the desks in the bullpen this morning. Dare looked up as I came in and beckoned to me. "Morning, Penny. How's the alternative suspect search going?"

"It's going."

"Who's at the top of the list this morning?"

I drew in a breath. "Well, Deputy Thompson, as a matter of fact, you are."

I braced myself, but his lips curved into a smile—a good smile, bordering on a grin. He should trot it out more often.

"I wondered if you'd see that. I also wondered if you'd have the brass to tell me."

"I've got brass to spare. Also, once you rule out Ty, which I do, your name pops right up, assuming Diana is somehow involved."

"I'll grant the assumption is not unreasonable. What's your theory? That I killed Roger during a jealous altercation?"

"Something like that. Or Diana killed him accidentally, in self-defense maybe, and called you for help." I kept the movie theory to myself. I doubted Dare watched chick flicks and had a feeling he'd balk at details like the minor fact that Louise was a waitress, not a deputy sheriff, and had a history that made her distrust the authorities.

"I see," he said. "And then I packed her off while I buried the body on her ranch, letting her brother take the blame, because that's certainly what she would want."

"She might not know. She might be somewhere far away, meditating or whatever she's doing, completely ignorant of the whole situation. Besides, Ty doesn't have to be convicted to suit your purposes. All you need is to confuse the issue."

Dare nodded. "Not bad, as theories go. You'd make a good detective, if you learned a little discipline."

Was that a compliment or an insult? I refused to be side-tracked. "You had opportunity. You knew when Ty would be gone. You know the keys to the Gator are kept under the mat. You're a trained investigator. You could have thought to send those fake emails to throw everybody off the track."

"Those emails from Roger are a problem, all right. My working theory is that Ty sent them himself."

That made no sense to me whatsoever. "Can't you trace them?"

"I've asked Peter Schmidzinsky to look into it, but I'm not optimistic. Ty's in the computer business. He must know all kinds of tricks."

Which hardly constituted grounds for accusing him of manslaughter. On the other hand, it might play with a jury from Long County; ultimately all that mattered.

"Isn't it possible that Diana sent them?"

Dare chuckled. "They look legit, as far as I can tell. I doubt Diana has that kind of skill."

He said her name without the worry that had been wrinkling his brow during the photoshoot. Something had changed. "Have you heard from her?"

"I have. A short note telling me not to worry, that she's taking a little time to clear her head."

"And that's enough for you?"

"It is." His calm agate eyes met mine. "I trust her."

I believed him. But while his faith was commendable, his commitment made him the best Louise on my list.

Time to lay my last card on the table. I looked Dare square in the eye. "Now you're in the catbird seat, able to influence the investigation into a crime you yourself may have committed."

His eyes crinkled with dry amusement. "I'm glad you feel safe enough with me to accuse me to my face. But I can put your mind at ease. I've got an iron-clad alibi."

"How is that possible? I thought y'all didn't know when exactly he died."

"Not on Friday, we didn't. But Ty has some influential friends. The medical examiner's office faxed the autopsy report to us this morning. Bainbridge died between 7:20 p.m. last Wednesday, when he was seen leaving the barbecue place, and noon the next day. We figure it was most likely sometime late Wednesday night."

"You have an alibi for that whole period?" The man lived alone and Lost Hat was not exactly Times Square at night.

"I have an alibi for the whole week. I was at a seminar in Georgia. The Internet Investigations Training Program at the Federal Law Enforcement Training Center."

"Sounds thrilling."

"After that business last January, the sheriff thought we needed to upgrade our skills."

"He's not wrong." I mulled that over for a minute while disappointment battled relief. Relief won. "Well, I had to ask."

"I would've been disappointed in you if you hadn't."

Sheriff Hopper walked into the bullpen, heading our way. He poked his head through the door, flicked a glance at me, and grinned at Dare. "Did she do it?"

"She did. She didn't pull any punches either."

"Goldang!" The sheriff pulled his wallet out of his back pocket, fingered through the bills, and tossed a five on Dare's desk. He looked at me like he was judging a heifer at a livestock show. "I wouldn't have thought you'd have the brass, Missy."

"You thought wrong. Sir." I sat up straight, torn between pride and humiliation. I had done the right thing. Did I deserve this mockery?

The sheriff laughed heartily, bending backward from the waist with his hands on his hips and his face tilted toward the ceiling. He looked like a paunchy model demonstrating the Laughter Pose.

Dare lifted up his butt and took out his own wallet. He tucked his winnings into it and restored it to his pocket, settling back into his wide chair. "Who's next on your list?"

I glanced at the sheriff. He had made himself comfortable, leaning against the window. What a good citizen I was, helping out the authorities by keeping them entertained on a Monday morning!

I didn't much like having him in the audience, but couldn't exactly ask him to leave. "Well, I've seen Hank Roeder out at that stone house, both times I've been up on Mt. Keno. Do you know the place?"

Dare's brow creased. "That old house on the hill across the road? Hank works on the 3C. Why wouldn't he be there?"

"I don't know. But he glared at me the other day in the parking lot at DeGroot's. Really hostile, like he wanted to scare me."

"Glared at you! Lock him up!" The sheriff's shoulders shook with amusement. "He was probably flirting with you."

"Not hardly," I said. "And then yesterday he shot at me."

"No, he didn't," the sheriff said.

I gaped at him. How the hell would he know?

Sheriff Hopper made a frowny face, shaking his head at me.

"Were you trespassing?" Dare sat forward.

"Well, sort of." I hesitated. This part wouldn't go over too well.

"Sort of yes, or sort of no?"

"Well…" I scratched my head and shifted in my seat. "I was taking some pictures, down there near Ty's southeast pasture. And suddenly there was this kudzu—"

"This *what?*"

"A reebok?"

Dare and the sheriff exchanged glances, like they were wondering if it might be time to break out the straitjacket.

"You know what I mean. One of those African deer things they have on the 3C."

"A gemsbok, you mean? Or a kudu?"

"Whatever. Something in the antelope department, with big spiral horns. Jake saw it too. He got under the fence and ran after it. So naturally I had to go after him." I told them the rest of the story, knowing it sounded lame, but hoping they would give me the benefit of the doubt.

They didn't. Dare summed it up. "You trespassed onto the 3C to get a look at that stone house, imagining you were going to find blood, I bet, take some pictures of it, and bring them back here to show us. That about right?"

"I didn't imagine anything and I wasn't going to go inside. Unless the door happened to be open."

The sheriff clucked his tongue.

"When did all this happen?" Dare asked.

"Yesterday morning."

"Oh, that's all right then," Dare said. "You went to a crime scene that hasn't been released and decided to add trespassing to your list of accomplishments. Is that when Hank allegedly shot at you?"

"Not allegedly. He shot at me." They kept focusing on the wrong thing. The point was not that I had trespassed; the point was that Hank made as good a suspect as Ty. More, since he hung around out there with a rifle and obviously had poor impulse control. Bainbridge hadn't been shot, but the general principle applied.

The sheriff unleaned himself and wagged a fat finger at me. "If Hank Roeder had shot at you, little lady, you'd be shot. He's the best damned hunter in this county. He was just trying to scare you, most like, to keep you off his land."

"Moral of the story," Dare said, "don't trespass."

"Folks don't like people wandering around on their property," the sheriff said. "You need to learn to respect those fences."

I hated being lectured, especially in Surround Sound. "I do respect them. But Ty said they used to play back and forth all the time as kids. I thought there might be something to look at over there. That little stone house is as close to the place where we found the body as Ty's house, you know."

Sheriff Hopper laid a heavy hand on my shoulder. "Best stick to the cafe and the beauty parlor for your investigations, Penny." He said "investigations" the way you might say "Tupperware party." He winked at Dare and left us.

I sank back into my chair, flopping my feet out in front of me, feeling thoroughly squelched. "You don't think Hank could be a suspect?"

Dare lifted one shoulder about a millimeter. "I can't see the connection. Hank runs hunts at the 3C. Good ones; I've been on a few. They get the fat cats from Dallas, business folks that have dealings with the Caines and such. They've got six thousand acres over there and they stock those exotics. Not to mention the feral hogs and lots of deer, including some mighty fine bucks. It's a year-round job and keeps him pretty busy."

"Hm." He made sense, but I hated to strike Hank from my list. He was the only suspect I didn't like personally. "Can't you at least check the alibis for the guys who live around there? Hank, for sure, and also Sid Matslar and

Carson Caine? They would know the terrain and whether Ty and Diana were home. Sid and Carson own land, so I'll bet they had cause to become annoyed with Roger Bainbridge."

Dare had started shaking his head before I finished. "I am not going to harass people like the Matslars and the Caines because they live within shouting distance of the crime scene, which is what your theory boils down to."

I pouted at my meager list. My Spidey sense told me Roger had been killed in a conflict involving Diana, pointing at an old flame or a secret lover, but I couldn't argue radioactive arachnid intuitions with Deputy Dare. I would have to dig up something more substantial.

I tucked my legal pad back into my backpack, getting ready to leave. "I will be going back to the Lazy H, you know. Ty wants me to keep working."

"He's an optimist."

"He's innocent. Which means you're going to let him go, sooner or later. You don't have much of a case."

"It's not a lot, but it adds up. It would help to find Bainbridge's car, but it's probably sitting on a back street in San Antonio or Dallas, stripped to the frame."

"If it is, Ty didn't put it there. He was at a meeting in Austin the very next morning. Wasn't he?"

"He did attend that meeting. And he dropped the dog off at the kennel at eight-thirty."

"Well, there you go. There's no way Ty could drive that car to San Antonio, drop it off on the wrong side of town, and then, what? Take a cab back? Ride the bus?"

"He had a week, Penny. That car could be anywhere. But it'll turn up, and then we'll see what we can see."

Chapter 12

I dropped by the studio to check on the dog before going to Ty's arraignment. Tillie had given him a big cookie and taken him out twice. She also had a message for me. "Ty's lawyer called. Ms. Courtney Chambers?"

I gawped at her. "Seriously? That's her name?"

"Can you believe it?"

"She sounds like a porn star."

"Or a furniture store." We laughed more than the joke deserved. "Anyway," Tillie went on, "she said she'd meet you here at one o'clock for lunch. And that you shouldn't be late because she has to get back to Austin. She sounded kinda, you know. Bossy?"

Something to look forward to. Maybe the judge would be impressed by a bossy out-of-town lawyer.

Turned out, he wasn't.

I sat in the fine old courtroom on the third floor of the fine old courthouse for over an hour, watching drunks and weekend brawlers get their bail assignments. When Ty's turn came, I got to look at him, clean-shaven and tidy in a dark suit, but not speak to him. His lawyer hopped up and did her bit, but this was apparently not the forum for trotting out alternative theories.

Judge Bogusch suppressed her with a contemptuous sneer at her designer suit. She looked absolutely *Law & Order*, in sharp contrast to the local prosecutor, who sported cowboy boots and an oversized belt buckle.

Only two questions were asked: how serious was the crime and how great was the risk of the defendant fleeing before the trial? The answers were very serious and very great. Ms. Chambers argued that Mr. Hawkins had strong ties to the community, but since he had hardly been seen in the county for nearly fifteen years before last Christmas, the judge didn't buy it.

He set the bail at one million dollars. I couldn't remember how it worked exactly, but I thought that meant Ty would have to scrape up a hundred thousand in cash. I had no idea if he had it or not, but the point was moot. He banged his fist on the table and said, "No way," loudly enough for everyone in the courtroom to hear.

His lawyer laid a hand on his arm and murmured something, probably trying to make him be quiet, but Ty pointed an angry finger at the judge. "That's outrageous. It's extortion. It's bogus, Bogusch! Bogus!"

The gavel banged. The judge added a new charge of contempt of court and sent Ty right back to jail.

* * *

At one o'clock on the dot, the bell on the studio door jangled and Courtney Chambers walked in. As slender as a snake with custom-made breasts, she wore artfully restrained makeup, a silk suit, and four-inch heels. Her bevel cut mahogany hair probably cost her a hundred bucks a month. She looked as out of place in Lost Hat as a ballerina at a rodeo.

"You must be Penny." She shifted her briefcase to her left hand and held out her right. Her grip was on the aggressive side of firm and her eyes glittered, wondering how I would take it. I gave as good as I got.

Her gaze took me in, from my cosmetics-free face to my Birkenstocks, though her smile stayed right where she'd put it when she walked in the door. The lip-liner probably helped hold it in place.

It was like meeting your top competitor before a race. You size each other up, but politely, so the coaches think you're good sports. I gave her my best *I-could-run-you-into-the-ground* smile. "And you must be Courtney."

She looked brightly around my studio. "Charming. A real Texas traditional."

"Are you from Texas?" Her accent was Modern Standard Television.

"Houston. Although I've been in Austin for nearly ten years." She shook her head. "Too long. I was on my way to D.C. for an interview when Ty called."

That didn't sound good. He needed a focused attorney, not a job-hunter. "You must have a lot of balls in the air right now."

She looked me dead in the eye. "I will give Tyler's case my full attention, until he is fully exonerated of these absurd charges."

"Good. But I'm worried."

"I am too." She sounded sincere. "It is literally unbelievable. Ty's got a temper." She paused to roll her eyes. "But I've never seen him strike anyone or even menace them. He'll pound a table, shove a chair, or go for a walk, but he does not hit people."

I let out a sigh of relief. She might be an uptight, uptown, overdressed climber, but she was definitely on Ty's side. We needed all the allies we could get.

"Shall we go eat?" I turned toward the door, making a face and wiggling my fingers at Tillie as I passed her. Courtney followed me out and stood for a moment on the sidewalk, gazing at the courthouse.

"Beautiful," she said. "A perfect example of baroque architecture."

The Long County Courthouse was one of the wedding-cake confections that were the pride of Texas counties, built in the early decades of the last century.

"Technically, that would be Romanesque." I had expertise too. "Having my studio on this square is one of the great pleasures of my life."

Courtney looked at me as though I had just confided to being a part-time bat wrangler. "It's charming."

We walked down to the Pearl Inn. "I hope the diner is okay with you. Ty's cousin owns the place. But there's Mexican or barbecue, if you'd rather."

"A diner is fine. I wouldn't expect to find a real restaurant out here."

"Maybe when we get Ty out of jail and he gets his spa built." I was trying, honestly. Food snobs were way down at the bottom of my list, jostling tailgaters and litterbugs.

We walked into the Pearl and enjoyed the little rush that comes from moving into over-cooled air from a sidewalk hot enough to fry fish. Courtney's jaw dropped as she took in the decor.

I braced myself. She was going to say *charming*.

"Charming," she said, struggling to get her face under control.

"Penny!" Perline sashayed through the tables to give me a hug. "And you must be Ty's lawyer." She hastily wiped her hand on her apron and held it out. She winced a bit at the Chambers grip and Courtney's smile regained its strength.

Perline hadn't wiped her hands before hugging me. That made me family. I grinned at her. She ushered us to a booth, handing a menu to Courtney, whose smile faded as she studied the options. Nothing even remotely Mediterranean. Whatever would she eat?

Perline watched her a moment, pursing her lips. "The special today is blackened catfish."

"Didn't the board say chicken-fried steak?"

"We ran out of that. It's the fish now. Fresh fish."

"Sounds great," I said. "With hush puppies?"

Perline beamed at me. "The best in the West."

Courtney read the menu through again, her plucked eyebrows furrowing with the difficulty of the task. At last, she looked at Perline and delivered her order in the clear tones of a tour bus traveler speaking to a retarded foreigner. "I'd like wheat toast, no butter. And an egg-white omelet with two slices of tomato. Can you manage that?"

Perline gave in and let herself look offended. "Of course." She whisked the menu away. "Anything to drink? Ice tea?"

"I never drink anything but water," Courtney said.

Perline rolled her eyes. She brought me my tea and plunked a glass of ice water in front of Courtney.

"Could I have some lemon, please?"

Perline put a hand on her hip. "I thought you didn't want anything but plain water."

Courtney flashed a smile that bordered on friendly. She might have realized that Ty's future jury probably ate at this diner and some of them might be here at this very moment. Time to be *charming*. "Just a bit of lemon, if it's not too much bother."

Perline sighed grandly and went to get a little dish of lemon wedges. Then she disappeared into the kitchen, no doubt to tell Cracker about the princess who had come to lunch.

"Really nothing but water?" I asked. "Not even coffee in the morning?"

"Oh, coffee, of course. I meant with lunch. Or maybe a glass of wine, but they wouldn't have that here."

"Certainly not. Ain't nuttin' but moonshine out here in the boonies."

She glared at me. I busied myself with the sweetener. This was not the time to bait the lawyer; we needed to get along, for Ty's sake.

"It's good to know you don't believe it," I said. "About Ty's temper, I mean. Since you were married to him and all."

She gave me a patronizing smile. If she called me 'child,' I would smack her right across her Maybelline cheeks. Then I swallowed a gasp of horrified shame. That was probably what had happened to Roger. I swore a solemn oath to myself: no more of that kind of thinking, not even as a joke.

"Ty and I had a perfect marriage," Courtney said, oblivious to the tiny battle in my soul. "For about five years. We met when I was in my second year of law school and he was in his last year of B-school." She batted her eyelashes at me. I was so surprised I batted back. "That's business school—the graduate program."

"I know." I might be an artist, but I didn't live in a hobbit hole. I knew what a B-school was. Although I had flashed on a capitol-sized apiary for a moment.

"We were both so ambitious," she said, with a fond smile for those long-ago days. "We had the same dreams, the same goals. He would rule the software industry in Austin while I ran for state congress."

Those sounded like different goals to me, although they both involved large amounts of money. They'd had that in common, then: greed and a lust for power.

"Sounds perfect," I said, with as much sincerity as I could muster. If I had met Ty a few years ago, I would have turned my arty little nose up at him, luscious eyelashes and lopsided smile notwithstanding. "But it doesn't sound much like the guy I know."

She shook her head. Her hair shifted with the motion and I caught a glimmer of diamond earrings. "He changed. He had made a substantial fortune by the time the bottom fell out of the software industry. He was a player; he could easily have moved into other venues. But somehow he lost interest in all that."

"He was as rich as anybody needs to be," I suggested. "And looking for something more meaningful."

She gave me a worldly-wise look. "Rich people always want to be richer. Don't let anybody tell you otherwise.

Believe me, if Ty goes through with his resort, it will be a money-maker."

"Hm." It wasn't only about the money; I knew it in my bones. He loved that ranch. He loved the Hill Country. That passion shone through everything he'd said and done. I remembered the joy on his face when he showed me the rare anacacho orchid tree he'd discovered deep in a canyon.

The kind of canyon that could be sheltering Roger's red Escalade at this very moment.

"Anyway," Courtney said, "Ty wanted to move back out here and I wanted to move to Washington. We argued about it for the better part of a year and then decided to call it quits and go our separate ways."

"It was an amicable divorce?"

"Oh, yes. Of course there were some harsh moments, but luckily, there weren't any children to worry about and we managed to get past the money part without too much bickering."

"That's unusual." Not in my circles, of course. In my circles, breakups meant divvying up the DVDs and deciding who got to keep going to Genuine Joe's for coffee.

"Isn't it? But Ty's a generous man. And that's another thing. He wouldn't be threatened by any partner, silent or otherwise, that Diana might try to recruit. He's as sure-footed in the world of investments as anyone I've ever met. He could dance circles around anyone she might bring in and make it work to his advantage in the long run."

"So the official theory of his motive is pretty much hogwash."

"Absolutely. I can demolish that in two minutes, if it comes to a trial."

"Is there any hope that it won't?"

"Absolutely. I'll have a chance to present alternative theories at the preliminary hearing. I'm hoping to get the charges dismissed. They're just so slow out here. The circuit judge only hears criminal cases in Long County once a week, can you believe it?"

I shrugged. Of course I could. We didn't get that much crime in the rural counties.

She tsked. "And the docket is full for Wednesday, so he has to wait until next week."

"How can you get the charges dismissed? That's the best thing, right? That would tell everyone he didn't do it?"

She nodded, smiling her patronizing smile again. Fine; let her patronize me. I wanted to understand this stuff. "That's right. Although, in a small town, there will always be doubters. What we really need is another solid suspect. Ty tells me that you've been working on that."

"I have a couple of possibles. The best at the moment is a guy named Hank Roeder. He lives on the ranch next door and he's a pretty unsavory character."

Courtney nodded. The earrings glinted again. "What was his connection to Bainbridge?"

"None, so far. But there could be something I haven't turned up yet."

"I thought everyone in a small town knew everyone else's business. But then, you're new here, aren't you?"

"I have friends," I said. "Friends who know things. Friends who are right in the center of the loop. Besides, I think this all has something to do with Diana."

Courtney lowered her voice to a whisper. "That bracelet."

I nodded. "Plus the location and the timing, and her being conveniently out of town and incommunicado."

"I'm not sure that's significant. Disappearing when things get tough is part of her *modus operandi*."

I liked that phrase. I repeated it in my head a few times, to get it into my working vocabulary. Maybe I could spring it at the sheriff's office next time I went. "My working theory is that whoever killed and buried Roger did both to protect her."

"If she's still the girl I knew, she'll have two or three men on her string. She'd come up to Austin to visit us sometimes. At parties, every man in the room would end up in a circle around her. She loved it, of course. She thrived on it."

That last remark held a sour note. It must be hard to put as much time and money into your looks as Courtney did and then be cast in the shade by your husband's hick sister. That was still true—the circle and the thriving—but it didn't bother me. It wasn't just about her looks. Diana had the gift of making everyone feel special.

"My best suspect until this morning was Dare Thompson," I said. "They've been dating for a while and it's pretty serious."

"*Deputy* Dare Thompson?" Courtney's eyes sharpened.

"Unfortunately, he has a really good alibi."

"Which is?"

"He was at a week-long training thingy in Georgia. Some law enforcement seminar on cyber-crime."

"How do you know this?"

"He told me."

She gave me a long look, the kind you give a dog who is standing in the middle of a well-strewn sack of trash. "Has anyone verified the deputy's attendance at this 'week-long training thingy?'"

"Deputy Penateka said the sheriff authorized the travel himself." My shoulders sank. "But I don't know if anyone actually talked to anyone who could actually say yes or no."

"Actually say it in a court of law under oath," Courtney elaborated. "As of this moment, as far as I'm concerned, that alibi is worthless. I'll have someone follow up. We'll need a credible witness to come out and testify that he saw Deputy Thompson in Georgia on the day and/or night of Bainbridge's death."

Now, that was more like it! I could tolerate the patronizing looks as long as she got my guy out of jail.

Perline brought out our lunches and waited for our reactions. Courtney poked warily at her omelet with her fork. It looked beautiful; Cracker had put some effort into impressing her. The eggs were a perfect golden color, with thick slices of red tomato peeking out at the ends. There was a pretty garnish of carrot curls with leafy parsley and two slices of cantaloupe. Even the toast was wrapped in a checkered cloth napkin and served on its own little plate.

Courtney sliced off a tiny portion with the edge of her fork and placed it cautiously in her mouth. Perline and I exchanged a look.

I cut my hush puppies in half to let the steam escape and started on my spicy fish. "Melts in your mouth," I said to Perline, knowing she would pass it on to Cracker. He'd also given me some fluffy rice pilaf mixed with diced vegetables. I caught Courtney eyeing my plate and smirked inwardly. Egg white omelet. Ha!

She smiled at me, gave Courtney a narrow look, and moved off to her other customers.

I had fresh fish and fresh hope, both sorely needed after the disappointing arraignment. "What happened with that bail business, anyway?"

"What a fiasco!" Courtney shook her head. "The whole thing blind-sided me. Yet another fun aspect of working in a rural jurisdiction. The judge can set whatever bail he likes. There are rules against excessive bail, but of course what counts as excessive varies from individual to individual. Even so, a million dollars is completely ridiculous for a manslaughter case."

"Can't you protest it?"

"I will request a reduction, but that takes time. I will also file a complaint against Judge Bogusch, who has a history of conflict with my client. That might get him a reprimand, but I doubt he'll care. Judges are elected, remember."

"How can he have a history of conflict? Ty's been in Austin for most of his adult life."

"That doesn't help him, so don't keep saying it." She sighed. "Judge Bogusch has a daughter Ty's age, who lost some competition to him years ago. Some high school agricultural event."

"Future Farmers of America?"

"Quite possibly. Anyway, the girl lost on points, according to the standard system, but a second set of criteria were introduced for her by the committee, which was chaired by her father, which bumped her into first place. Ty organized a protest against the unfairness and won, which does not surprise me."

"Me neither." A glow of pride warmed my heart.

"Anywhere else, that would be a minor incident, long forgotten. Not here."

"Small towns have long memories."

"So they say."

We ate in silence for a few minutes. I wanted to know if Ty had told her anything he hadn't told me, which of course he might have, especially if he had anything to hide. I couldn't ask straight out. First, because no lawyer would answer such a question and second, because of the added complication of us being the ex-wife and the new girlfriend. Plus it might look like begging, which is not among my skills.

I decided to try an oblique approach. "Have you learned anything about those weird emails?"

"I haven't had time to do anything yet." She scowled at the bit of tomato on her fork as if it were responsible. "The two from Bainbridge are certainly odd, if Ty's recollection is correct."

"Deputy Penateka said he asked Pete Schmidzinsky to examine them."

"We won't rely on that opinion. My firm has a tech expert we consult in such cases."

"That sounds good." It also sounded slow. The realization that this might all drag on for weeks, if not longer, began to sink in.

Courtney mopped up the last smear of tomato with the crust of her toast. She slid a glance with a trace of longing at my one remaining hush puppy. I forked it into my mouth and chewed it down, letting the pleasure of its cornmealy goodness show on my face. She poked a tongue in her cheek and favored me with a wry half-smile.

Okay, I didn't hate her. But she wasn't much older than I was. If she ran five miles a day, she could eat hush puppies too.

"I wouldn't expect too much from that direction," Courtney said. "I'm sure we'll find that either Ty misremembered the senders' addresses or Diana was playing some sort of silly prank."

"A very silly and pointless prank," I said. "Unless Ty's the Louise."

"The *what?!*" Her voice rang shrill, making heads turn in our direction.

"Shh!" I cautioned. I smiled as if nothing untoward had happened and explained the *Thelma and Louise* theory briefly. "So you see," I finished, "there is a remote possibility that Ty is covering for Diana. Maybe he even provoked that bail thing on purpose, to keep the attention on him for a while longer. But I'm sure he would have told you, in confidence, since you're his lawyer and everything."

She blinked at me, perhaps in some of sort of mascara-based Morse code. That was not the response I'd hoped for. I'd expected another *What?* or a swift and hearty *Nonsense!* Some assertive rejection of the whole idea.

Before I could press for a proper answer, Perline waltzed over and offered us dessert. We opted for the check, which Courtney took her time paying. She waited until Perline took the charge slip back to the register before granting me a bland, professional smile. "Don't worry,

Penny. I will give Ty the best defense any lawyer could provide."

Not exactly a vote of confidence.

Chapter 13

So far, I had precious little to offer Ty's defense. The Dare theory hadn't totally collapsed, but it had been suspended until further notice. The Hank theory only had one leg to stand on from the start. A good kick would knock it down.

That left me with the Ben theory, which I did not much like. Get Ty out of jail and put Tillie's husband in? But if I could spread the motives around liberally enough, nobody would sit in jail until real evidence came to light. I just needed to get that reasonable doubt going.

Tillie sat at the front desk, balancing the books on the computer. I pulled up a chair and told her about my lunch with Courtney. Then I asked, "I'm still wondering if Diana might not have had some side thing going. You know, a secret affair behind Dare's back. Have you ever gotten a whiff of anything like that at Dolly's salon?"

"For your investigation, right?" Her brow creased. "Digging up all the dirt?" She turned watermelon red the instant the words left her mouth.

I winced. "Possibly not the best choice of phrase."

"I meant, like—"

"I know, I know. And we really do need to dig. Don't spread this around, but it's possible that Diana did it and got an old flame to help her cover it all up."

Tillie loved it. Her face lit up like a flip-flash array at the prospect of dishing on Diana, especially when we came around to the boys in the old gang. "Sid Matslar?" She let out a happy shriek. "That is *so* perfect!"

She astonished me. Perline and Ty had both nixed the Sid theory. "You think there might have been something going on there?"

She shook her head, still beaming happily. "No, but wouldn't it be great? Diana, sneaking around on Dare, the Dishalicious Deputy, with Sid Matslar?" She sighed and the glee rushed out like air from a popped balloon. "But I seriously doubt it."

"You don't think she could have called Sid for help?"

She lifted one shoulder. "I guess it's possible that they're friends or something. He's in the middle of a super-bad divorce. My aunt says his wife is taking him to the cleaners. She says he'll be lucky if she leaves him with the clothes on his back."

In which case he wouldn't need the cleaners. "Sid sounds more like a doormat than a partner in crime. But maybe Diana was consulting him about the property thing."

"That, I couldn't tell you."

It didn't seem very likely either. Who would call their loan officer to help them conceal a body? Not even a full service bank would go that far.

"Anybody else on your list?" Tillie asked.

"Well," I said, "was Ben ever—"

She gave me a sharp look, almost baring her teeth. "Ben hasn't seen Diana since he married me. Not once. He doesn't love her anymore. He said so. He loves me." She picked up a stack of receipts and tapped them against the desk to straighten them. "Me."

"Of course he does. I didn't mean anything like that."

"Don't you dare put Ben on your list!" Tillie glared at me fiercely; at least, as fiercely as a short, round woman with a ridiculous pink streak in her hair can look.

"I'm noting anyone who ever had any kind of relationship with Diana. Only to show that someone else could have gotten in an argument with Roger on her behalf, that's all."

"No!" She shouted. Jake lifted his head and looked worriedly from her to me.

"You're scaring the dog, Tillie."

"Sorry, Jakey." Tears glistened in her eyes. She looked down at the desk, twisting the stack of papers awry with nervous hands. "Ben doesn't love her anymore. He loves me. He hardly ever talks to her anymore, you know."

"I believe you." I went around the desk to give her a hug. "I'm sure you're a hundred percent right."

But I didn't believe her. Cold ashes wouldn't put out this much heat. Some flames still flickered, if only on Ben's side.

"You'll take Ben's name off that list?" Tillie's voice quavered.

"I'll put him way down at the bottom, in the ancient history column." I smiled at her. "That's a pretty long column. There's about half of Lost Hat on it."

"More than half." Tillie sniffed.

"She was a regular man-eater."

"Totally. She was horrible to Ben. But like a zillion years ago, though."

"Two zillion."

She seemed more willing to talk, now that we'd established the antiquity of the affair. "She really broke his heart, he said."

"And then he got over it and wised up and fell in love with you. So, her loss, right?"

"That's right." Tillie managed a smile, but her lower lip still quivered.

Time to let it drop. I'd try to have a word with Ben when he came to pick Tillie up this evening.

I spent the afternoon at the computer, polishing the Caine photos. When five o'clock rolled around, I found a reason to sit at the front desk, so I could keep an eye out the window for Ben's truck. He drove a red Ford, easy to spot as it turned the corner around the square. I poked Jake with my foot, hard. He stood up and shook himself, jangling the tags on his collar.

"Look who's awake," I said. "Hey, Till. Would you mind taking the dog out one more time before you leave? I need to finish this letter."

"No problemo. Come on, Jakey."

She clipped on his leash and went out the back door. She usually took him into the alley to sniff up and down the block. That meant I had about five minutes to interrogate her husband behind her back.

Such planning; such intrigue. Wouldn't my folks be proud? But I had to do it. Ben seemed more likely to follow Diana's lead in the ill-considered shenanigans that went on after Roger died, however that happened, than level-headed Dare or Ty.

Ben had the shape of a former football player who spent more time on the couch than the field these days. His boyish face was turning to fat around the jaw line.

"Hey, Penny. Where's my wife?"

"She took the dog out for a spin. She'll be back in a minute."

"How're things going?"

"Can't complain. I took some nice shots of the Lazy H yesterday."

"You did? What'd you use, the Canon 7D?"

Ben was an amateur photographer who fancied himself a borderline pro, not entirely without reason. He'd entered a few photos in contests and won a prize or two. He'd gotten interested in black and white photography last winter and had even borrowed my darkroom a few times.

I showed him some pictures that I'd taken at the springs on Ty's ranch, turning the monitor his way so he could see.

"These are pretty good," he allowed.

"You ever been there?"

"To Leaping Springs? Sure." He looked at me like I'd asked if he'd ever drunk milk. "Probably everybody around here has, one time or another. They used to have people out for birthday parties and whatnot. And I used to date Diana, you know."

He sounded proud: a claim to fame.

"Back in high school?"

"Yeah, and after, for a while." His eyes narrowed. "Years ago. We broke up long before I got involved with Tillie."

A little more than a year ago. Barely enough time to heal a broken leg.

"It's horrible, what happened out there," I said.

"It's bizarre."

"We're not even sure Diana knows about it yet." I cocked my head. "When was the last time you saw her?"

"Me?" His eyes caught mine and then veered away. "I see her all the time. Here and there. It's a small town, you know. You see people."

"I mean to talk to." It was funny, in the sense of annoying, how people kept reminding me that Lost Hat was a small town, as if anyone with eyes could miss that central fact.

Ben wandered over to the wall and pretended to look at the framed pieces. "To talk to, huh?" He glanced at me again over his shoulder. "I haven't *talked* to her since I got married. I don't want to upset Tillie. She's always been kind of jealous of Diana."

"I can imagine. I wouldn't want an ex like that lurking in the background."

"There's no lurking," Ben said too quickly. "I've never done anything about it. I mean, there's nothing between us anymore."

Oh, there was definitely something. His neck had turned pink. The flush reached right up to his ears, showing even under the tan from his outdoor job with the electricity co-op.

"You must have talked to her sometimes, when you go out to the Lazy H to look after your father's cows."

"Oh, out there. Sure, sometimes." A smile flickered across his face. "We talk a little, now and then. You know."

He blinked, then turned and took a fast step in my direction, making me acutely aware of the hard muscles pulsing under the flab. "I know what you're doing." His hands formed fists at his sides. "You're trying to make out a case that I did it, that I had something do to with that guy's murder and why Diana took off."

"No, I'm not." I rolled my chair back an inch. "I'm just talking." I'd let myself get boxed in between the desk, the counter, and a large, angry man. *Stupid, stupid, stupid!*

"Yeah, talk. Women love talk." He said it like it was grounds for execution. "I didn't do it, but I'll tell you what. If I'd've caught that asshole trying to mess with her, I would've given him a taste of my fist." He smacked a fist into his palm by way of illustration. I got the point, but he wasn't done. "She's too trusting and so beautiful. She's the most beautiful thing I ever had in my life. I loved her, I'll admit it. Maybe in some ways, I always will."

I heard a gasp by the kitchen door. Tillie had come back with Jake in time to hear the last part.

Ben's head whipped around and his jaw dropped. He looked like a kid caught downloading a porn site. Then his face hardened into the stony look of a man who will never admit he's wrong.

"In the past, I meant. It's long over." He aimed his words at Tillie. She walked slowly toward the front desk, unclipping Jake's leash with fumbling fingers. "I meant it like an abstract thing, you know, like a fond memory."

Tillie's lower lip trembled and her eyes brimmed with tears. A bead of mascara rolled down her cheek. She cast a look of utter betrayal in my direction. She reached the desk and grabbed her purse from behind the counter without a glance at Ben. Then she lifted her chin with the dignity of a duchess and stalked past him out the door.

Ben glared at me, jabbing his finger in my face. "Now see what you've done." He followed her out, calling, "Till, honey! Tillie! Wait up!"

I hung my head in shame. Jake took it as an invitation and came over for a petting. I stroked his shiny fur, seeking undeserved solace.

"That went well, I don't think."

Chapter 14

The next day I zipped over to the grocery store before work to pick up dog biscuits and coffee for the studio. I wanted to put off facing Tillie, after the misery I'd caused her.

Alexis was at work already, a can of Diet Dr. Pepper handy by the cash register. I got the staples and then decided I needed extra chocolate in my diet, what with my boyfriend being in jail and all. I added a bag of chocolate miniatures and some cookies. Now I needed ice cream, because what good are cookies without ice cream?

I dreaded reaching the end of the aisle and having another troll encounter, but the freezers were back there. I squared my shoulders and pushed my cart around the bend. Colonel Trigg had not raised any cowards.

Sure enough, they had a full house: the three old farts and the Internet guy, sipping coffee and chomping doughnuts. Schmidzinsky had himself a chair today. He must have gotten a promotion.

I wondered if he'd made any progress tracing those strange emails. I stopped my cart in front of their half-circle. "Good morning."

They tilted their chins in greeting.

"How's the investigation going?" Schmidzinsky asked.

The skinny old fart giggled and slapped his knee. What could be more high-larious than a girl investigator?

"It's going. Ty will be out before you know it."

"Oh, really?" the fat troll asked. I couldn't tell if he meant it gladly or sarcastically.

Schmidzinsky smirked into his coffee cup and said, "I doubt it." Sarcasm, then.

He knew something and he wanted to be coy about it. Should I bat my eyelashes and try the flirtation route, or grab him by the collar and shake it out of him?

He was too tall for the collar gambit. I cocked my head in a casual manner. "Why's that?"

"There's some pretty strong evidence against him."

"If you're talking about those emails, anyone could have sent them. You said so yourself."

"Who would?" the old woman asked. "Besides Ty. Who would bother?"

"That's right," the skinny troll said. "Who'd bother? You'd have to be guilty to go to all that fuss."

We looked at him with exasperation. "That's the point," Schmidzinsky said. "Whoever sent email from Bainbridge's address is guilty. And they came from my ISP via Ty's account with me, so guess what that means?"

"I have no idea." I tried to sound loftily disinterested.

He treated me to a curl of the lip. "The messages supposedly from Roger originated from Diana's account, d.hawkins@hawkins-lazyh.com. There's no doubt about it. She or Ty obviously spoofed Bainbridge's address. I can prove that. It's not my job to speculate why they would want to send email from a dead man." He smirked at his circle of cronies. They smirked back, as if they were a circle of expert hackers.

My brain whirred like a truck tire stuck in deep mud. Why would either of them send email from Roger to Ty? If they wanted to make it look like the guy was still alive, why not send it to someone else, or better, a bunch of other people? It made no sense, other than to incriminate the Hawkins siblings. "Couldn't someone have hacked into Diana's account?"

Schmid gave me a pitying look, poor, ignorant, fool that I was. "They'd have to have the password. My systems are secure. After the mess y'all had last winter, I'm especially careful." He took a bite of doughnut, chewed it, and washed it down with a noisy slurp of coffee. "Of course, Ty could access it, easy. He's the admin for all the subaccounts."

I knew that part. Like me, Ty had set things up to keep business and personal matters separate. Unlike me, he actually managed to maintain the distinction. I'm a Photoshop wizard, but the Internet remains a place of unfathomed magic and mystery. I'm grateful for it, but do not try to understand it.

Schmid continued his lecture, the pomposity defeated by the powdered sugar dusting his brushy red moustache. "I advise my customers to set good passwords and change them frequently. It's not my fault if they don't follow my guidelines."

"I didn't mean to suggest it was your—"

The old woman interrupted me. "Of course it's not Schmid's fault. Ty Hawkins set it up to protect that no-good sister of his."

"That's right," the skinny guy said. "He set it up himself. He knew it all along."

"Knew what?" I snapped. "Nobody thinks this crime was premeditated."

The skinny guy stared at me mulishly. I'd lost him with that five-syllable word.

The old woman glared at me as if I had accused her of stocking out-of-date milk. "What business is it of yours anyway?"

That shut me up. What could I say? To my surprise, the fat troll came to my rescue. "She was there."

"That's right," the skinny one said. "And she's got the dog."

"Huh." The old woman frowned, then nodded, satisfied. Possession of the Dog must be a local rule of precedence.

"So, you're prepared to testify as to who sent those emails?" I asked Schmid.

"There aren't any fingerprints on them." He shrugged. "But whoever it was logged in as Diana."

"That's identity theft," the old woman said.

"That's right," the skinny guy said. "They spooked that dead guy's mail."

"Spooked email," the fat troll said. "That's a federal crime."

I couldn't take any more of their wicked nonsense. "Ty did not commit this crime. And y'all are all going to feel really bad when that gets proven in court."

I pushed my cart toward the freezer section, bumping roughly past the fat guy's chair. I knew they were watching me, but I really needed that ice cream now. I grabbed the first big tub I could reach and dropped it in my basket.

Alexis smiled at me sympathetically when I got to the checkout counter. "You shouldn't stop back there. Roll on by or don't even go all the way back."

"I wanted ice cream. What have they got against Ty, anyway?" I slapped the bag of chocolates onto the counter.

"Oh, nothing. They live for scandal. The Lost Hat Chair Committee. Nobody with any sense pays them any mind."

I glanced toward the back and lowered my voice. "Which one is Willie?"

She grinned. "The woman. The fat one is her brother and the skinny one's an old son-of-a-witch with nothing better to do. Schmid comes over for the free coffee."

She rang up my items in silence. I silently thanked her for not remarking on my culinary choices. But then a girl who drank Dr. Pepper for breakfast probably didn't subscribe to the *Healthy Lifestyles* newsletter either.

"How is Mr. Hawkins?" she asked. "Not everybody in this town thinks he's guilty, you know."

"Thanks. He's okay, considering. But if it goes to trial and those old trolls back there are on his jury, he could be in real trouble."

"Oh, nobody'd put them on a jury. Half the town would be in prison."

I paid her and put my stuff in the backpack.

"And listen," she said. "Next time, don't go back there. Ask me and I'll get the ice cream for you."

That was a relief. The next nearest supermarket was over an hour away, a heck of a schlep for a chocolate fix. And it looked like I'd be needing a lot more chocolate in the near future.

Chapter 15

I walked across the parking lot, worrying about those emails, half-blinded by the light reflecting up under my sunglasses from the white gravel. I blinked at the relative darkness of the shadow cast by the old bank on the corner. Another hot trot across the street and I plunged inside my cool studio. Only the dog greeted me as I walked in. Tillie wasn't there and it didn't look like she'd been in.

I went back to the kitchen to put the groceries away, then filled Jake's water bowl. I sat at the table drinking iced tea, listening to him slurping thirstily. He sloshed water all over the floor, but who cared?

What difference did it make? What difference did anything make?

Those emails had come from Diana's account, which was a subaccount or sub-something inside or under the Lazy H domain. I could never remember the right terminology for this stuff, but it didn't matter. The bottom line was that Diana or Ty—or possibly some mysterious third person who could guess Diana's password—had sent them.

It made no sense whatsoever for Ty to send them to himself, unless he had set the whole thing up, from throwing a punch at Dare to insulting the judge, to confuse the situation until Diana established herself safely somewhere south of the Rio Grande. I didn't know whether to applaud the loyalty, admire the scope of the plan, or be horrified by my boyfriend's willingness to go to such lengths to cover up an ugly death.

It did seem awfully elaborate. Maybe Diana had sent those messages in a lame attempt to convince everybody that Roger was still alive. She'd only sent them to Ty because she didn't have the nerve to try it on anybody else. That made more sense—marginally more.

Or maybe her secret lover knew her password. He could have sent those messages without consulting anyone named Hawkins. Except nobody knew about any secret lover. He probably didn't exist.

None of the pieces of this Bainbridge thing fit together. Trying to force them into a coherent picture made my brain hurt.

I went to the bathroom and splashed cool water on my face and neck. As I replenished my sunscreen, I studied my face in the mirror. I felt older, but it didn't show. Shouldn't there at least be a new line on my forehead?

The water revived me enough to get some work done. I turned on both computers and noticed a light blinking on the answering machine at the front desk. Carson Caine's secretary had left a message saying he would be at the bank all day, if I wanted to come by with his proofs.

Double-checking the images, making copies in different sizes, and burning CDs calmed my frazzled mind. Laughter might be the best medicine, but work was the best therapy. By the time I finished, I realized I could kill two birds with one disk that afternoon. There were two more names on my *Old Flames* list: Carson Caine and Sid Matslar. I could to talk to them and try to get a sense of whether either of them had been having an affair with Diana, whether sexual or financial.

I had a good excuse to talk to Carson. Maybe I could happen to pass by Sid's office and then happen to stop in and ask him a bunch of intrusive questions. At this point, I was willing to make a pretty big fool of myself.

The original Caine Bank building was the same vintage as my studio and catty-corner across the street. It didn't hold a bank anymore, though. A defunct title company still owned it, but *For Sale* signs adorned the plywood over the windows.

The new Caine State Bank and Trust was a generic 80's concrete and glass box at the corner of Pecan Street and Highway 88, complete with parking lot and drive-through ATM. Inside, customers were cocooned in soothing beiges and browns, with dull orange furniture squatting on the vinyl floors and generic bluebonnet paintings hanging on the walls.

The gal at the information desk made a quick call and directed me upstairs. I stepped off the elevator into a carpeted maze of beige walls. Having gone to Big State U, I knew how to navigate this sort of terrain and quickly found my way to the executive suite. The secretary greeted me with a smile and waved me toward the open door to Carson's office.

I walked into a world of color. Muted colors, mostly, but still a surprise after all that beige. Two walls of tinted glass overlooked the town. An enormous rug in Cubist rectangles of pewter, plum, and brown covered half the floor. A sleek curve of polished blond wood served as a desk, with a round extension at one end for conferencing. The surface was bare except for an open laptop, a photograph of a pencil-thin woman with two well-groomed children, and a perpetual motion toy in the shape of the solar system. Other high-tech toys stood between fat folders on the light oak bookshelves. The interior walls exhibited a few striking prints in an Abstract Expressionist style.

If the Jetsons made a raid on the Museum of Modern Art, this was what you'd get.

"I love your office!"

Carson rose from his ergonomic chair to shake my hand. "Thanks, but I'd trade you in a heartbeat. I have fantasies about restoring the old bank, at least for executive offices, but it isn't practical. So I go overboard with the modern to compensate."

"This is better. It's unexpected, which makes it more fun."

"I think it helps project an image of The Man of the Future. That's my campaign theme: 'Taking the long view for Long County.'"

"Catchy. And speaking of images—" I got out his CDs and he popped one into the laptop, sliding the computer onto the conference bulb so we could both see.

"Let's have a look." He started clicking through the thumbnails. "Oh, now, this one's perfect!" He tilted his head and leaned back in his chair to study it. "It makes me look a little older, don't you think? I'm a good bit younger than my opponent, which is not an asset."

"It looks great. You look mature, yet youthful; energetic, yet responsible..." He shot me a sidelong look and we both laughed. "Okay, I have no idea what a county commissioner should look like. What do they do, anyway?"

"It's an important job in a rural county, Penny. The Commissioner's Court sets property taxes, funds fire and ambulance services, reviews subdivision and wastewater plans, oversees road development. I'm running because I think we need some new ideas in this county. Agriculture is on the decline in central Texas."

"Global warming, right?"

"Partly, perhaps, but there are other factors. Whatever the cause, the result is that it's getting harder and harder for a family to make it on ranching alone. Tourism is booming in the Hill Country, but it's hard for the individual rancher to take advantage of that. The county could do more to promote the development of a tourism infrastructure."

I was impressed by his clarity and by his jazzy office. "You've got my vote."

"Well, that makes two. Three, if I can persuade my wife." We laughed again. It felt good. I needed a chuckle and a dose of optimism. I liked the long view.

Carson ended his laugh with a sigh and his face grew serious. "That's why this whole business about Roger Bainbridge is so bad. Apart from the tragedy of a man's death, of course. That project of Ty's is exactly what this county needs. He's got vision, along with the skills and the resources to make things happen."

"It will happen. You'll see." Saying it out loud helped me believe it. "Ty is innocent and sooner or later, they're going to find the real culprit."

"Let's hope you're right." He clicked open another picture, looked at it, and then turned back to me. "Any progress on his case?"

"Not really. Actually, things look pretty grim at the moment. He didn't get bail, you know."

"I heard."

"They still haven't found Roger's car. That could help us."

"Must be full of forensic evidence." He gave me an encouraging smile, like you'd give a kid with no talent who insisted on staying in the game. "Let's keep our fingers crossed."

"It has to be someone who knows the area pretty well." If I could get him talking about the old days, he might drop some useful clue. "Y'all's old gang used to play up on Mt. Keno, didn't you?"

Carson gave me a knowing look, but chuckled to take the sting out. "Indeed we did. Rangers vs. Banditos was my favorite." He put one palm on his chest and held up the other in the Boy Scout sign. "I did not kill Roger Bainbridge, Penny. Scout's Honor. For the record, on the night he died I was schmoozing a potential campaign contributor at the Riverhill Country Club in Kerrville. I must confess I drank a little too much of a very nice

Cabernet and ended up spending the night at the club." He hesitated, then gave a slight shrug. "I hate to speak ill of the dead, but Bainbridge was getting to be a problem. I had the idea that if he had some competition—someone smarter and more sensitive to local concerns—he might move on to some other county."

"That might have worked," I said. "Roger did seem like a shortcut kind of a guy. And I'm sorry to be so nosy. I didn't mean to—"

"Of course you did. It's common sense to consider anyone familiar with the Hawkins' ranch. I'm surprised the sheriff isn't double-checking along those lines. But you know, Penny, that old gang broke up when we graduated from high school. We all went our separate ways."

"But people came back. You're all here in Long County again."

"Now that Ty's back, you mean." He flipped his left hand in a so-what gesture. "Sid and Hank have been here all along. I was bi-municipal, you might say, between here and Dallas, until my grandfather died. My kids have spent every summer on the ranch since they were born. Both Sid and Hank work for me, so naturally we see each other on an almost daily basis. But it's not like we get together and play poker every Thursday night. Sid's got his family; I've got mine. Hank's got his hunting buddies and his Hat Trick girls." He shook his head at me. "I'm sorry, but you're on the wrong track. Not that I blame you for trying."

"I refuse to believe Ty did it."

"That's the spirit!" He gave me that look adults give teenagers when they know better, but don't want to squelch your youthful enthusiasm. "Have you talked to his lawyer?"

"I have."

"What's her plan? I hear she's well-regarded in Austin legal circles."

I hadn't heard that, but then who would I hear it from? I liked the sound of it, anyway. "She thinks we can generate a reasonable doubt. All we need is one good alternative suspect."

Carson's smile faded. "You're not thinking about Dare Thompson, I hope."

I gave him a sheepish grin. "He's the obvious first choice. He has an alibi. He was supposedly at a training seminar in Georgia. Ty's lawyer's going to follow that up."

"Well, I would hate to learn that one our law officers had committed such a terrible crime, but no stone should be left unturned. This is the legal system in action."

We contemplated that fact in silence for moment. Our meeting had plainly run its course, but I decided to take my last shot. "The thing is, Carson, I heard a rumor that Sid Matslar might be involved in an affair, and I sort of wondered if it might have been—"

"Sid and Diana? That's your theory?" Carson broke into a broad smile that would've looked great on his campaign posters. "Ty is doomed. Have you met Sid?"

"Not yet."

He stood up. "Well, let's go introduce you."

As we passed through the anteroom, Carson asked his secretary to cut a check for the portraits. We walked down the beige corridor to another office, about half the size of Carson's, with only one tall window at the back. No chrome toys or artworks livened up this doleful nook. It had been furnished from the same bland catalog as the lobby. A long desk covered by a computer and stacks of file folders filled most of the space.

"Hey, Sid, I'd like to introduce you to someone." Carson ushered me through the door.

A ramshackle bear of a man waddled forward to shake my hand. Now I understood why everyone was so certain Diana had not been having a secret affair with Sid Matslar. He was tall, which was good, but he was also wide; one might say, double-wide. His blue slacks and wrinkled white shirt barely contained his belly, even with the help of red suspenders. He sported a red bow tie, perhaps in an effort to look like an old-fashioned Southern banker. His oversized nose supported thick black nerd glasses.

He looked like a movie star: Woody Allen meets Orson Welles with a dash of Walter Matthau.

Carson smiled affably. "Penny, meet Sid Matslar. Sid, this is Penelope Trigg, Lost Hat's newest entrepreneur."

His fleshy grasp encased my hand briefly. "I've been meaning to get over to see what you've done with your studio. I hear it's quite a transformation."

I recovered my manners. "It is different."

The poor guy was such a shambles, his socks didn't even match.

Carson said, "Penny wants to know what you were doing on the night Roger Bainbridge died." He turned to me as if consulting on the details. "Last Wednesday, wasn't it? She has a theory that it was one of us guys from the old gang."

He was having a little too much fun with this. I took the hint.

Sid, caught totally by surprise, goggled, his mouth opening in a speechless O. He closed it and opened it again once or twice before he managed to get the motor running again. "Roger Bainbridge? Where did I—What was the question?"

I could identify genuine bewilderment when I saw it. This was not the guy.

Carson patted Sid on the shoulder. "It's just a theory and not a very good one. Penny has evidently heard some of the rumors circulating about your divorce and thought you might have been having a secret affair with Diana that went sour."

"Oh. Wow." Sid smiled at me, sadly, shaking his head. "That might have impressed my wife, actually."

"I'm sorry," I said. "It was stupid. I'm just..."

"She's turning over every stone," Carson said. "Trying to help old Ty."

"Sure. I wish I could help too." Sid scratched the back of his neck. "Last Wednesday you say?" He maneuvered his way back into the nest behind the desk, where he pondered the clutter, then shifted a stack of folders to unearth a diary. He flipped back to the previous week, frowning at the pages. "I probably worked late. I usually do, these days. Okay, here it is. Wednesday I was working on the Jameson project."

Carson asked, "How's that going?"

"Good. Good. We're almost there. Looks like we'll be closing on Friday."

"Excellent," Carson said.

Sid looked up at me. "After work, I would have gone home. I don't suppose that's much help to you." He looked mournful, as though he wished he could tell me he was guilty, but knew no one would believe him.

"That's okay." I had come prepared to make a fool of myself and I had succeeded. "I'm sorry to be so nosy."

"It's quite all right, Penny. It's such terrible thing, nobody can think straight." Sid shook his large head. "I don't suppose many people here will miss Bainbridge, but his death is still a tragedy. And for Ty to be in jail? I can't wrap my mind around it."

"None of us can," Carson said.

Sid heaved a sigh. "I had high hopes for that spa project. It would be such a great stimulus for the local economy."

"It'll happen," I said. "You'll see." I had one last question. "Did Diana ever talk to you about that project? About a mortgage or something for her half?"

"She did, actually." Sid flipped over another page on his diary. "A couple of weeks ago. I took her through the basics of equity loans, though I'm not sure she fully understood her options. She didn't know what she wanted, really." He glanced up at Carson again. "I had planned to give Ty a call, with Diana's permission, of course. We'd love to have a role in that project."

"Wouldn't we, though?" Carson smiled all around. "Maybe we still will. Let's set up a meeting with Ty when his avenging angel here gets him out of jail."

Enough, already! I could have sunk right through the beige carpet. "Look, Mr. Matslar—"

"Please, call me Sid."

"I really am sorry. I didn't mean to suggest that you had anything to do with any of this. I'm grasping at straws here."

"I'd do the same in your shoes." He walked us to the door and handed me a card. "And listen, if you ever need a small business loan to tide you over a rough patch or expand your operation, we have lots of expertise with businesses that have seasonal ebbs and flows like yours. Come on by and talk to me sometime. I'll fix you up with a great deal."

Chapter 16

Wednesday at eleven o'clock, I gathered my courage and optimism, what little I had left of both, and hiked on over to the Law Enforcement Center to visit Ty. I'd spent most of yesterday afternoon choosing and tweaking photographs to show him, but the guard wouldn't let me bring anything in. Doubtless he feared Ty would be so inflamed by the beauty of the great outdoors, he would make a break for it by holding a print to the guard's throat.

Paper cuts can be very painful, you know.

Ty looked puffy-eyed, like a man spending a lot of time sleeping. "Thanks for coming, Penny. The days get pretty long in here."

"No license plates to make? No cotton to chop?"

"I wish. I could use the exercise."

"I've got some great pictures to show you next week, when you get out."

That earned me a rueful grin. "That's optimism, isn't it? I vaguely remember what that feels like. You must have good news."

"Not exactly. I have been meeting new people, though. Meeting them and insulting them and thereby making a great fool of myself."

I told him about my visit to the bank and about wrecking Tillie's marriage. Ty assured me that they'd work things out and laughed at the idea of Sid as a suspect. He liked taking the role of Comforter and Advisor; it suited him so much better than Wrongfully Accused and Powerless Victim.

He studied my face for a long while in silence, as though he planned to paint it from memory. "Don't give up on me, Penny."

"I won't."

"And don't give up on my project either. Get out there and shoot the southeast pasture, like we planned. We need to document that zone before I get the cedar cleared."

"I'm on it." If the sheriff's department would let me back out there. Heck with it. I'd go anyway. Ty needed to know his life could still move forward.

I worked the conversation around to the gossip at DeGroot's. "The new Internet guy, Peter Schmidzinsky, sounded absolutely positive those emails came from Diana's account, from within your Lazy H domain, if that's the right way to put it."

"I understand you." He shrugged. "It's no surprise that Diana's mail came from her account. Where else would it come from?"

"Not just Diana's—the ones from Roger too."

That put a wrinkle in his forehead. "They think Diana sent those? That makes no sense. They were signed 'Roger,' with his business links in the signature."

"Not from her, like she wrote them. Schmidzinsky said they originated from her account. They were spooked."

"Spoofed?"

"That's it!"

"That makes even less sense, Penny. What's the alleged point of this?"

"One idea is that Diana sent them, to make it look like Roger was still alive."

"No." Ty had started his head at the word 'Diana.' "That's not within her scope."

"Is it hard?"

"Not for me or for someone like your brother, but for someone like Diana or you, who doesn't pay attention to how things work—"

"Hey!"

"Computer things, darlin'. No slight intended. You could do it, but you'd need guidance. There's probably a step-by-step out there somewhere, but it's definitely not her style." He thought about it for a moment. "Hacking Diana's account would be a piece of cake for anyone who knows her. Her login is 'lady_di'—same as her license plates—and her password is probably 'malibu.' That was her horse, growing up. She loved that animal more than she loved me and Dad. She rode him in competitions all over the county in high school, so pretty much everyone knows the name."

"That should help widen the pool." And make it deeper around Ty's ankles.

"Widen the pool," he muttered, catching my untrusting vibe. His brown eyes narrowed. "You think Diana did this, don't you? And for some bizarre reason she's trying to set me up."

"Not exactly." I drew in a breath and let it out in a rush. "Do you remember the movie *Thelma and Louise?*"

He listened patiently while I laid out the alternatives, only rolling his eyes a few times and managing to suppress most of the snorts and guffaws. He grasped immediately that we had cast him as the Louise.

When I finished, he ran both hands through his hair and frowned at the table for a moment. Then he said, "Well, your hearts are the right place. But that theory has holes a mile wide. In the first place, Roger wasn't shot."

"That's a detail." I made a big circle with my flat palm. "Look at the big picture. The Louise killed the cowboy to protect the Thelma. Then together they evaded the authorities. That's the main point of connection."

"Also nobody went to jail, as I recall. They drove off a cliff, didn't they? Which—" He stabbed a long finger at me. "Diana would never do, at least not in her custom pink

Mustang. She loves that car almost as much as she loved Malibu."

"Details, Ty! Details!" This man did not understand the concept of essentials.

"And they left the body in the parking lot, didn't they? They didn't lug it up to the highest hill and bury it with an incriminating bracelet around its wrist."

"All right, all right." I gave up. "Set the movie aside. The main idea is that Roger tried to rape Diana and either you or she punched his lights out and then the two of you buried him and came up with the whole scheme to cover things up and confuse the issue until she gets out of the country and you get off on reasonable doubt."

A muscle in his jaw pulsed at the words 'rape Diana.' The whole jawline had squared up by the end of my little speech, and his brown eyes had gone flat.

"You got one part right," he said. "If that son of a bitch had ever tried to hurt my baby sister, I would've punched his lights out. But that's where the similarities end. If he had cracked his skull, I would've called 911 on the spot. Same deal if I came home and found Diana standing over his body. I'd get her the best lawyers in the country and stick with her every step of the way, but I would not help her cover up a death. No way, Penny. Never in a million years. You should know me better than that by now."

"I do," I said, cheeks burning. "I honestly, honestly do. It's just, you know, in the interest of exploring all the possibilities. You are really protective of her and if you found her in mid-burial, for example, with the mess already made…"

"No way. None whatsoever." He gave a cold look that made me feel like I'd blown it badly; broken something valuable. I hadn't trusted him all the way and I should have.

He blinked and looked away for a minute. I caught a glimmer of moisture in his eyes, but he blinked again before he looked back at me. "Those spoofed emails prove that someone is trying to frame me. Why, I have no idea. I don't have any enemies, that I know of. But hey, if we're using movies to solve this case, let me throw another one out there. I don't see any resemblance between me and Susan Sarandon, but this past week I have been feeling a lot like Cary Grant in *North by Northwest.*"

"Ooh, good one," I said. "I can see it. Except weren't the bad guys chasing Cary Grant because they thought he was a spy or something?" I summoned up a memory of that plot. "They were trying to kill him, not frame him."

"Details, Penny! Details!" Ty's eyes glittered. "Screw Louise. You should be looking for James Mason."

Chapter 17

It had been years since I'd seen *North by Northwest*. The details were hazy, but the main story was unforgettable: an innocent man being wrongfully persecuted. I silently vowed to stop suspecting Ty, although I still thought Dare or someone could have pulled a Louise out there that night. I couldn't believe Long County had anyone as persistent and devious as James Mason's character. You'd have to be awfully damn cold.

I couldn't do much to patch things up with Ty, not while he remained behind bars. An hour a day of conversation with no touching wouldn't do the trick. But I could get back to work on the project and thereby demonstrate my faith in our mutual future. The man wanted the southeast pasture documented and by golly, that was what he would get. I wouldn't need to go into the house or up on Mt. Keno, so I wouldn't be crossing any crime scene boundaries.

I picked up Jake and went home to change into my outdoor gear and pack some sandwiches. Thinking twice, I grabbed a couple of towels. We would treat our shaggy selves to a swim in the springs after the work was done.

I parked under an old pecan tree near the gate on the western side of the pasture. My plan was to take macro shots of as many different plants as I could find, especially non-native species, and then do a series of mid-range photos to show the overall condition of the field.

I got lost in photography for a couple of hours, working my way from west to east across the pasture, playing with filters and lenses. I have a second tripod for a portable reflector that helps cut the glare when I'm working in full sun.

I reached the northeast corner of the pasture where I'd climbed over the fence on Sunday. I would not trespass again if a whole herd of kudus in pink tutus leapt out and danced the hokey-pokey right there in the road. But the juncture of the fences and the cliff and the road on the other side made good establishing frames for my context studies, so I switched to a wide-angle lens and focused in that direction.

I caught a flash of red under the oak woods inside the curve of the road. Not a kudu in a tutu; not unless there was something very peculiar in my water bottle. Not wildflowers either; not with that deep tropical hue. I zoomed in on it and got off a couple of shots when I heard Jake bark somewhere behind me to the north.

I straightened up, my back complaining about being bent over the tripod for too long. Off to the north, I caught sight of a man in a white straw hat jogging through the trees. One blink and he was gone.

Freaky. Who would be out here? Gooseflesh rose on the back of my neck and I shivered. Then I scolded myself for the mini-drama. A cloud had passed over the sun and lifted a little breeze. My sunbaked skin was so sweaty, even a shadow would feel cool.

"Jake!" I hollered. "Jako!" I turned in a circle, trying to spot a brown dog. Or a white straw hat.

I heard an indignant grunt at the end of the pasture that sounded nothing like a dog. I turned and saw Blackberry, Ben Jernigan Senior's Angus bull, standing inside the gate, looking back over his shoulder.

Another illusion? If I blinked, maybe he'd go away. I'd had my eye pressed to a viewfinder for too long and now my long-distance vision was playing tricks on me. I had animals on the brain, what with the kudus and my feral hog encounter.

Flash Memory

I closed my eyes and slowly opened them again.

Blackberry, large as life, stared right at me. The sun glinted off his short horns. He looked pretty damn substantial for a hallucination. He started moving in my direction; not fast, but definitely into my pasture, not out through the open gate.

I took two seconds to reconnoiter. The tripod with my camera attached stood a couple of feet from a broad prickly pear cactus. Blackberry stood between me and the gate. The nearest fence stood about a hundred yards away.

Florence Griffith Joyner ran a hundred meters in ten point five seconds. I figured more like seventeen for me over grass in my lightweight hiking boots. I didn't want to leave my camera, but I had been warned more than once to avoid the livestock.

Sound advice. Would they avoid me?

Trying to guesstimate the distance between the bull and the camera, I accidentally met Blackberry's eyes. Evidently, this was a major faux pas in bull society, because he snorted and glared at me with a disapproving expression.

The camera could wait. I needed to get my body out of that pasture. Should I walk casually, like a cowgirl going about her normal cowgirl business, or should I give FloJo a run for the record?

I took a few slow steps toward the nearest fence. Blackberry lowered his head and pawed the ground with one substantial hoof. It did not look like an invitation to play.

He took a couple of steps, his focus directed at me. His nostrils flared in an alarming manner—alarming in the sense that adrenaline spiked through my system like someone plunged a syringeful straight into my heart.

I ran.

In my panic, I lost sight of the fence for a moment. I needed three pairs of eyes: one to watch the ground for rocks, one to keep me aiming in the right direction, and one to watch Blackberry. I shot a glance over my shoulder and saw him picking up speed, head down, horns aimed and ready to gore.

My feet would have to look out for themselves. I set my sights on the fence and sprinted for all I was worth. The fence was four feet high; too high to hurdle. Could I vault a barbed wire fence or would the wire bend too much?

I veered sharply to the left, aiming for the T-juncture. I ran straight at it, got both hands on the top and bore down, flinging my legs to the side as high as I could, swinging them forward over the fence. I heard my pants rip and felt a burning pain along my thigh, but I cleared the wire. I landed a couple of feet beyond the fence, stumbled, and fell, rolling onto the caliche road.

I scrambled up and looked back. Blackberry skidded to a stop at the fence, puffing and snorting and shaking his big black head. If he'd struck that fence full on, he would have knocked it down, but I guess habit kept him off it.

Sing praise to the Goddess of Operant Conditioning!

I bent double, hands on my knees, breathing hard. I kept half an eye on Blackberry, careful not to look straight at him again. He watched me too. I coaxed my wobbly knees into a walk, glad to have a fence between me and certain destruction, but feeling a powerful need for more distance as well. Blackberry moved in more or less the same direction; idly, except for the occasional glance at me. Heaven knew he wouldn't find any grass in that degraded field to distract him.

How the hell had he gotten out of his pasture? And why had he wandered into mine?

I had left the gate open, which meant he could get out again and come after me if he wanted to. I should probably go around and close it, but not with Old Blackberry standing there waiting for me.

Flash Memory

I glanced to my left and saw the patch of red I'd been focusing on. Definitely not flowers. A shiny expanse of metal. Part of my mind thought, *Huh, that must be Roger's car*, but most of it still played the Blackberry Stampede episode over and over. My puny brain didn't have room for new ideas at that moment.

The ranch road terminated in a padlocked gate. I climbed over it and turned right onto the county road. Blackberry wandered back toward the center of the pasture. I let out a whoosh of air and settled into a walking pace.

Ben Senior must have neglected to close the bull's gate properly. Once out, Blackberry had ambled aimlessly downhill. That had to be it. No human being would deliberately put that bull into the field where I was working.

I'd done track in high school and had run almost daily ever since. If I hadn't been in such good shape or able to put on speed when I needed it, I could have been killed or maimed. Thinking about the impact of those horns and hooves on my tender flesh set my heart racing again, so I willed the images away and let anger rise in their place.

I'd had to leave several thousand dollars' worth of photography equipment in that pasture, not to mention the flash card with hours of shooting on it. If that damn bull trampled my gear, I'd have him barbecued and sliced into sandwiches! I worked up a satisfying image of Blackberry roasting on a spit over a bed of coals, savoring the details, considering the options for sauce.

Somehow I would have to go back in there to get my equipment. I couldn't leave it out all night. I had to find Jake too. That dang dog always managed to disappear when I had large animal issues.

I'd have to get my phone out of the truck and call somebody, but who? Deputy Penateka? If I called 911, the whole county would hear about my latest caper. More public humiliation. Unfortunately, I needed a bona fide cowboy to come corral that beast so I could rescue my precious gadgets.

I reached the entrance to the Lazy H and walked up toward the house, only to find Ben Jernigan Junior lowering the tailgate on his pickup. He wore a white straw cowboy hat like the one I'd caught a glimpse of through the trees.

The sight of that hat and the bland smile on his face as he raised a hand to wave at me made my temper rise so fast the hair lifted off the top of my head. I covered the distance between us in four long strides and punched him right in the gut.

"You son of a bitch!"

Ben sat down hard on the edge of the tailgate. "Shit, woman! What's come over you?"

"You sneaking, slimy son of a bastard, you let that bull loose in the pasture where I was working!"

"What? Blackberry? He's loose?" Ben stared at me like I'd come unglued. He was not wrong.

"I saw you. You were up there, you asshole, in the woods behind the pasture, right before Blackberry came after me."

It made sense; horrible, sickening sense. I must have scared Ben the other day when I asked him about Diana and he took the opportunity to get me off his trail when he caught me alone in that pasture.

God, poor Tillie! Leftover adrenaline fueled my righteous wrath. "I guessed right, didn't I? About you and Diana. So you set that bull on me to shut me up."

"Diana!" Ben's face paled. "What the hell are you babbling about?" He slid to his feet and eased around the tailgate, putting it between him and me. "No way, Penny! I just got here!"

"Prove it!" I banged my hand on the tailgate, hard. It made a big noise, which pleased me. I banged it again for good measure.

Ben flinched and backed up another step. He looked like he was afraid I might spring forward and bite him. I bared my teeth at him and he flinched again, backing up around to the front of his truck.

His hand touched the hood and he stopped. "Hey. Okay. I got it. Look, my truck's still hot. You can feel it."

I stopped snarling and narrowed my eyes at him. I walked around and put my hands on the hood. He scooted around to the far side, all the way back to the tailgate, watching me.

It was hot all right. Then I looked up. "You parked in the sun, you nimrod! It'd be hot no matter what!" But I caught a whiff of lingering engine smell. He could've driven up to the pasture and made it back ahead of me, but I would have heard the truck grinding on the caliche road. Also, he looked cool, with no sweat sagging his T-shirt, like a man who'd just climbed out of an air-conditioned vehicle.

Ben hadn't done it.

All the fire went out of me in a rush, leaving shame in its wake. "You're right; it couldn't have been you. I'm sorry."

A shaky grin curved on his round face. He swiped his hand through his hair, knocking his hat off. He caught it and settled it back on his head. "That's okay. That is Oh-kay."

He still seemed a little afraid of me, which took the edge off my embarrassment. I kind of liked being the scarer rather than the scaree.

He watched me warily for a minute, then he shrugged and raised his tailgate, latching the sides. "I gotta get that bull squared away."

"I'm coming with you. My camera and stuff are still out in that pasture."

"The Canon? You left that out there?" I glared at him and he said, "Whatever. I'll get it for you. Blackberry's used to me. He's not mean, you know. He just doesn't like strangers in his territory."

"He was in *my* territory. And I still think somebody put him there."

Ben shrugged. "Whatever." His expression said, *Don't argue with the crazy woman.*

He opened his door and got in. I got in next to him, and closed my door, but I kept my hand on the handle.

He scowled and reached behind me. I squeezed up against the door and he said, "Jesus, Penny!" He pulled out a ragged towel and handed it to me. "You're bleeding on my seat cover."

I hadn't even noticed. There was a five-inch tear in my pants leg showing a bloody scratch. "Crap!" I dabbed at it, then looked at the grime on the towel and decided the blood was cleaner. I tucked the towel under my leg to protect the seat. Now I'd have to get a tetanus shot on top of everything else.

We drove back up to the pasture. I sat in the truck while Ben went in, shutting the gate behind him, and gathered up my equipment. He walked out of sight for a few minutes and I caught no sign of Blackberry.

Ben came back out and closed the gate securely. He handed my camera through the window, which I cradled in my lap while I took the bag and the tripod from him. I put the camera back in its case and tucked it away safely in the bag.

"Isn't he in there?" I had a moment of total weirdness. What if I'd imagined the whole thing? No bull, no guy in a straw hat, just crazy Penny having a big pink fit out here all by her lonesome.

"He's there." Ben swung back into his seat and started the engine. "Standing looking off toward the 3C, waiting for you to come back and play with him." He started to chuckle, but cut it off when he looked at my face. "All right, I know, it's not funny. It must have been hellacious.

And I'll tell you something. From where that camera was to the nearest fence—you must be hell on wheels."

"All State Girls' Champion, hurdles." We chewed on that interesting statistic in silence for a moment. Then I relented. "Thanks for getting my stuff."

He waved it off. "Let's go see how he got out."

"Wait." Poor Jakey! I'd forgotten all about him. "I need to find Jake. He ran off right before I saw that—before I thought I saw that guy in the hat."

"Ty's dog?" Ben leaned out the window and put his fingers between his teeth, letting out a whistle so loud every dog in Long County must have heard it. Jake came streaking out of the woods. He circled the truck, huffing like a steam engine. I opened my door and he jumped in, squashing me comfortingly.

"Jako!" Tears stung my eyes and I buried my face in his fur.

We drove north and west to the pasture where Blackberry normally lived. The gate hung wide open. Ben pulled up in front of it and jumped out. I got out too this time.

Ben slid the latch on the gate back and the thing fell off into his hand. "What the hell?"

I studied the dirt around the post and sure enough, there were two screws lying in a clump of grass. I pointed them out to Ben.

He growled under his breath. "Looks like my dad's getting sloppy. He should've fixed that right off, instead of letting it get this bad."

He got some tools out of the box on his truck and repaired the latch. We closed the gate, now that the bull was gone, and drove back down to my truck. I moved my gear and my dog into the Hulk, hopped in, and buckled up. I'd had enough danger for one day.

Ben put a hand on the edge of the open window. "Look, Penny. I'm real sorry about what happened. But you can see it was an accident, right? The old man needs help out here. He oughta hire somebody to pitch in a few hours a week, but he's kinda stubborn."

"Why can't you help him?"

"I got my job. Full time job. And I'm studying for a real estate license so I can go into business with Tillie's Uncle Ed. If I still have in-laws, after what you did."

"Hey! I didn't put the words in your mouth. You got yourself into trouble there, pal."

"Well, you stirred things up."

"Things are already stirred up, Ben, in case you hadn't noticed. A man has been killed and somehow Diana is involved, probably along with somebody who loves her. If you're hiding something, you'd better come clean. Because all the secrets are going to come out before this thing is over."

Ben's eyes narrowed and he pursed his lips, like he was sucking on a sour candy—or a bitter secret. Did he have the courage to spit it out?

Nope. He said, "Someone who loves her, huh? You mean, like a brother?" He tipped his hat and went back to his own truck.

I stopped at the clinic on Highway 331 for a tetanus shot on the way home. It hurt and put a dent in my checking account to boot. They told me I should have gotten one the day I started working on the ranch, even to do photography, and that I should be able to deduct it as a business expense. Even so, I would have to keep that job to cover the costs of doing the job.

They recommended a warm bath to soothe the wound, instructions I would follow with pleasure. I was up to my chin in lavender bubbles, letting my muscles relax and my thoughts unravel, when I suddenly remembered that flash of red in the brush beside the road.

"Great balls of fire! Roger's car!"

Chapter 18

Evenings are long at the end of June. The sun finally drops below the hills around seven-thirty, drawing off the blanket of heat and brightness that presses on the landscape all afternoon. As the day wanes, everyone perks up, people and animals included. Breezes stir under the trees and the air takes on that indefinable golden haze that induces a sense of bliss when you're sitting on your patio with a cold drink and an old friend.

I couldn't appreciate the glow period tonight. The Mexican takeout I'd picked up on my way home from the clinic did a mambo in my gut as I drove back out to the county road along the Lazy H and 3C ranches. What would they find in his car? Would finding it so close to Mt. Keno help or hurt Ty?

I parked behind a county car and met Penateka standing near the gate to the 3C. We had to wait for the owner to come unlock it, to do everything legal and by the book.

Another county car rolled up and parked on the opposite side of the road. Dare got out and crossed the road, hitching up his pants as he walked. Penateka tilted his head, like he was about to say, *No, sir*, but he held his peace. Dare met his eyes and said, "I'm only here to observe, Rob. I gotta know."

Penateka gave him a short nod. I frowned to show my disapproval, but they ignored me. Now Dare could put his fat fingers on everything they found and muddy up the evidence.

Another car pulled up and parked. This time the sheriff and Deputy Freshwater emerged and crossed the road to join us. Sheriff Hopper frowned at me. "I thought we were pretty clear about the trespassing, Penny."

"I wasn't trespassing, sir." The sheriff cocked an eyebrow at me. "Okay, *technically*, it might be construed as trespassing, but there were circumstances." I told them about Blackberry and my run for glory, leaving out the part about the disappearing guy in the straw hat.

"You must be one quick cookie." He looked more concerned than aggravated now.

"All State Girls' Champion, hurdles, two years in a row."

He tucked his chin, impressed. The other guys made admiring sounds.

What is it about men and sports? I gained a few points on their credibility scale just for being faster than a half dozen other teenage girls over a decade ago.

What the heck. If it saved me another lecture on respecting the rules, I'd take it.

"Looks like Ben Senior's getting too old to keep up with things on his own," the sheriff said. "We'll have to get a caretaker out here to mind the fences while Hawkins—" He broke off. He and Dare both shot me worried glances, and then they all turned together to study the gate.

Is in prison, he'd been about to say. I heard the murmur of the deputies' voices behind me, as though they were far away and under water. They seemed to be taking this new find as evidence against him already.

A smoke gray Land Rover with tinted windows and a 3C logo on the doors stopped in front of the gate. Carson got out with a large ring of keys in his hand. He looked tired, like he'd had enough troublesome revelations. I felt the same way.

"Sorry it took me so long. I had to ask Skip which key to use. We don't use this gate much." He thumbed through the keys, selected a small steel one, and clicked open the lock. "It's not as sticky as I would've expected."

"Who has keys to this gate?" Sheriff Hopper asked.

"Well," Carson said, "there's this ring hangs in the office. Hank has a key, I believe. He uses that old building up there to store deer corn and other hunting supplies."

"Nobody else? Former employees? Neighbors?"

"Neighbors!" Carson snapped his fingers. "Now that you mention it, I believe the Hawkins have a key, or they used to. In case one of their animals got through the fence somewhere, or one of ours got onto their spread. You know, emergency access."

The sheriff glanced at me briefly as he turned to his deputy. "Freshwater, whyn't you trot over there and have a look around. Mr. Caine, could we borrow that key?"

Carson worked it free of the crowded ring and handed it over after a moment of hesitation. "At the risk of sounding argumentative, Sheriff, don't you need a warrant to search Ty's property?"

"Since we don't yet know where Bainbridge was killed, the whole of the Lazy H is considered a crime scene. So no, sir, we do not." The sheriff grinned. "But you're right to ask. We do things by the book in Long County."

Freshwater took the key, got back in his vehicle, drove a few yards, and turned in to the Lazy H entrance. I had the sinking feeling he would find that key hanging on a nail in a shed somewhere.

"What happens if he finds it?" I asked. "Having a key doesn't prove Ty's the one that used it."

"One step at a time, Penny." Sheriff Hopper smiled at me in a kindly way that raised the fine hairs on the back of my neck. That advice only made sense when you knew where you were going.

Another sheriff's department SUV pulled up and two guys in uniforms got out, lugging a couple of cases. The crime scene team had arrived. "Let's get busy," the sheriff said.

We all trooped up the road, the sheriff leading, Carson and me trailing behind. Neither of us had any further contribution to make, but we felt we had a moral right to watch. Besides, we were curious and they hadn't told us to go away.

We walked down the road in silence to the curve under Stone House Hill. And there it was, a shiny expanse of red metal, glinting darkly in the lowering light. Without the run-for-your-life adrenaline blurring my vision, I could clearly see the sheen of window glass.

The SUV lay nose down in a shallow gully under the scrub oaks, close to a towering cliff face of limestone boulders blocking the view from the county road. Cut branches had been spread around the sides and back in an effort to conceal it, but some of them had slipped, toppled by animals or the wind. The rear third of the passenger side was now plainly visible from the ranch road and the pasture where I'd been working.

Dare shook his head, anger hardening his glare. "Y'all should've seen that when you searched this side of the Hawkins place."

"Must've been better covered back then," Penateka said, unruffled.

Dare paced a little way around the bend in the road, sighting in every direction from where the car lay, plainly intending to press his point. Penateka ignored him. He stepped over to the place where the car had gone off the road and stood with his hands on his trim hips, studying the scene. He'd probably been taught to review the general layout, establishing the context, before diving into the details.

Same as a nature photographer.

Carson and I took up positions at a discreet distance. His light brown eyes shone gold in the evening light. "I kept thinking they'd find the car under a highway in San Antonio or Dallas and the guy'd turn out to be some hot-headed husband Bainbridge had…" He cut that off with a sigh. "Now I don't know what to think."

"I don't either." But I did know. I just didn't want to be thinking it.

They would find the gate key in Ty's shed and draw a straight line from it to this car, adding another strike against Ty. He'd be in jail until his trial now. No way would the judge let him out at the preliminary hearing. Even if Courtney could make a good case for involuntary manslaughter, the jury would be sickened by the sneaky covering-up.

I felt a little sick myself.

The sheriff's phone buzzed. He swiped the screen and said, "Yep. Uh-huh. Good work. Come on back." He put the phone back in his pants pocket and said, "Freshwater found the key, all right. And a small axe with leaf matter still stuck to the blade. He's bagged both items to print back at the station."

Dare came back to stand between the sheriff and us civilians. He pointed his thumb at the sky. "The roof is clearly visible. If we'd had a helicopter, we'd've found it Day One."

The sheriff smiled. "Try selling that to the commissioners." He shot a wry glance at Carson, who made a who-me grimace.

"I hope this doesn't happen often enough to justify that kind of expense." Carson's voice was light, but tension around his eyes betrayed anger. I couldn't blame him. Somebody had made free with his property to cover up an ugly death. Somebody he'd grown up with. Somebody he'd trusted.

Somebody I'd trusted too. Hard as I tried to tell myself other stories, my faith crumbled a little with each new discovery.

One of the crime scene guys opened a case, rummaged around in it, and said, "Dang it, Dave, where's the camera?" The other guy went over and rummaged through the other case, both bickering all the while in low voices they must have thought we couldn't hear.

Penateka watched them with his tongue poked into his cheek. Then he turned to me and jerked his chin at the camera around my neck. I'd brought it just in case. "You up for it?"

I nodded and moved out of the observer zone and into the crime scene. We fell easily into our old routine. Penateka pointed at what he wanted and I snapped two or three shots from slightly different angles. The other guys lifted the branches away, setting them in a neat stack on the other side of the road. The sheriff, Dare, and Carson stood together and watched.

The passenger's side was free of brush, since it would only be visible to someone crazy enough to scramble down the pile of boulders. Nobody ever would. There might as well be a sign hanging over it saying, "Here There Be Rattlesnakes." Apparently snakes are not curious creatures, because they stayed inside their snake holes, to my huge relief.

We started with an overview, working around the car, opening each door and assessing the contents we could see. Penateka opened the passenger side front door with his gloved hand and gave a low whistle at the tan leather upholstery. The stuff looked expensive, even in the glare of my flash. The darker tan carpet still showed the stripes of a vacuum cleaner. A Bigfoot air freshener hung from the mirror, but its pine scent failed to mask the stink of rotten organic matter.

Penateka and I glanced at each other. "Might as well get the worst over with."

We went around to the back. Penateka lifted the rear door and gave a little grunt. Everyone moved closer to observe the rumpled towel, once white, but now heavily streaked with red, and the dark stain soaked into the carpet.

Otherwise, the cargo zone was empty; plenty of room for a man with his knees folded up to his chest.

I took a few pictures, letting the flash blind me. Then Penateka directed the crime scene guys to bag the towel and the carpet and beckoned me to do the rest of the car.

He opened the back door, took a long look, and then stood back. I snapped pictures of a black plastic file box, a black hanging clothes bag, and a brown leather briefcase. Then I took a nice photograph of a pair of fancy-looking cowboy boots sitting on the floor behind the driver's seat.

Penateka picked up one of them, holding it by the heel so I could get a good shot. "Guess we found that missing footwear."

"Why would anyone steal his boots?"

"You don't bury boots as fine as these, Ms. Trigg. Genuine alligator. Ten thousand dollars, remember?"

I couldn't begin to fathom that, but I did know one thing. "Ty wouldn't keep those, Detective. No matter how much they're worth. That's more like something Hank Roeder would do."

"Which might be what Hawkins is trying to suggest."

I pressed my lips together. He had a point. "Let's see what's up front."

"One thing first." He motioned away so he could reach in and open the briefcase. "Ha," he said, as he extracted a black cellphone. He swiped a few times, tapped a few times, and then said, "Huh."

He walked past me over to the sheriff's group. "Mr. Caine? Can you verify that this is your number?" He showed Carson the phone without letting him touch it.

"Yes, that's mine."

The sheriff asked. "What'd ya got?"

Penateka showed him the phone. "The last three calls were made to the same number, which Mr. Caine confirms is his." He turned the tiny screen back his way so he could read the data. "The last two were between 10:30 and 12:00

on the night Bainbridge met his death. Each of those lasted only a couple of seconds. The third lasted a couple of minutes and took place at 7:23 p.m."

Everyone turned to Carson, who looked surprised. "Oh, that's right. I do remember that call. Bainbridge wanted to discuss his ridiculous idea for an airstrip again. I'd already turned it down once, but he didn't seem to understand the word 'no.' He wanted to set up a meeting, but frankly, he sounded more than a little drunk and I put him off." He grimaced apologetically at the sheriff. "I'm sorry, Sheriff. I should have remembered that call sooner."

"Easy enough to forget. It couldn't have made much of an impression on you at the time. Do you remember anything about the other two?"

Carson drew in a breath, shaking his head. "No. Sorry again. But if they were that brief, he must have gotten voice mail and hung up. My phone would have been turned off at that hour." He flashed a smile. "My wife has a strict no-work policy during family time. I don't remember noticing those missed calls..." He pulled out his own phone and fiddled with it. "No, I'm sorry. My recent calls only go back to the seventeenth."

Sheriff Hopper said, "It doesn't matter. At least this helps us narrow down the time of death. Had to've been after that last call, unless—" He cut himself off with a quick glance at me.

Carson opened his mouth to say something, but then shook his head and focused on his boots. They were nice boots, a supple brown with fine tooling across the toe. Nothing like Roger's alligator marvels, but still nice.

I understood. Those last calls established the time of death only if Roger had made them. If they'd been made by someone else, meaning the person who had perhaps just finished burying him, they didn't do much narrowing. Roger had left the barbecue place not long after seven.

Under that interpretation, what they mainly did was make sure Carson's phone number stood out bright and clear. Like a big highlighter, underscoring the location of the vehicle. "Look, look," it said. "This here is all the work of Carson Caine."

A loud horn blasted the cavalry charge, making us all jump. "What the devil?" Sheriff Hopper glared at the car.

One of the crime scene techs was half-sitting in the front seat, caught in a guilty cringe with his fingerprint brush poised over the steering wheel. "Sorry, Sheriff," he called, but in half a minute the charge sounded again.

The sheriff folded his arms across his chest. "If you boys can't examine that vehicle without making Tom fools of yourselves, you let me know and I'll find someone who can."

A chorus of meek voices answered, "Yes, sir."

The sheriff returned his attention to the cellphone. "Anything else of interest there?"

"I'll log the rest of the calls from that day when I get back to my desk," Penateka said. "Looks like there's some papers in the passenger seat."

He opened the door and I took some pictures. A manila folder labeled "3C" lay on the smooth leather. Penateka removed the folder, revealing a dark gray arrowhead about three inches long. I took a couple of pictures of it, my heart sinking.

For two seconds, I considered withholding my tidbit of information, but knew it wouldn't help. "That's Ty's, I think. He keeps it in his desk drawer. He told me he found it on Mt. Keno years ago."

"Is that the story now?" Carson's voice held a bitter edge. "In point of fact, I'm the one that found it, when we were, oh…must have been about thirteen. Ty claimed it as belonging to Hawkins land. We kept it up on Mt. Keno under a rock."

The sheriff asked, "How did it come into Bainbridge's possession?"

"I have no idea. I haven't seen that thing in years." Carson smiled sadly. "We used it for oath-taking, all the way through high school. We'd say, 'I swear by the arrow that I will take Charlene to the prom,' or whatever the great deed was supposed to be. Maybe Ty gave it to Roger as a promise of some sort?"

Deputy Penateka said, "More likely Hawkins put it here to implicate you."

Carson frowned. "It's a little obscure, don't you think?"

Penateka shrugged. "He didn't have much time and he might not have been thinking clearly. He had to come up with something to supply a motive for you. Maybe this was the best he could do."

"Doesn't seem up to Ty's standards," Carson said. "Although, since there's no conceivable connection between me and Bainbridge, I suppose he had to improvise."

They all shot glances at me again, perhaps checking for signs of impending hysteria. I calmly placed the camera in front of my face and took another picture. Something not unlike hysteria bubbled up in my chest, but these guys weren't the ones I wanted to rail at. My mind boggled at the extent of Ty's deceptions.

Get that pasture documented, he'd said. *I want a complete record, from fence to shining fence.* He might as well have added, *And wait until you see the fun surprise I left for you to find, when the time was right.*

Whose idea had it been for me to do sunrise shots on Mt. Keno last Friday? Mine? Or Ty's? I couldn't remember. But how convenient for me to be there with my camera equipment when Ty brought Jake up and let him nose around.

He'd given me the clue himself. Look for James Mason, he'd said. A criminal mastermind, not a couple of scared women improvising on the run. He'd been controlling the timeline from the outset, deciding what would be discovered when.

He'd played me like a grand piano. *A Symphony in Stupidity.*

He'd overplayed his anger at the scene though, or underestimated Dare's temper. He'd gotten arrested, limiting his ability to direct the rest of the drama he'd staged. Lucky for him, he had me to run around and turn up his cleverly planted clues on schedule.

"What's in the folder?" the sheriff asked, in an oddly gentle tone.

Penateka opened it on his gloved left palm and flipped through its contents. I spotted a sheet of yellow paper. That caught his attention too. He slid it out and put it on top to show it to the others.

Dare got out his phone and found a flashlight app. Very handy. We gathered around the cool glow to examine the hand-drawn map of the Lazy H, showing the major features and roads. The neat labels were in Ty's handwriting. Someone else had drawn bold lines across the northwest corner, with the word "airstrip" penciled down the middle. Ty had written over it, "Compete or collaborate?!"

I could hear him saying the words, his voice dripping with sarcasm, his meaning plain. *How dare this buffoon threaten me with such nonsense!* Then my disloyal brain produced another reading, turning the threat around. *Watch out, Bainbridge! I can screw you before you screw me.*

Which was it? I didn't know how to decide anymore.

Dare said, "That's Hawkins' handwriting, except for that one word there." He moved the light over the striped lines.

"Is Ty thinking of building an airstrip out here?" the sheriff asked.

"No," Dare and I answered together.

Dare picked it up. "Ty hates the idea. He told Bainbridge there was no way he'd allow such a thing to be built on his property. That strip there's on Diana's half, but of course she'd never do anything that big without his approval."

"Bainbridge tried to get me interested in the scheme," Carson said. "I turned him down too. Planes are noisy, smelly, and expensive."

The sheriff grunted his agreement. "So, what's the idea here? That Bainbridge threatened to build on Hawkins' spread instead of yours and you got into an argument about that and killed him?"

"That doesn't make much sense to me," Carson said. "All I had to do was say no, which is actually what I did."

Dare said, "It would threaten Ty's plans, though, if he believed it."

"That reinforces the motive we had before," Penateka said. "I'd say this set up here pretty well seals the deal."

"We'll talk about this back at the station," the sheriff said, tilting his head toward me, signaling his men to shut the heck up in front of the killer's naive girlfriend.

The four men exchanged worried looks, glanced at me, shook their heads, and frowned at their feet. It was ridiculous. I had half the lawmen in the county, plus a future county commissioner, trying their best not to ruffle my girlish feelings. Maybe I should sit in the front row of the courtroom at Ty's hearing, looking all fragile and shocked and pitiful. Maybe the judge would give him a break and let him go, for fear of wounding my bitty baby heart.

Maybe I wouldn't want him to.

"I'm not going to explode." I faced the men, turning the lens cap on my camera around and around. "I'm not going to cry either. Not now, anyway. I get it, I do. Y'all think Ty set all this up to implicate Carson. Then he sent me out here to find it, on schedule, to get himself released and get Carson locked up in his place."

My voice sounded shrill in my ears, but I did not cry. The top of my head might fly off and my hands might shake themselves free of my arms, but I would not cry in front of these men.

"Now, Penny," the sheriff said, stepping toward me with his big, flabby palms up, no doubt to pat me on the shoulder and say, "There, there."

I waved him off with a broad sweep of my arm. "I'll bring you the photographs tomorrow." I turned away from their worried faces and stalked down the road—walking, not running. Tears began to stream down my cheeks, but I held my head up and my back straight and I did not run.

Chapter 19

Thursday was a dark day. Not outside, of course. Outside it was a typical, sunshiny, June day in Central Texas, full of bees and birds and flowers and happy trees, dancing and singing nature's unending song of joy. Inside my house, however, a deep, depressing gloom prevailed, especially under the covers with pillows heaped over my head.

My thigh hurt where the barbed wire had snagged me. My arm hurt too, where they'd jabbed the needle for the tetanus shot. But neither hurt as much as my pride, whenever I thought about my stupid *Old Flames* list and my deluded investigation.

What a towering fool I'd been! Penelope Trigg, the Queen of Fools; the Empress of Idiots; the Nabob of Nincompoops.

At some point, Jake rousted me out of bed and made me take him for a walk. We went to the studio. Where else would we go? I wore a floppy hat and walked fast to avoid having to talk to anyone. We didn't meet a single soul, but I did stub my toes on a lamppost, thanks to the hat.

The unlit light on the answering machine signaled the lack of messages, but someone had propped a folded sheet of notepaper in the keyboard at the front desk. Tillie, of course.

She wrote that she wouldn't come in today because she needed to think. She might or might not come in tomorrow, depending on how the thinking went. She didn't want to quit, not yet, but she was very definitely not happy with the way her boss had meddled in her marriage and wanted me to know that.

Wonderful. Perfect. I'd lost my boyfriend, my only paying gig—which also happened to be my dream photography job—and my best friend in one fun-filled, action-packed week. Less than a week. With a whole week, maybe I could break a leg and burn down my house as well.

* * *

The next morning I woke up aching for a good, hard run through the leafy lanes of Lost Hat to burn off my crying hangover. Running gave me energy; maybe I'd keep running. I could be packed in an hour if I took only my own stuff, not Aunt Sophia's antiques. I could load up the Hulk and go to Austin and stay with a friend, if I could find a friend with a fenced back yard. I had a dog, now. My housing requirements were stiffer.

But what about my studio? My beautiful studio, whose floors I had sanded with my very own hands? My artwork framed on the walls, my darkroom, my computers? I'd trapped myself in this town, investing my savings and a sizeable chunk of my soul.

I didn't like feeling trapped. Now we'd have to run twice as far.

I opened the front door with Jake at my side and nearly barreled into my brother Nick. "Wha-huh!" I backed up and trod on Jake's foot. He yelped and barked at Nick, placing the blame where it belonged.

"Pardon me, Ma'am," Nick said. "I must have the wrong address. I was looking for a sister who doesn't have a dog."

"He's a guest. I mean, I'm taking care of him for a friend. Or he was. A friend, I mean." Even my relationship to my dog was complicated.

I backed into the living room. Nick gave me a one-armed hug as he negotiated the screen door and the dog and entered my humble abode. "You look awful. Rough night?"

"Thanks ever so."

When I didn't elaborate, he took himself on a mini-tour of my cluttered living room. "Holy Yard Sale, Penny! How can you live with all this stuff?"

Nick had given up swearing two years ago, along with the speed, the coke, and the booze. Now every time I saw him he was trying on new interjections. He appeared to be on a Batman kick at present.

"Hey, it's a lot better than it was. I've moved at least half the kitsch into the back room."

"Half, really? Yowza." He turned a lime green fluted vase around in his hands, frowned, and put it back on the shelf like a man distancing himself from an unsavory object. "Could be hazardous, you know. A single woman, living alone in Little Old Lady Land. Might be catching."

I rolled my eyes. "Busy. Artist-entrepreneur, remember? I'll get around to the house one of these days. Besides, what am I supposed to do with all this junk?"

"Give it away. There must be needy people out there with no kitsch to call their own."

"I can't do that, not without an appraisal. What if that little shepherdess thingy is an original Whatsis? It could be valuable."

"Right. Because the Whatsis thingies are worth so much more than the non-Whatsis thingies."

We grinned at each other. I needed a friendly face right now more than anything in the world. And his face was so much like mine, with the brown eyes and the wide smile, topped by wheat-blond hair. I invented the look, being the firstborn, but he did a decent masculine version.

"Want some coffee? Or would that mangle the alignment of your chakras?"

Nick chuckled. "It might, but reaching for perfection is more challenging, and thus more satisfying, than maintaining the exalted state. Besides, the dark brew is legal, so thank you, I will indulge."

I led him to the kitchen. He sat at my chrome dinette and held his hands palms out between his knees for Jake to inspect. "What's the dog's name?"

"Jake."

He ruffled the dog's ears and thumped his shoulders. "Jakerino, what a fine brown dog you are." He looked sideways up at me. "He's the dog of our childhood dreams."

"Isn't he?" I took two of my infinite supply of Holland America Cruise Line coffee mugs out of the cupboard and set them on the table. "I guess he's my dog now."

"You guess?"

I shrugged. "He's Ty's dog."

"Ty, your boyfriend? Is he the one who's no longer a friend? What's the what, Penny?"

I gave him the Cliff Notes version of recent events in Lost Hat while the coffeepot chuffled and dripped. Then I asked, "What brings you here? Not that I'm not glad to see you. Your timing is perfect."

He flashed me a grin. "I came to lend you money."

"I'll take it." He owed me, who knew how much. He used to show up at my doorstep at all hours, wasted, hungry, and broke. Back then I was Responsibility Gal, the one with the steady paycheck. Now he was pulling in big bucks designing mystic mojo video games and I was the one living hand-to-mouth.

"Seriously? Whenever you need it. But I'm here because the folks called me. You have failed to return Mom's calls, not once, but twice. Nor have you answered her email in a day and half. She's assuming you're lying in a ditch or unconscious in a hospital. I needed a break, so I said I'd buzz over and look at you with my own two eyes."

"Mom called *you* because she was worried about *me?*"

"And the wheel just keeps on turning." At least he had the grace to recognize the irony.

Enough coffee had dripped through for two mugs, so I poured and sat down opposite Nick. I doctored mine with cream and sugar; he took his black. He tasted it and smacked his lips. "Ah. Coffee from a can. It's been a long time since I've had anything so regulation."

"You can't get fancy coffee in Lost Hat. You have to order it online or bring extra bags from the city." I sipped and stared out the window. I loved my little breakfast nook. It had windows on two sides of the table, so I could look at my green back yard while I drank my coffee. I liked thinking about what I could do out there: build a patio or a deck, plant some native shrubs, hang a hammock or two.

I'd never owned a back yard before. It made me feel rooted, like I'd unpacked my last box. And now I had a dog to run around in it and everything.

"I'm okay, physically. And fiscally, holding my own. But this situation…Roger's murder. I think Ty really did it. And worse, I think he set me up to find the body and tried to frame his neighbor."

Nick whistled softly. "That's harsh, Penny. I'm sorry."

"Thanks." Sympathy without scolding—this is why we have siblings. "It pretty much sucks all the way around. The worst part is I've made such a fool of myself, barging around town hassling people, trying to come up with alternative suspects."

"Detective Trigg, eh? You're all, 'Where were you on the night of June the twenty-first?' Tell me, do you have a magnifying glass or do you rely on your finely-honed intuitions?"

Mockery, but with sympathy. Some of the knots in my chest loosened and I laughed. That brought a prickle of tears to my eyes, but good tears, like a release of emotional toxins. "What was I thinking?"

"You thought someone would break down under the power of your penetrating glare and confess."

"Nobody did, though. And meanwhile the evidence kept piling up against Ty." The laughter died, replaced by another stab of humiliation. "He really played me, the son of a bitch."

"You're loyal, like the rest of our tribe. Your motives were good. You're not responsible for his deeds, Penny."

"A fool, but an honest fool. I know. But all that sneaking around, planting incriminating evidence, sending those phony emails…It doesn't seem like the guy I thought I knew."

"Whoa-ho-ho! Back up! 'Sneaking around planting incriminating evidence?' You didn't mention any of that." He got up, stepping nimbly around Jake, who had sprawled across the middle of the floor. He grabbed the coffeepot and refilled our mugs. "You'd better tell me the story in full detail."

"It's a long story, Nickelodeon."

"I got all day, Penny-lope. That's why I'm here."

So I told him the whole story, starting from the beginning, when I first met Ty. He'd heard some of the early parts, but he let me establish the context in my own way. Nick was a good listener, a skill he'd probably acquired in Narcotics Anonymous meetings. He didn't interrupt until I got through the part about finding Roger's body on Mt. Keno.

"Let's go out there." He stood up and did a Half Moon to stretch his back. "I'd like to see the scene. I'll do my *Monk* impression and catch something everybody else missed." He held his hands out like he was framing my kitchen counters. Mr. Monk does Tai Chi in an over-kitsched kitchen.

I groaned "I don't want to go back out there. Bad things keep happening to me on that ranch."

"Yeah, but this time you'll have me with you. I'll stun the villains with my Warrior Pose." He demonstrated, standing in the channel between the sink and the range, feet planted close around Jake's body. Jake's eyebrows twitched anxiously, but he stayed down. "We can't sit around here all day. I drove all the way out to the boonies; I want to get outdoors. Let's go swim in that spring you told me about."

"Oh, you don't know, Nick. There's bulls and hogs and rednecks out there. Mean ones. I haven't even gotten to the exciting parts."

"You can tell me in the car. Besides, what good is a nature photographer who's afraid to go out in the country?"

He had a point. So we packed up all the snacks and portable beverages we could find. I put my swimsuit on under my hiking clothes and grabbed a stack of towels and my sun hat. And my camera, of course.

"I get to drive the Hulk," Nick said. "Let me move my car."

His iridescent blue sports car was parked in my driveway behind the Hulk. It looked like a dragonfly nudging a cow patty.

"I want to drive the jazzy little sports car," I whined.

"No way, Bay-bay. I'm not risking the Corvette on your ragged ranch roads. It's the Hulk for us."

We climbed into the cab, dog in the middle. Nick twisted the wheel and made boyish vrooming noises while I stowed the towels and pack behind the seat and buckled my seat belt.

"Hey, Pen. Do you realize this truck is older than we are?"

"I know. It's my new mentor. Sturdy, reliable…"

"Low maintenance, resistant to change…"

I told the rest of my long story on the way out to the ranch. As we drove past Ty's house, Nick clucked his tongue. I thought he was commenting on the crime scene tape still sagging around the front porch, but he said, "It's hard to believe Starmaker Tyler Hawkins lives in that dump. I'd pictured him in something more *Architectural Digest*. He isn't one to scrimp on image."

"You've met him?"

"I wish. He's a legend in Austin technology circles. If Hawkins agreed to come in on your project, you were almost guaranteed to get uber-rich. You broke out the champagne and did the Victory Macarena up and down the hall."

He made a trumpet noise with his lips, doing the Macarena in his seat. I begged him to stop. We Triggs are a visual people. We are not gifted in the musical domain.

We stopped long enough to change places. I took Nick on the ten-dollar tour, pointing out features of interest as we passed. One major feature was Old Blackberry, back in his own pasture, placidly browsing the sparse grass. He didn't even glance at us as we idled in front of the securely fastened gate. He was totally faking it, though. He was way too casual, larruping up lashings of grass with his fat tongue, like he didn't even know I was there.

I kept my eyes on the bull as I told Nick about the guy in the white straw hat. "I barely saw him, *if* I saw him. I probably imagined it."

"If you think you saw it, you saw it. You've got a camera in your head."

He looked past me, surveying the terrain to the west. He turned and looked through the rear window and then moved his head to intercept my line of sight. His eyes gleamed and his lips curled in a smug smile. "What's wrong with this picture?"

"What picture?" I shifted my head to look past him at the bull again, but he countered my move, holding my eyes. "*What?*" I hated this game.

"Where's the glitch in the story?"

"Nick, if you have an observation to make, make it. I'm too stressed out to play guessing games."

"If I were a big black bull and my gate magically opened before me, would I walk up that dusty road—" He tilted his head toward the road behind us. "Around the bend, and down to the one pasture guaranteed not to have any grass in it? Or would I mosey across that lush swale right in front of me to go visit those nubile young heifers over there?"

I turned my head to follow his gaze and saw the rest of the herd grazing within sight of the gate, beyond a gently rolling swath of knee-high grass and wildflowers.

"Maybe he doesn't like that kind of grass."

Nick rolled his eyes.

"Or maybe he doesn't like girls."

"Of course. He's gay. That explains everything. He's bound to be conflicted about it, since bulls are the very symbol of masculinity. That's why he walked away from the tasty grass and the luscious heifers and attacked you. Overcompensation. It makes perfect sense." He flapped a hand at the steering wheel. "Drive on, James."

"No, you're right. It doesn't make sense. But why didn't Ben notice? He should know something about animal behavior. More than we do."

"Hm, let's think. Could it be because he's the one that let the bull out and led him down to your pasture? Because he's Suspect Number Two and he wanted to scare you out of asking any more questions?"

I closed my eyes and groaned. "Back to the ping-pong match. And it's Ty; now it's Ben; no, wait! Hawkins is pulling back into the lead."

"I know one person who definitely didn't let that bull out."

"Really, Mr. Monk? Who?"

"Man, you must be stressed. It's staring you right in the face. The guy in the slammer, dimwit. Your boy Ty."

Chapter 20

I'd parked in the sun and between the two full-sized adults and the fur-bearing mammal, the truck was getting a mite stuffy. Gusts of wind tossed tree branches around on the hilltops, but precious little breeze made it inside the cab. The coffee had laid a veneer of jitter over my crying-jag headache and sweat glued my T-shirt to the seat.

I put the truck in gear. "No more thinking. Let's go for a swim."

Leaping Springs was a secret paradise, hidden in the northwest corner of the Lazy H. The limestone cap of the hill had collapsed, creating a wide circular well backed by sheer walls, about thirty feet in diameter and about twelve feet deep in the center. The water shimmered an inviting Coke-bottle green. Knotted roots of an ancient cypress formed a miniature pier into the pool, perfect for bare feet. The water bubbled up from a spring at a constant temperature of sixty-eight degrees. It flowed east into a creek that eventually fed into the Mariposa River.

Jake hit the water first, having no clothes to shuck. I was seconds behind him, leaving my outerwear in a heap on a flat rock above the beach. When the water struck my toes, a welcome chill flashed through me. I eeked and squealed until the water reached my knees and I couldn't stand it anymore, then I dove in and swam underwater. The cut on my thigh stung at first, but the cool, clean water soothed it, dissolving my headache and the knots in my back as a bonus.

I found a spot where my toes barely touched the sandy bottom and stood moving my arms in slow arcs to stay upright. The water smelled like fresh rain.

Nick had climbed up on the ledge that ran part way around the back wall. "Banzai!" He cannonballed into the middle of the pool, splashing water in my face and rocking my bliss. *Banzai* was the battle cry we'd adopted during the year we were stationed in Japan. We'd kept it going for a couple more years in the Philippines, where we liked to play Forgotten Soldier, stumbling around on the beach, discovering strange modern inventions like plastic cups and flip-flops.

The three of us paddled around, exploring the pool. "This place is awesome," Nick said. "I totally get the spa idea now. This pool alone will draw people like—"

"Bees to a bake sale. I know. Except now there isn't going to be a spa."

"Sure there is. Or there could be. A little prison time doesn't slow down your modern CEO. In some circles, it counts as a recommendation."

"Are you serious?" In all my miserable imaginings last night, it never occurred to me that Ty could serve his time and come back to start over as if nothing had happened. "Don't they take your property away when they convict you of a felony?"

"Not unless you stole it." Nick pulled himself onto a rock and stood in one smooth motion. When had my brother gotten so buff? He used to look like a scrawny junkie; now he was all sleek muscles and glowing skin. I needed to get some updated pictures of him.

He struck a Pioneer Pose with one hand shading his brow. "It's the land, young Penelope. The Land is Our Heritage." It would have been more impressive if he hadn't been wearing sopping wet boxer shorts with pink and yellow fishies on them.

He performed a flawless Sun Salute and then grabbed an apple out of the snack pack we'd dropped by the towels. He sat on the edge of his rock, dabbling his toes in the water. He launched a splash in my direction and I splashed him back.

Nick said, "Ty probably won't be gone for more than a couple of years. He's charged with manslaughter, right? You should ask that lawyer, but I think the max is only something like fifteen years."

"Only!"

I undid my braid and dove under the water to smooth back my hair. I waded out, re-braiding as I walked. Jake followed me and pawed up a cool patch of sand in the shade for himself. I grabbed a couple of towels and spread one of them over my rock. Lying back with my head on a folded towel and one arm crossed over my eyes, I let the sun warm the gooseflesh from my skin.

The only sound was Nick crunching his apple and the riffle of wind in the tops of the trees. The sun was pressing me into the warm rock, smoothing out the kinks in my back.

"Can I throw this apple core in the woods, or do I have to pack it out?"

"Throw it," I murmured. "A critter'll eat it."

I heard the swoosh-plop of the apple core landing in the woods above the creek bed and Nick's feet shifting pebbles in the direction of the snack pack.

"He won't get the max, though," he said. "He'll have an extreme lawyer. Say he gets six years. He could be out in three."

"That's not much."

"It's nothing. He might not even get six. If they can paint it as an accident, he could be out this time next year."

"No way." I sat up. Hot now. "It wasn't an accident. The autopsy report will show that. He hit the guy more than once, Nick."

"Ugh. Was he drunk?"

"He doesn't drink; not much, anyway. Shades of the old man and all that. Plus Diana's trying to stay sober, so they don't keep booze in the house." I waded back to my spot in the pool, making circles underwater with my arms.

"It's hard to picture," Nick said. "I don't know the guy, but I've never heard any gossip about Ty Hawkins having a bad temper. And that kind of thing gets around. The year before I started at MageMatica, they had this manager that used to pitch these major fits. People said he used to get so mad his face would turn bright red and his neck cords would stand out like a Cardassian."

"What happened to him?"

"He got fired. You can't let the suits go rampaging around, rattling the talent. It slows up the work."

Now I was cold again. I snagged a bottle of water from the snack pack on the way back to my sunning rock.

"Which is why I don't get it," Nick continued. He tucked the Clif Bar wrapper back in the pack and started in on the cookies. "Ty Hawkins is famous for being cool in a crisis. Here we are, the night before the big demo and nothing works. Does he go around knocking people's heads together? No. He sends out for pizza and pumps everybody's energy up, telling them what geniuses they are."

"That sounds like the guy I know." I settled back into Sloth Pose. "Or thought I knew. But people can be very different at home from how they are at work."

"True. You could keep working for him, though."

"Three years from now?"

"He can keep the project going from the inside. He could hire a manager or work through his lawyer. The grass is going to grow, wherever he is. I'll bet he'll want you to keep on documenting."

I sighed. "I don't know what I'm going to do. Last night I seriously considered packing up and leaving town."

"A time-honored strategy for the Army brat. But I thought you liked it out here in Hicksville."

"I love it. Having the run of this place, cruising out to shoot whatever I want, whenever I want, with no crowds or admission fees."

"Hard to beat."

"I like the town too. That's why I kept coming back to visit Aunt Sophia. I love running around the square every morning. I love walking to work. And I deeply love my studio."

"You took a risk, moving out here. Money-wise, I mean."

"I know. Believe me, I know. But so far, so good. I think I can make it, even without Ty's job. The portrait business is going okay and I have an inkling that commissioner guy might hire me to do a photo spread of his ranch. It's big, they run hunts and stuff. He says he wants to promote tourism, which sounds like a photo op to me. And I can design websites and start going around the Market Days fairs with posters and stuff."

"It's a living," Nick said, "but is it art?"

"I find time for the art." I turned sideways, propping myself up with a folded towel under my elbow, working on that well-rounded tan. "More here than in Austin, and on my own terms. I had to work overtime at Monster Wedding Studio to make the rent and commuting gobbled up the best part of the day. The traffic gets worse every year."

"You should try it on a bike. Seriously scary!"

"Mostly though, the noise in my head from other artists drove me batty. Trends sweep through the art world, but most people are oblivious to how fashion-driven their own work is. 'It's pretty, Penny, but it's not political enough. It's not provocative. Where's the anger?'"

Nick grinned. "You're facilitating the capitalist hegemony by pandering to a bourgeois conception of beauty."

"Exactly. I need to find my own vision. There's something…I don't have it yet, but there's something in the intersection of the natural, the agricultural, and the creative…"

"Something like an eco-dude ranch and spa."

"Well, yeah."

I suddenly remembered that I didn't have any sunscreen on my chest or legs. Enough roasting for this little white girl. I got up, put on my T-shirt, and stood with my feet in the water, letting the chill rise up my body.

"This project has been incredible for me already. I'm seeing things I never noticed before. It's intriguing and challenging. I thought I might even get a book out of it."

"You don't have to be sleeping with the guy to do your book."

I turned smooth pebbles with my toes, considered Nick's words. I truly did love this place—the pool, the county, the town. I still had faith in the dream of making a living and making my art, my way, in my own studio. Even if I could afford to move, even if I could find another situation as good as this one, I would always know I had run away when trouble turned up, instead of digging in and defending my dream.

"Okay," I said. "If there's still a job when all this gets resolved, however it gets resolved, I'll do it."

My tummy rumbled. Life-changing decisions burned a lot of calories. I searched the pack, but there was nothing left but an apple and a couple of Milk Bones. "You ate everything."

"You had cereal."

"That was hours ago." I considered the Milk Bones—they were crunchy and nutritious—but opted for the apple. "Let's go."

Jake jumped to his feet, shook the sand off his back, and splashed back into the pool with his tail held high.

"Oh, great," Nick said. "I vote the wet dog rides in back."

I studied the light reflecting off the green pool onto the gray rock wall. "Someday, I'm going to get the perfect shot of this place."

Nick raised a finger high over his head. "But it is not *this* day. Let's go look at the scene of the crime."

* * *

We parked in the middle of the field on top of Mt. Keno. Nick did a slow three-sixty with his arms spread wide. "Now *that's* a view!"

His reaction pleased me as much as if I had built the landscape myself. Sunrise and sunset offered better light. The noon glare tended to flatten the contours of the hills and valleys. But cloud caravans cast shifting shadows and the wind sent riffles through the trees and turned the blades of the windmill, which added interest.

"Ty's going to build a yoga pavilion up here."

"Sweet." Nick looked up at the windmill approvingly. "Hey, I should check my mail." He pulled his phone out of his pocket and waved it at me. "Got my own Blackberry."

"Very funny."

He typed rapidly with his thumbs and I took a few pictures of him. He looked so urbane in his high-fashion shades, his ethnic cotton trousers, and his hip Hawaiian shirt, standing on the top of the windswept hill with his sleek black gadget. He could have been in one of those ads that are so suave you can't figure out what they're selling.

He flipped his phone shut and flashed a big smile at the camera. "One for the folks."

"Do you have unlimited data?" I liked to hear about the latest toys, even though I couldn't afford them. I'd switched to basic service, calls and text only, pay as you go.

I didn't miss the extras—much. "You must have a good service provider. People say the signal is pretty dismal out here."

"Not on Ty Hawkins' home place." He jerked his chin at the windmill. "See that little black zigzaggy thing? That's a wireless antenna."

"I thought it was a lightning rod."

Nick laughed heartily. "Foolish girl. Why would you care if lightning struck your non-functioning windmill?"

"Wait a minute. Are you saying you can send email from up here, through Ty's service?"

"Of course."

"How did you log into his account?"

"I didn't. I logged into his guest account."

"Guest account!" I gaped at him. "Guest account! Why didn't anybody mention a guest account before?"

Nick gaped back, but then he said, "Ah! The messages from the dead guy."

"Could someone have sent them from the guest account?"

"No, they'd have to log in as Diana, if they came from her account. But they wouldn't have any trouble connecting or finding the login page."

Ty had said it wouldn't be hard for someone who knew her moderately well to figure out her login and password. "Do you have to be right under the zigzaggy thing?"

"No, it's line of sight. If I can see the antenna, I can connect. If that's your key piece of evidence, you need to go back to the storyboard. Look." He pointed back up at the windmill. "There's your antenna, on top of the highest hill in the area, right? Pretend it's a bird—a far-sighted eagle. What can it see from up there?"

He didn't wait for me to answer. "That house down there." He pointed at Sid's half-built house. "If that guy's a cheapskate, he'll put a repeater in his attic and coast off Ty's service."

"And the stone house too, right?" I pointed east.

"And the gate down there and Ty's house. Pretty much everywhere we can see."

Something cheerful turned a back flip under my heart. "All this communication stuff has been driving me crazy. Supposedly, Ty made some calls on Roger's phone to Carson Caine, not leaving messages, to make it look like Roger tried to call Carson, presumably to demonstrate some connection between them."

"What's supposed to be the point of all that? To keep people from looking for Roger?"

"I guess. But in that case, why make sure Jake and I dig him up?"

Nick shrugged. "He would have made the calls when he stashed the car. Then sent the emails sometime later. Maybe he changed his mind about his strategy."

"Twice? First, frame Carson. Then, make it look like Roger's out of town. Then, no, oops—let's go back to Plan A."

We stared at each other for a long moment.

"I also don't understand the car business." I walked toward the eastern edge of the hill. Nick and Jake followed me. "Look." I pointed down toward the road and the trees behind. "You can see the crime scene tape where the car was." They had wound yellow tape all around the area with cut branches and car-crushed shrubbery. That stuff was getting to be quite a feature around here. I snapped a couple of shots for the heck of it.

Jake wandered down the slope, following the path we'd taken a few days ago. Nick stood with his hands resting on the small of his back, looking from Ty's house to the place where the car had been and back up to the stone enclosure under the windmill.

"What's the theory? That Ty and the real estate guy had a big fight down there at the house and Ty hit him, knocking him dead? Then he brought the body up here in the Gator. They didn't find any blood in the house, right?"

"Right. And they looked; up here too. There was a lot in the back of the car, though. He must have been put in there right after he died."

Nick drew in a sharp breath. "Sad. Poor guy. Then he was buried that way, right? You found him with his knees drawn up."

"Yeah." Then it struck me. "Why would there be blood in the car *and* in the Gator?"

"Maybe he put him in the car for a while, while he figured out what to do."

"And then moved him to the Gator, wrapping the towel around his head."

"But he wouldn't be bleeding anymore by then, because, hello? He'd be dead."

We blinked at each other. "Things do not add up."

Nick grinned at me. "They really don't. Your boyfriend may be innocent after all."

I felt like dancing the Dance of Victory. So I did, holding on to my hat to keep it from blowing off while I hopped and kicked. Jake galloped up the slope to help me celebrate.

Nick watched me with a dry expression. "I'd stick to photography. Let's walk through the whole scenario. Here I am, a wealthy venture capitalist, planning to build a high-concept resort on the old family homestead. My useless space cadet of a sister is giving me grief and getting in my way. We have a galaxy-class fight and she storms out of the house."

He paced around the barren field while he talked. Jake trotted alongside him, trying to get the hang of the new game. "Then the biggest pain in my butt drives up and starts getting in my face. We argue. I haul off and let him have it. *Pow!* I knock him to the ground, where his head happens to land on a handy rock."

"And then you pick him up and do it again, twice."

Nick shook a finger at me. "That's right. Luckily, there are rocks a-plenty, everywhere he falls."

"Which there aren't, if this is happening in the yard in front of Ty's house. It's all mud and gravel and leaves. The big rocks get chunked into the woods."

"Also, you'd think there'd be blood thick on the ground somewhere."

"Which they found no trace of."

"If they looked. Doesn't sound like these yokels have been doing their jobs very well."

"They're not yokels, Nick." My brother still had authority issues. "The sheriff isn't stupid and the deputies have good training. But they're used to crimes where the guy is standing right there saying, 'Oops.' This is Penateka's first big case and he's determined to do everything right. He said they looked and I believe him."

"Ms. Citizen, so trusting. But okay, let's say they looked. Has it rained?"

"Nope."

"Then where's the blood?"

I couldn't answer that.

Nick raised both hands in an elaborate shrug. "A major point, but what the heck? Let's move on. Here I am, with a dead developer on my hands. What to do? What to do? Should I call 911? Get an ambulance? Because, dammit, Jim. I'm a businessman, not a doctor. He might still be alive for all I know."

I groaned. "Poor Roger! I hope he wasn't. Still alive, I mean, while they were doing all this."

"Ugly business, however it went down. Anyway, I suffer some sort of brain fusion and decide that no, I must hide the body, so that no one should ever know what evil lurks within my seemingly placid breast."

"So you say, 'Aha! I'll put him into his own car!'"

"It is right in front of me, here in my own front yard. Maybe I'm thinking I'll get rid of both the car and the body in one fell swoop. I can dump them into a nearby arroyo and walk away, dusting my hands and cackling with fiendish glee."

"But you don't do that," I said. "You wait until rigor sets in and the body is stuck in a fetal position. I wonder how long that takes?"

"Let's find out." Nick whipped out his phone and flicked his thumbs across the keys. In a few seconds, he said, "According to Wikipedia, rigor mortis sets in about three to four hours after clinical death, with full rigor being in effect at about twelve hours, and eventually subsiding to relaxation at about thirty-six hours."

I scowled at his luxury device. "I wish I could still afford a smartphone."

Nick chuckled as he tucked the phone back in his pocket. "You do have a birthday coming up. But if I solve your crime for you, you won't deserve another present."

"I'm solving the crime. You're my technical assistant."

"The faithful sidekick?"

"No, that's Jake. You're more like the outside consultant, except that you don't get paid."

"Hm. I need to talk to my agent. Now, where were we?"

"Roger was curled up in the back of his car for three to four hours. Longer maybe, if full rigor means he can't be budged out of that position by the time he gets buried."

"I think it does. Okay. Here I am, Mr. Big Shot, worried about my reputation, with a stiff tucked away in a big red vehicle. What do I do? I chill for three to four hours or maybe longer." He shook his head. "I'm having trouble with my motivation here, Boss. What do I do for three to four hours?"

"Maybe you take a nap. You're exhausted from the stress of it all."

"More like I'd be pumped up with adrenaline. Murder never makes people sleepy in the movies." He stared down at the yard in front of Ty's house. "Maybe I get a shovel and dig up the blood-soaked dirt to scatter it in the woods, and then tramp around smoothing out the mess. That could take a few hours, if I were thorough about it."

"And you pick up the bloody rocks, which weren't there in the first place, and carefully wash them with soap."

"Yes, I do. Because I'm a tidy guy."

"Okay, we've found something for him to do. Not plausible, but possible, in a pinch. But the clock is ticking. You've got a meeting in Austin at nine o'clock and it's a three hour drive. And you have to drop Jakey off at Doggy Day Care on the way."

"Doggy Day Care! Aren't we the pampered pet?" He bent to pat Jake on the head. "Okay, let's see. Somehow, I am stricken with remorse and decide not to leave the obnoxious developer deep in some lonely canyon for the rest of eternity. Instead, I will bury him properly in a place with a view. So I take him out of the car and load him onto the Gator."

He started making putt-putt noises, turning his hands like he was driving, and jogged over to the stone enclosure. The yellow tape still sagged around the irregular broken wall. Evidently nobody was in a hurry to clean up the scene. Maybe the authorities left it for the land owners: one last, sad task.

Nick walked around inside the enclosure, stepping carefully over the tape. Jake sat and watched him with his head cocked to one side.

Nick looked at me over his shoulder. "I must have quite a sentimental streak to bury a guy I famously did not like here in the old Indian graveyard, scene of so many happy childhood games."

"How long would it take, do you think?"

Nick stared at the ground. "I have no idea. I've never dug a hole in my life."

"Me neither." That seemed funny somehow. Did normal people—by which I mean non-Army—know about hole-digging? "Let's say an hour. Ty's in great shape."

"What time did the sister leave?"

I shrugged. "Sometime after nine. Say nine-thirty, to give her time to get clear. Unless the theory is that she was on her way out when Roger turned up and assaulted her in the driveway, with Ty watching, which sounds really awkward, now that I walk it through."

"Uh-huh." Nick nodded. "Now you're getting it. I can't see the sister anywhere in the Ty-based scenario. Unless we roll all the way back to the house, before she leaves. Then Roger could come into the house and they have a free-for-all."

"But then there would be blood in the house, which there isn't."

"If you believe the cops, which you are apparently willing to do. Okay, I'm not believing any of it anymore, but let's take it all the way to the end. It's now around nine thirty. I crack the guy's skull and take my four-hour nap. That puts me up here after one a.m., digging by the light of the moon, assuming there was a moon, or the headlights of the Gator would do. I put the body in the hole, hold my hat over my heart, and say a few words."

"But first you clip Diana's charm bracelet around his wrist and remove his boots, although you probably took the boots when you put the body in the car."

"You didn't mention any bracelet. That's very weird. Why would I do such a creepy thing?"

I shrugged. "All I can think of is that it drags Diana into the picture. Like she's the reason Roger was killed or maybe to implicate her…"

"This is the theory? That Ty tried to frame his own sister?" Nick blew out a long raspberry. "How is he still in jail?"

"He did shove the sheriff and say rude things to the judge during his arraignment."

Nick grinned broadly. "I like this guy! I can't wait to meet him."

"Let's hope you don't have to wait three years." I grinned too. Ty would not go to prison. Once we spun this story for his lawyer, she'd be able to get a reasonable doubt on the grounds of sheer unbelievability.

"Okay," Nick said. "One last thing. I've buried the body, so I go back down in the Gator to figure out what to do with the dad-blasted car."

"It's after two by now," I pointed out. "You don't have time to drive it to a canyon anymore, not if you have to walk back."

"Really? It seems like there's canyons everywhere out here."

"On private property. You'd have to drive around via the county road and get through a gate somewhere."

"But I have my own private property, acres and acres of it. Why can't I hide the car somewhere out here and deal with it after my meeting in Austin? I've hidden the body. I've had my clever idea about the emails, even if I haven't sent them yet. People will think old Roger's left town. What's the rush?"

"I don't know." I paced around the windmill, looking north and west. The country grew more rugged between here and Leaping Springs. "You could drive the car into a canyon off that way and then later dump boulders on top of it. It'd never be found. You could make sure of that, because it's your place and you control what gets developed where."

Nick shrugged wide, raising both hands. "How is that not obvious, especially to me, the owner of this fine land?

Instead, I put the big red SUV on my neighbor's ranch beside a road to a hunting cabin where someone is bound to see it sooner or later."

"That's what I was thinking last night—that Ty put it there on purpose, to make sure I would be the one to find it. He sent me to that particular pasture to take pictures. He practically told me to go find the damn car."

"But why?"

"He told me that too, sort of. He said someone was trying to frame him, when in fact, he was trying to frame Carson. Or that's what I thought yesterday. And I think it's what the cops still think."

"A strike against the cops," Nick said. "Why not leave the body in the car, in that case? Why hide the body and leave the car?"

"The new idea is that he engineered the whole event. He planned for me to find the body and then later for me to find the car. But maybe he didn't figure out what to do with the car until after he buried the body."

"He had at least four hours to think it through." Nick shook his head. "No way, Penny. None of this adds up. You're not going to convince me that Tyler Hawkins, the Wizard of Silicon Hills, spent the whole night spazzing around without once stopping to have a cup of coffee and think the plan through. 'I'll push the car and the body off a cliff somewhere. No, I'll bury the body and hide the car somewhere else. No, I'll make it look like the neighbors did it. Oh, no! Now somebody has to find the body or the story will never unfold as planned!'"

"When you put it that way…"

Nick shook his head again. "If he was tripping, maybe. Otherwise, *fuhgeddaboudit*. And why would he send email to himself if he was framing somebody else? Hawkins is in the industry, for crying out loud! You think he wouldn't know better than to use his own account?"

"Even I would know that."

"No, you wouldn't."

"Okay, no, I wouldn't. But I wouldn't do the email in the first place. I wouldn't do any of it. I'm in good shape too, but just walking through this wears me out. He would have been up all night shifting dirt, lugging a stiff corpse around, finding the key to the 3C in the shed, driving vehicles hither and yon, cutting branches. And then a three hour drive to a meeting where everybody said he looked the same as usual."

"He didn't do it. I'll bet you a Blackberry he didn't do it."

I tucked my tongue in my cheek. "You do mean a phone, right?"

He chuckled.

"You're on." I crossed my fingers. I couldn't afford to pay up if I lost. "But we don't have another suspect who makes any more sense. Dare is a smart guy too, and also a trained law enforcement officer. He loves training, in fact. He's probably had courses in rigor mortis, identity theft, you name it. If he wanted to frame someone, he'd be consistent about it."

"What about the BullMeister?" Nick asked. "His marriage was on the line. Let's say he's having a secret affair with Diana. She gets mad fighting with Ty and runs off to meet Whosis—"

"Ben."

"Ben, in their secret love nest, wherever that is. Somehow Roger the Developer is there too. The men fight over her and Roger falls down dead. Ben can't call 911, because then the secret love affair would come out and his wife would leave him."

"Worse than that." I'd forgotten a crucial detail about Ben. "He told me he was studying for his real estate license, so he could get a job with Tillie's uncle. If she divorced him, he could kiss that career goodbye. Along with half the town. The Espinoza clan is large and closely knit."

"Even better. He's got a lot to lose. So they're off somewhere that's not here when he kills Roger. Now it makes sense for him to hide him in the car and wait for hours before he buries him."

"He has to wait for Ty to leave."

"Yes, he does. Because Jake the faithful watchdog would bark if anyone drove past the house, wouldn't you, Jako?" Jake wagged his tail in the affirmative. "But why does he send the bogus emails?"

"To confuse things and make people think Roger is still alive."

"Exactly. The more delay, the better for the BullMeister."

I should have done another victory dance, but I wasn't up to it. Get my guy out and put Tillie's guy in. Is that what friends were for?

A shadow fell across the field as a long bank of clouds moved over the sun. "We may actually get some weather," I said. Rain in June was a treat, unless it turned into hail or tornadoes.

"I hope it doesn't rain on me on the drive home."

"You're not going to stay the weekend?"

He shook his head. "Gotta work. Worlds to build, monsters to slay. I came to a stopping point yesterday and decided to take a personal day."

A gust of wind nearly tore my hat from my head. It carried a foul stench with it. "Ugh! It smells like cat piss up here." I hoped it wasn't really cat piss, because it would have to be a mighty big cat. I'd never heard of any cougars out around here.

I turned toward Nick, holding my hat on with my hand on top of my head. He was staring at the stone house with his eyes narrowed and a grim smile on his lips. "Let's get the hell out of here."

"Huh?"

"Let's move. Get in the truck."

"Why?"

"Isn't that the house where the redneck was? The guy that shot at you for no reason?"

"Yep."

"He had a reason." He whistled for Jake and headed for the truck. We climbed into the cab and I started the engine.

"That's not cat piss, Penny. It's anhydrous ammonia. You've got a meth lab upwind from your yoga pavilion."

Chapter 21

I used Nick's phone to call Deputy Penateka when we got close enough to town. He said he was on his way over to the diner for a late lunch and that we should meet him there. We parked at the studio to leave Jake in the air-conditioning.

Nick took himself on a tour, making complimentary noises, stopping to reminisce in front of familiar pictures. When he pointed at the ceiling and said, "Let's go up and look at the junk collection," I knew he was stalling.

"He's not going to arrest *you*, coward. You haven't done anything."

"Neither has Ty." He had a point. A tiny pinhead of a point.

We walked down the street in silence. As I laid my hand on the door to the cafe, I turned to him and grinned. "You're in for a fun surprise."

I got the reaction I wanted. Nick's jaw dropped and his eyes popped as he took in the decor. "Holy SeaWorld, Batman! We're underwater!"

Perline met us with a tight little smile that relaxed into a welcoming grin when I introduced my brother. Had she thought I was stepping out on Ty with a near-identical twin? I waved at Cracker behind the pass-through, pointed at Nick, and mouthed the word "brother." He grinned and saluted us with a spatula.

Three of the tables were occupied by Lost Hatters lingering over pie and coffee. They all seemed to be having trouble with their eyes: lots of blinking and darting glances. I said, "Howdy," in a general way as I followed Perline and Nick to the round table in the corner in front of the window. Penateka was getting his hands around a three-story Pearl Burger.

I made the introductions, while Nick and I sat. We ordered chicken fried steaks with all the trimmings. Perline brought our iced teas and stayed to listen while I told Penateka about the stink coming from the stone house that Nick had identified as methamphetamine production.

Perline gasped, put her hand to her mouth, and scurried off to tell Cracker.

"How would you know what a meth lab smells like?" Penateka asked.

Nick met his eyes squarely. "I have a checkered past. Let's leave it at that."

"Fair enough." Penateka quirked a micro-smile. "Well, I can't say I'm all that surprised. We've had our eye on Hank Roeder for a while, but haven't been able to get anything solid on him. We can't snoop around on the 3C without a warrant and if he's selling around here, we haven't been able to catch him at it."

"He probably goes to the cities," Nick said. "Bigger market, less risk."

"More important," I said, "it gives Hank a motive to kill Roger. He could have found out about the meth lab the same way we did. Or maybe he was a customer and they got into a fight about money or whatever."

Penateka frowned and nodded. "He might have threatened to sell him out."

"Or maybe the guy assumed he would," Nick said. "Meth heads are totally paranoid."

"If Hank killed him," I said, "burying him on Mt. Keno makes perfect sense. It makes sense he would be in that curled-up position too. He could've left the body in the car while he waited for Ty to leave. He wouldn't want to bury him on the 3C for fear that dogs would find him come hunting season."

"It's always hunting season on the 3C," Penateka said. "You can shoot feral hogs and exotics on your own land whenever you want."

"There you go, then. Signed, sealed, and delivered." I sat back in my chair and smiled. I felt pretty clever, solving the biggest crime in Lost Hat history. And soon Ty would be back out in the world where I could play with him.

Penateka worked on his burger and home fries in silence for a while, his gaze turned aimlessly toward the window.

Nick flicked me a what-did-I-tell-you glance, and then leaned back in his chair with his arms crossed and his lips buttoned tight. He looked like a guy in an interrogation room waiting for his lawyer. I sipped tea and watched the heat shimmer on the street, trying to be patient.

Finally, Penateka finished his hamburger and wiped his hands clean. "It's not bad."

I grinned happily. "Will you go arrest Hank? And let Ty go? Soon?"

"It's not that easy, Penny. I have to get a warrant to go onto the 3C and Judge Bogusch is mighty keen on hunting. If Hank goes to jail, it could put a stop to the good times out there for a while."

"You can't let him go! If you went out there right this minute, you could catch him red-handed."

"I have no intention of leaving him be, but I have to have a warrant." He thought a bit. "Meth labs are a plague in Texas and Sheriff Hopper hates 'em worse'n poison. Which is what they are. That house and the land around it will have to be decontaminated by guys in moon suits. I'll ask the sheriff to call the judge today."

"Then you can charge Hank with killing Roger, right? The evidence against him is as good as the evidence against Ty."

He shook his head. "I don't think so, Ms. Trigg. There's still the blood in that Gator."

Flash Memory

I huffed my disbelief. "Hank could've put that there, rubbed it on with that towel in the trunk, to implicate Ty."

"That'd be pretty crafty for Hank Roeder," Penateka said.

"Not if he was high," Nick said. "Believe me, meth can do wonders for your ingenuity. He'd have the energy. He could've snuck around planting clues everywhere all night. Y'all haven't found half of them because they don't make any sense."

Penateka narrowed his eyes at him. "Must have been some checkers."

Nick held up his hands. "I never did any crimes, besides the drugs. We did get into some weird situations. Your brain goes into overdrive, that's all I'm saying."

Penateka caught Perline's eye and made a scribbling motion with his hands. She brought his ticket and he paid, counting out exact change plus a decent tip. As he stood up and put his hat on, he said, "Don't y'all go back out there until I find a way to bring Hank in. I don't doubt this's why he was shooting at you the other day."

"You said he wasn't shooting at me." That trespassing lecture still stung.

Penateka's lips tilted a mite at one corner. "Dare said that, not me. But we were right about the trespassing. Keep yourself busy in town until we get things sorted out."

As soon as he left, Perline brought our chicken-frieds with mashed potatoes and cream gravy. Hard core comfort food. We ate like orphans who had been lost in the wilderness for a week. Solving crimes was hard work, but Cracker's chicken-fried was not only the most delicious in the state of Texas, it had magical soul-restoring properties as well. Every bite made me feel better.

When our plates were clean, we leaned back in our chairs and patted our full tummies. "Oh, man," Nick said. "That was worth driving out here. This place must be the best kept secret in the state."

"It's no secret, honey." Perline set our plates on the pass-through to the kitchen and poured us more tea. Then she sat down at our table with a hearty sigh. "When Ty gets that spa built and we start getting more people in here, I'm going to have to hire some help."

"I like the way you say 'when,' not 'if.'"

She gave me a know-it-all look. "I never had a shred of doubt."

I had only doubted for one night, but I guess that made her the winner in the faith division.

Cracker came out from the kitchen with a Shiner Bock in one hand. He waggled it at Nick by way of an offer. Nick shook his head. Cracker shrugged and joined us with a hearty sigh of his own. His chef's shirt was unsnapped, revealing a T-shirt that read *Everything's Bigger in Texas*. Including T-shirts, since that one must be an XXXXL to cover Cracker's mighty midsection.

"Perline tells me Hank Roeder's been cooking up drugs out there on the 3C." Cracker frowned, his shaggy red eyebrows diving toward his bumpy nose. "I saw a show about it on the TV a while back. That boy hadn't ought to be bringing that mess into Long County."

"It's everywhere," Nick said. "Anywhere you can hide a lab. More in the country than in the city, because it's easier to hide the smell."

"Bad business," Cracker said. "But I gotta tell you, I'm not all that surprised. Hank's always fancied himself an outlaw. All that Confederate rebel bull corn."

Perline said, "If Hank's bringing drugs into our county, I hope they lock him up and forget where they hid the key. What I want to hear about is Ty. We heard about y'all finding Roger's car and that frame-up business they found in there. That's all anybody could talk about last night."

Nick and I glanced at each other. "You tell," he said.

"We're pretty sure Ty didn't do it. There's too many holes in the story. But Hank is a strong possible." I told them the way we'd worked it out, step by step.

"Oh, my heavenly Lord," Perline said.

"Man, oh, man," Cracker said. "That is one heck of a tale, though you kinda lost me with that antennae part. You're telling me old Hank Roeder is sitting up there by his lonesome with one of those laptop computers, sending fake emails to Ty?"

"It wouldn't have to be a computer," Nick said. He pulled his Blackberry out of his pocket. "He probably has one of these little beauties."

He handed it to Cracker, who turned it around, studying it. It looked tiny and strange in his big, rough hands. "I can't picture Hank with a gadget like this."

"Oh, he's got one," Nick said. "I guarantee it. Every drug dealer on this planet has a smartphone. They have to let their customers know when the goodies are on the way. If he's got illegal money to spend, he'd buy the fanciest phone he could get."

Cracker handed the Blackberry back to Nick. "I don't know. I'm thinking that drug deal could be a whole separate thing from Bainbridge's death."

Perline spanked him on the shoulder. "Graham McCrocklin, whose side are you on? We're trying to save my cousin Ty."

"I'm on your side, honeybunch, and I always will be. But it doesn't do us any good to pretend we know something that we don't." He took a swig from his Shiner. "I was sort of rooting for Sid Matslar, myself. I never liked that guy. He's always pushing those small business loans with that greedy gleam in his banker's eyes. Get us tied up in debt 'til the bank owns us, right down to the flatware. And everybody says he was having an affair, which is why his wife is divorcing him."

Perline and I looked at him like he had sprouted antlers. "It was her, not him," Perline said. "And it wasn't even a real affair. They're just sick of each other. Sid's a nice enough guy, for a banker."

"Sid's pretty much the last one on my list," I said. "Even if he had been working on some kind of secret deal with Diana, I can't imagine him being so madly in love that he would help her hide a body."

"I'm not so sure," Cracker said. He had a mulish look on his face now. "That woman could sweet talk the rattle off a snake."

"It doesn't take much to piss off a meth head," Nick said. "Hank's the most likely guy. After him, I put my money on the boyfriend, good old Deputy Dawg."

"Dare," we all said in unison. Perline gave him a quelling glare.

"Don't make fun of him," I said. "He's the best we've got. Besides, he has an iron-clad alibi."

"Iron-clad, like the *Titanic*?"

That shut us up for a second.

"We can't do anything about it, though," I said. "I can't call the Federal Whatsis Center in Georgia and ask them if he was really there last week."

"You can't," Nick said, "but the Colonel can. I'll bet Dad's got a friend who has a friend who knows somebody. You know how officers scratch each other's backs." He twitched his eyebrows at me with that smug look that always made me want to put ice down the back of his shirt. I scooped up a cube with my spoon. He eyed it warily and scooted his chair back a fraction.

Cracker watched us with a wry smile. "I take it you don't think much of the officer class."

"Do submarines have screen doors?" Nick asked.

"Army submarines, maybe. See, kid, in the Navy—"

Perline whacked him with her towel. "Hush, you." She leveled her gaze at Nick. "Around here, we respect the law and our officers. Dare's the best deputy we've ever had."

"I'm sorry. I take it back. I'm sure he's a great guy and a terrific officer." Nick gave Perline his very best please-forgive-me smile. I'd seen it too many times to be susceptible, but she bought it.

I said, "Dare is the most likely Louise, coming back around to the movie theory."

Nick raised a finger. "Y'all realize you're casting Thelma and Louise as lesbians, right? Not that I mind, personally."

Cracker chuckled and they both got quelling glares.

"I've never seen anybody be as patient as Dare is with Diana," Perline said. "Helping her get sober, encouraging her in that new job. He would do anything for her."

Cracker shook his head. "I'm still rooting for Sid. I doubt Diana is going to marry Dare, not once Ty gets that fancy resort going. Diana likes the good life. She'll be setting her sights a whole lot higher than a small town deputy living in a trailer on the wrong side of the tracks. Dare must be able to see that himself. He wouldn't risk his career for her."

"I'll call my father to see what he can do about that alibi," I said, "but I'm not going to hold my breath. Y'all think the email thing is too sophisticated for Hank. I think it's too artistic for Dare. He knows the best way to keep a crime unsolved is to wipe the fingerprints and leave the body in the car by the side of the road in a big city."

We sat and nodded at each other, satisfied that we had alternatives, but not knowing which was best.

Perline got up to fetch the pitcher of iced tea. "Y'all want pie? Cracker made chocolate meringue this morning."

Nick and I sat up straight and put our hands on the table like good children who deserved pie. "Is the Pope Catholic?" Nick asked, spoiling the effect.

She went into to the kitchen and came back with generous slices on chilled plates. She and Cracker beamed as we took our first bites and made chocolate ecstasy noises.

"Y'all're going to make a fortune," Nick said, winning complete forgiveness from Perline. "Ty's spa people will climb the walls and hike into town to eat this pie."

"I can do spa pie too," Cracker said. "A nice lemon chiffon with chocolate curls on top, so they feel like they're cheating on their diets." I couldn't think of anything more unlikely than this burly man concocting delicate treats for the ultra-fussy. But then, Lost Hat had turned most of my former ideas about country folk upside down.

"If we get to vote," Perline said, settling back in her chair, "I vote for Carson Caine. He always was a sly kid. He'd say anything to anyone to get what he wanted."

"You don't like his wife," Cracker said, "cuz she won't come in here and chew the fat with the rest of the gals."

"Fat! Her? Ha! She hardly comes into town at all. We're not good enough for Little Miss Dallas High Society Prancey Prance Prance."

That was quite a title. I'd love to photograph the next contest.

"He has an alibi too," I said. "He was at a country club in Kerrville Wednesday and Thursday, schmoozing another developer guy."

"Another one?" Cracker asked. "What's going on around here?"

"He said it was a potential campaign contributor, a green builder from San Antonio that Carson thought might act as a counterweight to Roger Bainbridge."

"Set one developer against the other," Nick said. He mimed a couple of boxing punches. "It might work, if the second guy is bigger and faster than old Roger."

"More likely they'll knock the rest of us out of our homes," Perline said. "I want to change my vote. I think the second guy did it, out of pure greed. I want him to be the one that goes to jail, not my cousin or our best deputy. We don't need a bunch of rich snobs waltzing around chasing after our land and whining about how countrified we all are."

"Good enough for me," Nick said. "The developer did it. Case closed."

Chapter 22

I let Nick pay for lunch with his platinum credit card. Now he only owed me 999 meals. Alas, he had get back to Austin, so we picked up the dog and walked back to my house.

Nick aimed the clicker at his car and gave me a long look. "It wasn't the green builder from San Antonio."

"I know."

"It might not have been Hank either."

"I know that too."

"You got your guy a reasonable doubt, which is more than he had. But it'll have to go to trial before he's really in the clear."

"I know. I do, honestly. The main thing is that now *I* don't think he did it. That's the part that was killing me."

Nick slung himself into his seat. "Keep your chin up, Penny-lope. And don't forget to call the parents."

Jake and I waved him down the street. After the shiny blue sports car turned the corner, I felt disconnected, at loose ends. Restless.

My Kit-Kat clock said five after three. Too late to call the folks in Germany. I'd just had lunch at the diner, I couldn't do that again today. I could go hang out in a coffee shop for a while, except that—oops! We didn't have one in Lost Hat. No movie theater either. Also no museums or friends' studios to hang out in when I didn't feel like working. I could go shopping for a new outfit, but we didn't have an Academy Superstore or a Goodwill and besides, I hated shopping.

I couldn't even go out to Ty's ranch and do photography, not while Hank the Raider was lurking out there cooking up redneck cocaine.

I stood on the grass in my front yard under the shade of the live oak tree, studying my house, pondering how I'd ended up here. Somehow over the course of this rackety couple of days, I had come to a decision to stick it out, come what may, and put down roots right here in Lost Hat.

My house was a small three-bedroom ranch model, white with brown trim. It had a front porch where I could read the Sunday paper and wave at the neighbors. Great Aunt Sophia had kept it up, so it had a relatively new roof, sound siding, and level gutters. I mowed the lawn and trimmed the box hedges around the foundations as needed.

I'd never owned a house before and had mixed feelings about it. On the one hand, it was comfortable and it was mine; I could do whatever I wanted with it. On the other hand, I hadn't had time to do anything, apart from carting most of the knick-knacks up to the second floor of my studio and unpacking my few boxes of clothes. I mostly owned photography stuff, which lived at the studio. I hadn't done anything to make the house really mine, to make it a place that said "Penelope Trigg, Artist-Entrepreneur, lives here."

Maybe I should, now that I'd had my little epiphany. I could at least do something about that boring brown trim. How wigged out would the neighbors be if I painted my house turquoise with neon yellow trim?

Pretty darned wigged, more'n likely. But a whole spectrum of colors shone between blah-blah brown and Caribbean bright.

A sudden surge of energy made up my mind. I could at least get some paint chips and ask the hardware guy how to go about it. I walked back to the square to pick up my truck, then drove over to the Benson Hardware Store on 331.

Ray Benson, the owner of the store, called, "Howdy, Penny," as I walked in the door. I had been in here a lot when I was fixing up the studio. He told me about the paint preparation steps, listed the supplies I would need, and offered to rent me a sander. He thought I should paint the whole house, since it had been a good ten years.

Another upside to small town living. Nobody at a big box store knows how old your paint is. Plus Ray never gave me any of that "little lady" malarkey. He knew I was handy; most artists are. We use a lot of tools in unusual ways in art school.

I went to the paint department at the back of the store and fell into a Technicolor dream. Did I want to go tropical with hot pinks and ice blues? Or perhaps something more sophisticated, like sage greens, burgundies, and mustards? My brain whirled, trying colors on the house in my mind's eye, when I smelled stale smoke and sour sweat and heard a gravelly voice in my ear.

"Look out, look out! Big black bull's a'coming."

I froze, stiff as a possum cornered by the family dog. *Hank!* I didn't dare look at him. Ray's voice talking on the phone sounded a thousand miles away.

Hank chuckled and I unfroze enough to take a step backward, bumping my heel against the paint chip display. I held the color brochures in front of me, as though I could defend myself with good taste.

I screwed up my courage and took a peek. Hank's close-set eyes were bright—too bright. The dilated pupils and the bloodshot whites reminded me of that feral hog. No doubt his bite would be every bit as nasty. He held a case of Sterno cans under one arm.

"Shoo!" I said. It came out in a whisper.

Hank recoiled, curling his fingers in front of his scraggly moustache. "Ooh! I'm so scared!" He leered at me. "You got balls, girl. I'll give you that. But you need to learn to mind your own business. I thought old Blackberry'd teach you that lesson, but you're one zippy little bunny."

He took a step closer and I leaned back into the display, trying not to tremble visibly. But he was a hunter. He could smell my fear as clearly as I smelled the cigarettes on his skin.

"I'm a wily coyote and I eat bunnies for breakfast. Best you remember that when you're out there with that nosey camera of yours."

"How's it coming, Penny?" Ray's friendly voice melted my fear. I met Hank's eyes and summoned a tense smile. He chuckled and slipped around the corner.

I stood in front of the paint display, shuffling color cards aimlessly with shaking fingers, waiting to hear him pay for his Sterno and leave.

The front door chimed. I made my way to the front of the store. "That guy gives me the creeps," I told Ray, as I paid for my house-washing soap and sandpaper. "He snuck up and scared me."

"Hank?" Ray chuckled as he bagged my stuff. "He's an odd duck, all right. He was probably just flirting with you."

Why did people keep saying that? The day I thought Hank Roeder was flirting with me was the day I'd start wearing a burka.

"I wish he'd get rid of that Confederate flag, though," Ray said. "Gives people the wrong impression of us. I keep telling him the Hill Country counties voted against secession, but he's not interested in the real history."

I took my purchases and went home. I put on a pair of old gym shorts and my oldest T-shirt and found a pair of blown-out running shoes in the back of the closet. Add a ball cap and sunscreen and I was ready to rumble.

I got out the big ladder and started in the front, scraping loose paint, banging in the odd nail, scrubbing the siding and trim with a weak soap solution. Good, hard, physical labor tires the body, loosening mental knots and washing away the frustrations of the week. I felt safe outside in plain view of my neighbors, although for a while I kept getting a prickly feeling that made me look up and down the street for a black pick-up with red flame decals.

Hank Roeder had put the bull in my pasture. Every time I thought of it, I got so steamed I had to climb down from the ladder and run the hose over my head. I could have been killed! Worst of all, that son of a bitch had made me afraid to go out and do the job that I loved best.

At least now I knew Ben hadn't done it. Somehow, in time, I'd find a way to persuade him and Tillie to forgive me.

When I took my supper break, I called Deputy Penateka and told him about the Sterno. He said, "We're working on it, Penny," and advised me to stick close to home in the meantime. I asked him how long a meantime was in Long County and he said there was some hang-up about the warrant.

That made me so mad I got out the clippers and whacked away at the box hedges around the base of my front porch. Then I decided I didn't like the dumb things anyway, so I got a shovel and dug them right out. Boring little old lady hedges. I wanted flowers—lush, wild, exuberant flowers.

I worked until dark on Friday night and then got up early Saturday and started in again. Neighbors wandered over to see what I was up to and give me contradictory advice. It made me feel like a real home-owner, standing all sweaty in the yard yakking about caulk and how to keep skunks out of the crawlspace.

I was fixing myself a peanut butter and peach sandwich for lunch when I suddenly realized I'd forgotten about Ty's visiting hours. I used to think about him every hour; heck, I used to think about him every other minute. Could one night of believing him to be a killer have pushed him that far out of my mind?

I licked peach juice off my fingers and called the jail. They said I could visit him Sunday at four. They couldn't bring him to the phone right then, because he was teaching a class in Windows Basics to the other inmates.

A model prisoner. Somehow that made me feel guiltier. Would our relationship survive this experience? Other people managed to get through bad patches and stay together, didn't they? That revelation that peels the paint from your illusions, that shows you your lover wasn't the man you thought he was. People adapt and go on.

It could be worse. I could be finding out that Ty was a freelance art critic.

I finished the prep work late in the afternoon. I had gotten wet and dirty from head to toe and still hadn't decided which colors I wanted. Most of the neighbors liked the muted shades. Only Mr. Muelenbach, the retired high school English teacher who lived next door, voted for the turquoise and pink scheme. Marion, who dropped by to bring me a plate of health food cookies and critique my work, told me bright colors would compete with the landscaping, if I really ever planted flowers, which she very much doubted.

I shared the cookies with Jake, who liked them more than I did. I decided to go to the studio where I could try on the colors in Photoshop, so I put away the ladder and the tools and got cleaned up.

The studio was deliciously cool and dim with the front shades drawn. It felt like I'd been gone for a month. When I booted up the Power Mac and popped the flash card out of my camera, I remembered that I hadn't yet uploaded the pictures from the car scene. Another whole card from Blackberry Day sat forgotten in its pocket in my camera bag.

I started uploading the photos, but didn't want to look at them quite yet. Thinking about the southeast pasture made me think of Hank and thinking about Hank made me paranoid. I got up to lock the front door. Then I went into the kitchen to check the back door. I had to fight the urge to go check upstairs. In a horror movie, that's where old Hank would be, crouched in the shadows among the antiques, drooling while he licked his long hunting knife.

Enough! I had a faithful watch dog; let him do the watching. I turned on all the lights and put on the one sure cure for the wiggins: Tito Puente's *Mucho Cha-Cha*. I danced back to the computer, opened a picture of my house in Photoshop, and started trying on colors.

Tito favored the hot tropical schemes.

By seven-thirty, I'd moved on to Alejandro Escovedo and the contemporary yellows and grays. Jake reminded me that we hadn't eaten anything but cookies, so we took a break and went to the Seven Sisters—Tillie's mother's restaurant—for enchiladas and refried beans.

Somebody should have told me not to feed beans to a dog.

I stepped out to the sidewalk for a breath of fresh air and a look at the sunset. The concrete still radiated the day's heat, but a light breeze ruffled the leaves of the trees in the courthouse park. I could almost hear them sighing with relief. Another summer day survived; a warm, soft night for recovery.

I put Jake on the leash and locked the front door. Might as well take him for a spin before knocking off for the night. We walked toward the Law Enforcement Center, since I figured that was the last place my arch-enemy would choose to spend a Saturday night. We were rounding the corner of the bank when a police siren bleeped behind me.

I startled and pulled Jake back against the old bank building.

Two—no, three—cop cars went whizzing past, lights flashing and sirens blaring. There was big trouble somewhere in Lost Hat tonight.

We jogged down to the corner of 88 to look, but the trouble must be outside the central business district. We cut across the bank's parking lot back to Pecan Street and bumped into Sid Matslar coming around the corner.

"What's going on?"

"I don't know," I said, "but it must be big. Half the sheriff's department just raced past."

He looked at me with a boyish sparkle in his eyes. "Let's follow 'em."

What the hey. We country folks take our entertainment where we can find it.

Sid's car, a well-worn Kia Rio, was the only car left in the bank's lot. He didn't mind having a large dog drooling over his shoulder. Points to the loan officer in the wide suspenders.

He gave me a sidelong look as he turned the key in the ignition. "You're not afraid to get into a car with me? That must mean I'm not a suspect anymore." He didn't sound like he'd taken the notion very seriously.

Neither had I; not him, anyway. "Well, I got my dog."

Jake chose that moment to give Sid an ear-washing.

Sid groaned, then focused on speeding down 88 without hitting any of the other cars following the cops.

The sirens ahead of us muted into random bleeps as the cop cars pulled into the parking lot of the Hat Trick Saloon. Being Saturday night, they had a full house. We pulled over at the edge of the lot and jumped out of the car, following the other sightseers to a spot near the door.

"Let us through, please," I said, edging my way through the bodies, "I've got a dog here."

People parted to let me through with Jake. This dog thing worked like magic! Sid followed us, mumbling, "I'm with them."

We made it to the front of the small crowd in time to see Dare coming through the front door with Hank Roeder in handcuffs, lecturing him in a low voice. I couldn't hear the words, but I knew them from TV: "You have the right to remain silent…"

He marched him to a county car, where another deputy had the back door open. Hank looked demented in the flashing colored lights: bony as a grasshopper, beady eyes glaring, that death's head grin under the Confederate moustache. As they tucked him into the car, he spotted me in the crowd and bared his teeth like a wild beast.

I bared my teeth right back at him, happy to be fear-free again. Also, of the two of us, which one would be spending Saturday night in jail?

Chapter 23

I presented myself at the desk at the Visitation Center promptly at four o'clock on Sunday afternoon. I'd spent the morning helping Mr. Muelenbach with his vegetable garden, hauling mulch and stacks of weeds. I'd also called the folks to ask Dad if he could find a way to confirm Dare's alibi. He said he'd make a few calls, but recommended that I not hold my breath in the meantime.

He hadn't decided if he liked my getting involved in murder investigations. On the one hand, it brought me into regular communication with the peace-keeping authorities, in whose mission he wholeheartedly believed. On the other hand, it also brought me to the attention of people who considered violence an effective coping strategy.

I took some pains with my appearance this morning, using the mirror time to try to resolve my feelings about Ty. I didn't get any farther than I had with the color schemes yesterday. We'd moved past the hot, tropical phase of fresh romance, but were we ready for the muted tones of mature disillusion?

Surely not. This trouble, once we got past it, would only strengthen our relationship. I pulled on my purple linen pants and a plain white T-shirt with a scoop neck that showed a little cleavage. I found a string of amber beads in Great-Aunt Sophia's jewelry box and looped those around my neck while I stepped into my dress-up sandals. I even polished my hair with an old silk scarf and left it loose. I decided against lipstick, for fear Ty would think I'd been possessed by an alien entity.

The desk sergeant waved me through to the visitor's room, saying "It's a regular old home week in there."

I didn't know what she meant until I walked in and found Carson sitting across from Hank and Ty. They had pushed their chairs back from the table so they could see each other over the fixed plastic dividers that were supposed to provide privacy for each visitor-prisoner pair. Ty sat in our usual bay near the visitor entrance; Carson and Hank sat at the opposite end. Dwayne, the guard, stood at the door to the jail corridor with his hands behind his back. He kept his eyes on Hank, with occasional glances at the other two.

The three old friends lounged in the hard plastic chairs with the air of neighbors passing the time at a backyard barbecue. But tension hung in the air strong enough to prickle the hairs on the back of my neck.

"Penny!" Ty showed me his businessman's smile. "Look who's here! My old pal Hank, come to keep me company, and my other old pal Carson, come to keep him company."

"Penny, what a delightful surprise," Carson said, half-standing until I got myself seated opposite Ty. "I'm checking up on Hank and taking the chance to visit Ty. I should have come sooner, but with the campaign on top of everything else…" He produced his politician's smile.

Hank did not smile. The loose jumpsuit made him look scrawny, like a blond monkey with a scraggly moustache. The pink fabric accentuated his bloodshot eyes and the grayish tinge of his skin. He looked thoroughly miserable, but he managed to pull himself together enough to bare his teeth at me again.

"Oh, stop," I said. "You can't scare me anymore."

"I'll be out on bail Monday morning. Then you'd best watch yourself, Missy." His voice sounded like he'd been gargling spackle.

"Are you threatening me?" I glanced at Dwayne, who stood up straight and looked as authoritative as a twenty-year-old with freckles and jug-sized ears could.

Carson made a pacifying gesture at me and gave Hank a stern look. "Now, now. Of course he's not threatening you. We're all friends here."

Hank rolled his eyes and stretched his thin lips into an unnatural smile far less pleasant than the sneer.

Carson shrugged at me. "Manners are not Hank's long suit. He really is all bark though. He thinks it's funny to tease the girls."

Very funny. I was laughing so hard it almost showed.

"It appears Hank has been up to no good in our old club house," Ty said. He gave him a cold smile. "It's hard to believe he could have been cooking his messes right under our noses, so to speak. I'm surprised you never noticed it, Carson."

"It's no surprise, Tyler," Carson said. "My spread is a lot bigger than yours, remember. And I have staff to work the fences. I rarely get out that way myself."

The two men sat and grinned at each other. I sensed treacherous undercurrents, but had no clue what drove them. Were they old friends or old enemies?

"Besides," Carson said, "the Raider is innocent until proven guilty, isn't that right, Dwayne?"

Ty said, "Like me, right, Dwayne?"

Dwayne didn't answer. Wise kid.

Ty said, "I heard they caught old Hankerino red-handed last night, selling meth out at the Hat Trick."

Both Ty and Carson gazed at old Hankerino as if considering a hound that refused to go hunting. I expected the next words to be, "What are we going to do about that dad-blame dog?"

"A friend wanted a few hits," Hank grumbled. "A little two-bit dealing. That's all they got on me."

"Oh, I think they've got more than that." Ty's voice thrummed with menace.

The tone penetrated Hank's foggy condition. He twisted in his chair to face Ty squarely. "I did not kill that guy." He put a hand over his heart. "I swear by the arrow."

The old boyhood oath. Ty held Hank's eyes for a long time. "Huh," he said at last. "I almost believe you, Raider."

"I don't." I glared at Ty. Hank was far and away our best suspect and I personally wanted to see him locked him up in a high-security prison in another part of the state.

Hank rolled his bloodshot eyes at me. Then he gave a rasping cough. "I want a beer."

"They don't give us beer, old son," Ty said. "But you've got a scoop of chicken salad, two slices of wheat bread, and canned fruit cocktail to look forward to for lunch."

Hank made a gagging gesture. "I'll be out on Monday, right, Boss?" He gave Carson a hard look.

"Do my best." Carson's tone was neutral, not promising anything. A good sign for my team.

"Dealing less than an ounce," Hank said. "That's nothing. You'll bail me out, a little bargaining, I'll get what, three-to-five? Good behavior, I'm out in half that."

"What bargaining?" I asked. "Once they get into that old stone house, they'll have everything they need for both charges. They're probably out there right now."

"Not without my knowledge," Carson said. "I haven't seen a warrant yet. And nobody has said anything about charging Hank with Bainbridge's murder."

"Manslaughter," Ty said. "That's the charge against me, anyway. But now we've got my old pal Hank to rearrange that picture."

"I honestly don't think Hank did it." Carson looked at me as he spoke. "It's too sophisticated, especially that bit about the email messages. And I should hope I'd be the last person he would try to implicate."

"My lawyer told me about the stuff they found in the car," Ty said. "That doesn't sound sophisticated to me. In fact, Hank is the person most likely to salvage those alligator boots. Anyone who knows me would know I prefer ostrich."

He flicked a glance at me and I bravely looked down at my hands. He knew, I could feel it. He knew I'd given up on him after we found the car.

I took a breath and met his eyes. "I believed it was you for one night. One long, terrible, sleepless night. I don't believe it anymore and I'm sorry I ever doubted you."

He smiled that lopsided smile that turned my insides to mush. "It would have worried me more if you hadn't."

Hot, tropical feelings washed over me like warm paint. We beamed at each other, telepathically crossing the plastic divider in a big, smooshy hug.

Hank groaned. "Oh, spare me."

Carson said, "That's so touching, really. Except that I'm the one that you were trying to frame, Tyler, which I must say I resent."

Ty leveled his gaze at Carson. "You really think I did it, don't you?"

"Put all the pieces together and yours is the only picture that emerges."

"I can't believe you think I'm capable of hitting a man hard enough to kill him. I've never hit anybody in my life."

"You hit me," Hank said.

"What? When?"

"That time I put that hog snake in Diana's backpack."

"You scared the shit out of her! She was in tears, you asshole!"

I chuckled.

"See," Hank said. "It's funny."

"I'm laughing *at* you, not *with* you, moron. The more you try to defend yourself, the deeper you dig the hole. I can't wait to see you on the witness stand."

"She's got a point," Ty said.

"No, she's proving my point," Carson said. "Hank doesn't have the smarts, except when it comes to hunting, which must be some kind of *idiot savant* characteristic."

"Hey!" Hank said.

"Idiot savant is better than just plain idiot," I explained helpfully. Hank glared at me and I stuck my tongue out at him.

"Children, please," Carson said. "I am presenting a considered argument. Hank isn't capable of sending those misleading messages or of setting up the false story with the car and the call to my campaign line. Even if he were, he wouldn't hide the thing right downhill from his meth lab." He winced—one step too far.

"Got that part right," Hank said, missing the point. "That car's a beaut. Brand new Cadillac Escalade with leather interior and chrome detailing? Must've cost a boatload." Hank jerked his chin at Ty. "It'd been me, I'd've took that car and sold it, and then they would've found it, and then they would've got me. Case closed." He sat back with his arms folded and a satisfied sneer on his face.

We stared at him, silent for a long moment.

I broke first. "So your defense is basically 'Not guilty by reason of stupidity?'"

Ty and Carson frowned at him for a long moment, then traded nods. "That ought to do it," Carson said.

"Pretty much," Ty agreed.

I stared at him, flabbergasted. "That's the most unreasonable line of reasoning I've ever heard!"

He shrugged at me. "We've got other suspects, right? On that list of yours?"

"Yes."

"I'm on the list," Carson said, as though it were some kind of local honor. "Unfortunately for you, I have an alibi. Quite a good one."

"Aren't you the clever jinx," Ty said.

Carson smiled thinly. "I'm a busy guy with a good secretary. I could probably provide an alibi for any time last month. Between the campaigning, the bank business, the ranch..."

"You're turning into your grandfather." A spark glimmered deep in Ty's green eyes. I didn't get the joke, but Carson plainly didn't like it.

Hank laid his forehead on the table with a long, croaking groan. "I'd give my right nut for a smoke."

Carson clucked his tongue. "You'll live. It's less than twenty-four hours."

"If he makes bail," Ty said, "which he won't, if my lawyer does her job. Hank's a menace to the community, whether he killed Bainbridge or not." Ty looked at me. "You should meet with her when she comes back out and go over your list of suspects."

"I will," I said. "I'll keep at it right up to the trial, if necessary." Although I was eighty-five percent certain that the man who'd killed Roger Bainbridge was sitting right here, moaning for a cigarette.

"You're very diligent," Carson said. "I have to admire your work ethic."

"I'm motivated." I flashed Ty a tropical smile.

"You've done a good job already." Ty smiled encouragement, but worry shadowed his eyes. "You're a better investigator than any of our deputies."

"Yeah," Hank growled. "She's a regular Girlock Holmes."

The rest of us gaped at him in astonishment.

"What?" His lip curled, pleased with the result. "Y'all think I don't got cable?"

Chapter 24

As I walked out of the building, an argument against Hank's stupidity defense struck me like a blast of hot air. No, wait—that was just heat rising off the sidewalk. But the argument worked. Hank could have hidden that car near his lair to keep an eye on it until things cooled down, planning to sell it in San Antonio, like he'd said, along with the ten thousand dollar boots. Why waste such valuable commodities?

It was still stupid. Possibly stupider. A case of delayed stupidity, which perhaps displayed some degree of maturity, but still did not invalidate my version of how things had happened.

Thinking about the car set a memory flickering in the back of my mind. I'd seen something related to that set up, something useful…Something important.

I needed to spend an evening in the studio getting my latest batches of photographs in order. I hadn't even delivered the car scene photos to the sheriff's department and that package included an invoice. I zipped home to change into my everyday clothes and pick up the dog, then back to the studio for an evening of work.

I'd uploaded everything the day before. Now I sorted the car scene pictures into their own folder and made the six-picture proof sheets. I printed those, made a CD, and brought it all up to the computer at the front desk. Someday it would be nice to network these two computers, but I didn't know how. Maybe Nick did; I'd have to ask him.

I opened up QuickBooks to do the invoice and stared at it stupidly. Tillie usually did this part. She'd set the

Flash Memory

system up and I had never troubled myself to learn how to use it. It had menu options galore; not as bad as Photoshop, but I'd learned that one at school.

I fiddled and clicked and backtracked and deleted. How could this be so hard? I didn't want to screw up any existing thing, that was part of the problem, but I didn't know how to make the existing things line up with the new thing. Frustrating!

How could Tillie walk out on me like that? I'd hurt her feelings, yes, but in the service of Truth and Justice. Things were looking pretty dire for Ty, in case she hadn't noticed, and more importantly, Roger's killer was still out there walking around. Possibly even dancing little steps of glee, since nobody but feeble Girlock had so much as asked him where he was on the night in question.

I'd worked myself into a fine state of righteous indignation when the object of my ire pulled up in front of the studio with a screech of tires. She struggled out of the truck, slammed the door, and stomped across the sidewalk, clutching a manila folder. She banged through the studio door and slapped the folder onto the reception counter. "There's your goddammed secret! This is what you were fishing for, interrogating my husband and following him around. Are you happy now?"

I started to point out that I had not followed Ben around, although in fairness I had considered it. Tillie had turned pink with fury, so I let it slide.

I got up and stepped cautiously toward the counter. I could take the Tillster in a fair fight, but a woman in a rage was a dangerous animal. I opened the folder gingerly. Its contents rocked me on my heels. "Whoa ho ho!"

I could never have predicted this, not in a million years. The folder held photographs—rather good ones, all black and white—of Diana frolicking at the spring, wearing nothing but her birthday suit and a big, shiny smile.

Al fresco. In the buff. In other words, stark naked.

She did not frolic alone. A man appeared in some of the photographs, but never full frontal. Not even his face; just part of an arm or a leg and that much only in a few shots. The best one caught him climbing out of the pool with his back to the camera.

Ben, the sly dog, had been doing a little covert photography in his spare time, producing a fine series of ex-girlfriend nudie pictures, something to cherish over the years as he and his wife grew older and fatter.

"Oh, me, oh, my." I leafed through the photos again. "Oh, Tillie."

"Awful, isn't it?" Tears shimmered in her eyes, but didn't fall. Judging by the redness and the smudged mascara, she'd been doing a lot of crying. Now she seemed ready to move on to the next stage: retribution.

"Awful that he took them," I said, "but they're pretty good photographs." I held up one where a band of light from the setting sun striped across the frame, lighting up Diana's head, shoulders, and breasts like a Madonna in a Renaissance painting. "This one is good enough to show."

"Penny!" Color rose in Tillie's cheeks again.

Not the best moment for a critique. "Sorry!" I shrugged sheepishly.

She glared at me and growled in the back of her throat. That pink streak in her hair gave her a wild aspect. She clenched her fists and shook from head to toe. I took a step back, actually afraid she might charge over the counter at me.

Then she drew in a huge breath and let it out in a long growly huff. "I'm not mad at *you*. Not really. If you hadn't stirred things up, I never would have gone looking for Ben's stupid secret, and I never would have found these—these—Rrraaahhh!" She shrieked at the ceiling, shaking her fists.

"And that's better?"

"Of course it's better! You think I want my husband keeping his own personal stash of his own personal pornography in *my house*? Now it's out, now I know, and now I can make him pay for it for the rest of his miserable, rotten, lying, cheating life."

"Sounds fair to me." Poor Ben. "So you're going to stick it out? Stay with him, I mean?"

"Oh, he doesn't get off that easily. No way. I want revenge, with a capital Grrrrrrrr."

"You go!" I grinned at her, or rather gave her an apologetic grimace grin. "Are you sure you're not mad at me?"

She thought about it, then shook her head. "Nope. All the mad belongs to Ben."

"Want some tea? Nice and cold. And there's health food cookies from Marion."

"No ice cream?"

"I ate all the ice cream. It's been a rough week."

Jake led us to the kitchen. I brought the folder. We needed to study those pictures, however hard it might be for her, to figure out when they were taken and who the guy was. We might be able to recognize something about him, if we put our minds to it.

"We're a little low on supplies," I said. "I didn't get to the store on Friday."

"It's my job to keep the kitchen stocked."

"It's been a weird week." I opened the plastic container of cookies and stood by the counter, holding it in my hands. "I am so sorry about last Monday, Tillie. I should have found a better way."

"You couldn't help it and it turned out you were right. Ben really did have something to hide."

"I could have tried to head him off or change the subject or something."

"Nope." Tillie shook her head. "This is his fault. Not yours and not mine."

She got the Flintstones glasses out of the cupboard and filled them with iced tea. "I don't know what I was thinking with that stupid note. This job is the best thing that ever happened to me."

"Let's forget about the note," I said. "Let's forget about Thursday. Let's forget about Monday. In fact, let's screw the whole damn week."

"Screw the whole damn week!" Tillie shouted. Jake tucked his tail between his legs and scooted under the table. "Not you, Jakey." Tillie bent to coax him back out with coos and smooches.

We sat. Tillie gave Jake a cookie and then looked at me sideways. "Can I have my job back?"

"You never lost it, because none of last week happened, remember? Except for Hank getting arrested. We keep that."

"What! How?"

Points to the new girl, beating Tillie in the gossip division! I caught her up on events since the last time I'd seen her. She *oohed* and *oh, no-ed* in all the right places. When I told her about seeing Ben right after the bull chased me, her eyes narrowed. I hastily assured her that Hank had practically admitted to letting Blackberry out. Not in front of anyone else, but good enough for me.

"I am so glad he's the guilty one," she said. "Now nobody we like has to go to prison."

"The thing is, it might not be Hank. The drugs, yes. They caught him red-handed. But maybe not Roger. So, Tillie, if you can stand it, we kind of need to look at those photographs. That guy, whoever he is, could be the Louise."

"The who?"

I stared at her for a moment. More than anything, her non-knowledge of the *Thelma and Louise* theory exposed how deep the rift between us had been. Normally, we would already have examined it from all possible angles. I filled her in, briefly setting out the variations. She hummed and nodded, getting the point immediately and with way more enthusiasm than Ty had shown.

But when I got to the end, she cocked her and said, "I didn't realize Thelma and Louise were gay."

"They're not. They weren't. It's more like an overlay than a direct match. Think of it as sort of thematic."

"Thematic. Got it." She pulled the folder toward her and opened it with tightened lips. "Let's do it." Let it never be said that Tillerina lacked courage when courage was required.

I scooched my chair over so we could look at them together. "First, let's see if we can figure out when they were taken."

She studied the photos one by one, a grim look on her face. I admired her. It had to be hard, looking at Diana's magnificent figure, knowing yourself to be built on the hefty side. It was hard enough for me and I'm in good shape. Not Diana's kind of shape; there are limits to what running can do for the womanly form.

I concentrated on the non-Diana aspects of each picture. Ben must have been higher than the pool, probably hidden in the rocks along the path. He must have been shooting slightly from the west, judging by the angle of that beam of light and the shadows on the right sides of boulders. "Close to sunset, I guess."

"Hm."

One picture showed a champagne bottle and a pair of plastic glasses leaning against a rock at the edge of the pool. Another caught the edge of a rumpled pile of clothes.

"Look." Tillie pointed at a picture of Diana posing on a rock with her head thrown back. She tapped her finger on a bunch of wildflowers. "See these flowers?"

"Yes?"

"Those are Mexican hats. I remember them because they don't look like hats."

"They really don't," I said. "But I like them anyway. They come out later, after the bluebonnets are done, when the hot colors start to predominate. May—mid-May—maybe June. I think they go on all summer, but at least we have one endpoint. Good call, Tillie!"

"I want to get to the bottom of this as much as you do. More."

"Speaking of bottoms, who the heck is this guy?" I pulled out the best photo of the mystery man, a clear shot of his backside from the shoulders to the knees, as he climbed out of the pool.

"It can't be Hank," Tillie said. "Not skinny enough."

"Plus if it was Hank, there'd be beer cans lying all over the place. Can you imagine going skinny-dipping with Hank?"

We shared a horrified shudder and recovered by eating more cookies.

"It could be Dare, maybe." I turned the photo from side to side. "But I think he's a bit stockier."

"It can't be Dare." Tillie tapped the photo of the champagne bottle. "No way."

"Good catch. Hm. When did they start going out?"

"Way before May, if these are from this year."

I looked at the back, suddenly remembering a lab would've dated each print. Blank. "He developed these himself, in my darkroom, so these are definitely from this year."

Tillie stared at me, eyes round, mouth open. "He made these here? In my place of work? Right under our noses?" She started looking around the kitchen, eyes catching glassware, dish towels, odds and ends, like she was going to get up and start throwing things.

I grabbed her hands and caught her gaze. I spoke in a low, calm voice. "He's barred for life, don't worry. But first we catch the bad guy. Then you punish Ben. Okay?"

She pressed her lips together and nodded. "Okay." She turned back to the photos. "Okay."

I gave her a few seconds, then picked up where we left off. "So she's been dating Dare for many months at this point. Which means she's cheating on him, as well as falling off the wagon."

"And there's Ben hiding in the bushes taking nudie pictures like the most pathetic loser fool of an asshole that ever lived!" Tillie shook the photo at me. "This is so pitiful!"

"It really is." I laughed. "Poor Ben. Trapped in the past, taking his sneaky photos, worrying about you finding them. Then here comes Detective Trigg, backing him into a corner saying, 'Confess! Confess!' He must have walked around with his boxers in a bunch all week long."

Tillie giggled. I giggled. We fell into an all-out giggle fest. After a while, we tapered off and sat there wiping our eyes, trying not to look at each other, to keep from starting up again.

I said, "I'll bet this whole picture thing was one of those last gasps, you know? When a guy realizes that he's married and his life has changed and he can't quite get a grip on it. Now that it's out in the open, I'll bet he gives it up without a whimper."

"Oh, there will be whimpering," Tillie assured me. "Whimpering, wailing, begging for mercy. It used to be me trying to please him. Well, the spur's on the other boot now."

I toasted her new position in her marriage. "But I feel sad for Diana."

"What!"

"I do. It looks like she's having fun here, and probably she thought so too, at the moment, but this isn't what she wants. I know it. When she thinks about this day, if she ever does, she must cringe. She's worked so hard to get sober and be good at her job. Dare might not be the One, but he's a giant step in the right direction. Whoever this guy is, he's no good and she knows it. But he's got some kind of hold on her, some special draw…"

Tillie had listened to my defense of Diana with a slight curl to her lip. Now she conceded one small point. "He's got a great butt."

Fair enough. "It is a mighty fine butt."

"I might keep this one," Tillie said. "Cut out the Diana part and pin it up on the fridge. Between you and me, Ben's rear view is nowhere near this good. He's got love handles out to here." She illustrated with her own figure.

And a sizeable beer gut, but we didn't have a shot of this guy's belly, so that was neither here nor there. I doubted Butt Guy had a gut. His trim back and toned legs suggested a man who got regular exercise of a structured variety.

"Could it be Roger Bainbridge?" I tried to put imaginary pants on the man, but it wasn't easy.

"He was pretty fit, I think," Tillie said. "It would help if there was one with them standing side by side so we could see how tall he is. Bainbridge was kind of tallish."

"Not as tall as Ty or Ben."

"But we know it's not either of them anyway."

"True." I sighed. "Well, there's only one thing to do. We'll to have to get out and look at the bare butt of every single man in this county."

Tillie shrieked with glee. "Like Cinderella, only men's backsides instead of ladies' feet!"

That set us off again, howling with laughter.

"Drop 'em, pardner!" I tried to sound like the law. "Show us your rear or we'll haul your ass in for questioning."

"We could have a Wet Boxer contest at the Hat Trick."

"Hey, that could make money! We have the contest here and take pictures. We could do a calendar."

"Line 'em up and strip 'em down."

I sobered up again. "This doesn't necessarily help us, though. Help Ty, I mean."

"Yes, it does," Tillie said. "For one thing, it proves Diana was two-timing Dare with someone who is *not* Ben."

"Not Ben. Not Hank. And not Sid."

"Definitely not Sid."

"That leaves one guy on my list—Carson Caine."

"Carson Caine is on your list?" She picked up the butt picture again and studied it closely. "I have a naked picture of Carson Caine?"

"Except he's got an alibi. Or also it could be Roger Bainbridge, which is where the not helping comes in."

"Oh, right. Except that no, it does. If Dare found out about this, the jealousy would make him crazy." She spoke with authority. "That gives him the perfect motive to kill Bainbridge. Any little thing might set him off."

"He's got an alibi too, although nobody's checked it. But jealousy does make the most sense as a motive. Jealousy or loyalty, in the alternative where Diana killed Roger in self-defense."

"I vote for the jealousy." Tillie's eyes took on a fiery gleam. "If I'd caught Ben out there skinny-dipping with that tramp, I would've pushed him off the nearest cliff."

Chapter 25

After Tillie left, I popped a frozen dinner in the microwave and took Jake out back for a short stroll while it cooked. The sun had set while we'd been yakking, leaving a dark red stain along the horizon between the low buildings of the downtown area. I decided to take a spin around the courthouse, stretch all six of our legs and catch a breath of warm air. I loved the quiet of Lost Hat after everyone else closed up shop. No hum of traffic, no sirens wailing, no airplanes roaring overhead. Instead we get crickets, the occasional dog barking, maybe a truck rumbling past on a side street.

Jake inspected some fascinating shrubbery, while I gazed at the Law Enforcement Center, wondering if Ty had gone to bed already. They probably didn't have much to do in jail in the evening, other than watch sports on TV. Would he be in the same cell block as Hank? That wouldn't be pleasant.

Would Hank really get out on bail in the morning? That would be even less pleasant. I should be careful about locking my doors, going in as well as going out.

"Come on, Jakey. Back to work."

True to my new resolution, I locked the back door behind me as we went in. I let Jake off the leash and went up to lock the front door too. All secure. Back in the kitchen, I poured dog food into Jake's bowl and sat down to eat my equally simple fare.

That took ten minutes. Then I made a pot of coffee, put on some loud music, and settled down at my computer.

Ben's photos added a few pieces to the puzzle, enough that a picture finally began to emerge. Diana had been fooling around with a man who could tempt her into a relapse. I'd bet the relapsing was actually a big part of his appeal. Getting sober and finding the right balance for your life is hard. Sometimes it feels like a never-ending, joyless drag. Working with Marion and spending evenings with Dare gave Diana a daily double-whammy of earnest rectitude.

So when Mr. Good Butt came calling with his bottle of bubbly, she must have jumped off the wagon with a shriek of relief.

I had two good candidates for the man at the springs: Carson Cameron Caine, the boy next door and her teenage heartthrob. Everyone described him as a solid citizen, married with kids, but politicians and infidelity went together like cream and sugar. They could've been skinny-dipping at Leaping Springs ever since she was sixteen, for all anyone might know.

But Carson had the least motive of anyone in this situation. Say Diana was his little bit of extra-marital naughty. A man wouldn't get into a fight to defend his mistress. And even if he did, he certainly wouldn't set things up to frame himself for the crime. Besides, he had an alibi.

Roger Bainbridge made a better candidate for the secret lover. He had been new to Lost Hat, but had made a beeline for the county belle, who coincidentally happened to be co-owner of the second largest ranch in the area. I hadn't liked him, but tastes differ. Diana, like her mother, might long for a taste of the fine life. Roger, with his upscale vehicle and his fancy boots, might have made her offers she couldn't resist. Maybe he'd taken her to Mexico for a weekend of luxury, buying that silver heart charm as a secret reminder.

If Roger was Mr. Good Butt, then his killer was mostly likely Dare. He'd caught them hanky-pankying out at the springs and lost his temper. Then he'd sent Diana away and covered up the death, framing Ty with Carson as a backup story. Dare had the skills and the smarts and the tightly wound temperament. He had the best alibi, but also the strongest motive: good, old-fashioned jealousy.

Jealously could easily have lit Ben Jernigan's fuse. I would never say it to Tillie, but those photographs gave him a stronger motive, rather than exonerating him. They proved he'd been stalking Diana. Maybe Roger had caught him sneaking around and put the screws on, or maybe Roger had pushed too hard and Diana had struck back. Then Ben and Diana did the covering up together.

That was the only story in which the bracelet made any sense. I could see Diana being sentimental enough to make that burial offering, but why would any of the men do it?

The boots had value; so did the car. Burying a guy on top of the hill might have made more sense in the moonlight. Then once you got started, you might as well frame somebody else: Ty, Carson, take your pick. But that bracelet...

I clicked open the folder with the crime scene photographs and found one that showed all the charms. I cropped it so I wouldn't have to look at anything yucky and zoomed in to study the heart, the capital D, the Texas, and the horse. Nothing new struck me.

Then I remembered the silver archer I'd found in the road outside the old stone house. I opened that picture beside the one with the bracelet. It looked about the same size as the others and there seemed to be a gap between two charms where it might have hung.

Good enough for me. Now, what did it mean?

Diana had been a horsewoman in her younger days, but I'd never heard anyone talk about archery. Nor had I seen evidence of the sport anywhere on the Lazy H. No bows, no arrows, no straw targets left rotting in a field.

Didn't astrology have an archer in it somewhere? I googled "significance of archer" and discovered that it represented Sagittarius. So I googled "Sagittarius" and learned that these people loved freedom and disdained routine, might suffer illnesses of the muscles and thighs, and had birthdays between November 22 and December 21.

I googled "Roger Bainbridge birthday" and got nothing useful. It must be Dare's or Diana's birthday or surely he would have asked her about it. I hadn't been here last year, so I would've missed the party. Or it could represent Mr. Good Butt. If asked, Diana might have laughed and said it was Malibu's birthday or something completely unrelated.

Alcoholics do keep secrets; it's part of the disease. They're supposed to come clean, but hey—one step at a time.

I poked around in my folders of photographs, avoiding the ones of the burial site, while I pondered the archer in the dirt. I wondered if it still lay unnoticed in the road. I hoped so and quickly scribbled a note to mention it to Deputy Penateka. At the very least, it proved Diana had been up there since the last time it rained. We could safely bet she hadn't been delivering deer corn. She had a key to the gate too—the same key Ty supposedly used to hide the car.

The car! Something about that set up nagged at me. I opened the folder of photos from the car scene and studied the thumbnails. I'd gotten one good establishing shot from the road, with stacks of boulders on either side of the car lying nose down in the gully.

I opened up more folders and browsed the thumbnail images. I found a clear shot of yellow crime scene tape wound around the trees where the car had been, taken from Mt. Keno two days ago, when I'd been up there with Nick. Now the rock pile rising behind the trees set my spider sense tingling. When had I seen that configuration before?

A thrill of excitement shimmied along my spine as the connection clicked into place. I'd taken shots of that rockscape from Mt. Keno on the morning we found Roger's body. I opened the folder of pictures from my sunrise shoot and there it was: a photograph of the antelope creature standing at the edge of the road in front of Rattlesnake Terrace, the very same spot now liberally decorated with yellow tape.

I positioned the two images side by side. Sure enough, they were nearly identical in terms of location, which did not surprise me. I tended to favor certain framing devices, like curves in roads and distinctive rocks. The antelope stood slightly east of the car, but the pictures had substantial overlap. Anyone, including a judge and a jury, would recognize the similarities.

Except in Photo A we had a four-legged animal with tall curving horns, whereas in Photo B we had a strew of yellow crime scene tape. Most significantly, no big red Cadillac gleamed behind the beautiful beast. The roof of the car had been exposed to the sky. Dare pointed out that a helicopter would have spotted it right off; so would a camera with a 50mm lens on the top of Mt. Keno.

If the car had been there, I couldn't have missed it. That red metal stood out from the gray-green brush like a cardinal in a flock of sparrows. That car had not been there last Wednesday morning and I had the pictures to prove it. Somebody had moved it, sometime during the past week— a week during which Ty had been snugly locked up in the county jail.

Ty could not have moved that car. And if he didn't do that part, he didn't do any of it. My guy was innocent, provably so.

I got up to stretch, walking over to peer out the window at the darkened courthouse square and the glow of the Law Enforcement Center beyond. I could walk over there right now and present my evidence to whichever lowly deputy got stuck with the night shift. Or Deputy Dare, who might be whiling away his nights without Diana at the office.

I wished Dad would call about that cyber-crimes seminar. Could Dare have done both? How long did it take to get from here to Georgia? The nearest airport was in Kerrville, but he'd have to change planes in Houston or Dallas and probably again in Atlanta, with hours of driving on both ends. That added up to the better part of a day each way, in the middle of the work week too. But maybe he'd never even gone. He'd had a week to set up an alibi. He'd taken so many of those seminars, he probably had a good buddy in the training center who would vouch for him on his word alone.

I looked at the clock over the kitchen door—a little after nine, making it four in the morning in Germany. Four hours before I could decently call Dad. Then he'd have to wait six hours before he could decently call anyone in D.C. Ten hours to get that ball rolling. By then, it'd be seven a.m. here. The sheriff probably got to work by nine.

I wouldn't show these pictures to anyone other than Sheriff Hopper, to be on the safe side. So I might as well go home and catch a few Zs. Once I got Ty out, the rest was the sheriff's problem anyway. I would not personally help to put Tillie's husband in jail.

"One more night, Jakey. Then our guy will be back and you'll be sleeping on the floor again."

Chapter 26

I got to the studio early and called my father first thing. He promised to do what he could about Dare's alibi and congratulated me for producing solid evidence in Ty's favor. "It's out of your hands now, honey."

That might be true, in point of fact, but it didn't feel right. I wanted to know who had killed Roger Bainbridge and set my boyfriend up to take the fall. I itched to go out to that old stone house to scout around for more clues, in case Hank made bail.

I drummed my fingers lightly on the keyboard, wondering if I dared to go or if it would even be worth the risk. Then the front door opened and Perline came in. She closed the door firmly behind her and leaned against it with her hand on the knob, thrusting her head forward to project her whisper across the room. "I know who killed Roger!"

Her eyes were early-morning puffy, but brightened by green shadow and she'd swept her hennaed hair into a snug chignon on the top of her head.

"Me too," I said, walking up to the front counter.

"You do not!"

"I figured it out last night. It has to be either Dare or Ben Jernigan."

She folded her arms across her chest and smirked at me. "No and no. I was right all along. Carson Caine did it."

"He has an alibi."

"Unlike your favorite, Dare? I knew it had to be Carson. Mr. Slippery Sly. I've never trusted him. So I called my friend Rhonda who works at the Riverhill Country

Club. That one where Carson supposedly spent the night last Wednesday?"

"He wasn't there?"

She snapped her mouth closed. "Do you want to hear it or don't you?"

"I'm sorry. Please go on."

"Well, I called Rhonda and she said she worked that Wednesday night and Mr. Big Shot was nowhere to be seen. She would've remembered him too. He's a big tipper, which is good, but he always brings in an international crowd, if you know what I mean."

I shook my head and she giggled. "Roman hands and Russian fingers?"

I groaned. I couldn't take stale chestnuts this early in the morning.

She clucked her tongue at my lack of humor. "Anyway, Rhonda called a friend who works days, and she said he wasn't there Thursday morning for breakfast either. So his alibi is a crock, which means he lied about it, which means he must be guilty." She nodded once to rest her case.

"He could have been lying for some other reason," I said, not believing it, but needing time to digest the news. "Surely Sheriff Hopper would have had someone check that alibi."

"Nothing sure about it," Perline said. "They probably called that San Antonio feller and asked him if he had dinner with Carson Caine. Those guys always stick up for each other. He would have said yes without even thinking."

"I believe that. But what about the stuff in the car and the phone call? Why would Carson make it look like someone had tried to frame him?"

"Mr. Slippery Sly? He would think that was all kinds of funny, making it look like Ty was trying to make it look like he did it. That's exactly Carson's style."

I remembered the toys in his office and the undercurrents in the conversation between him and Ty at the jail. It kind of made sense, in a twisted way.

"Okay. I can kind of see that. And I can believe he and Diana were having an affair. He was her oldest old flame, after all, and I have proof she had been up to that old stone house recently." I told her about the archer charm, but not about Ben's photos. I might as well send them to the *Long County Communicator* for everyone to enjoy as let Perline see them. "But why would he kill Roger?"

"Carson's running for commissioner. An affair would ruin that little plan. Maybe Roger found out about it. What do you think a guy like that would do with such a tasty little tidbit?" She glanced up at the clock. "And now I got to get to work. There's hungry people out there wanting their breakfasts."

And people would soon be arriving at the courthouse for Hank's arraignment. If they let him out on bail, he'd go flush that stone house out with a fire hose, destroying any evidence of what had happened to Roger along with his meth lab.

I needed to get out there with my camera while everyone involved was at court. I caught Perline's arm as she opened the door. "Don't tell anybody else about this yet. Let me talk to the sheriff first. We don't want Carson to get a head start."

She tossed her head. "I think I know when to hold my tongue."

* * *

She wouldn't be able to hold it for long. I needed to roll, to be back before Hank's arraignment ended.

I went to the bathroom and braided my hair, good and tight so it wouldn't get in my way. Then I went into the kitchen to fill Jake's water bowl and make sure the coffeepot was off. I unlocked the equipment closet and got out my camera. Then the doorbell jangled again.

"Penny?"

Marion stood beside the reception counter, dressed for work in one of her sensible navy pantsuits. "You shouldn't leave the front unattended like this."

"I'm on my way out, Marion." I got my wallet from my backpack and put it in the side pocket of my pants. I slung my camera around my neck. "What's up? I'm in kind of a hurry."

"Where are you going?"

Oops. "Nowhere. Outside, here and there. Morning light is best."

She rolled her eyes at me, exasperated. "I just talked to Perline at the cafe. She told me about Carson."

"No way! She said she wouldn't tell anybody yet."

"Of course that doesn't mean me. You're going out there right now, aren't you? To snoop around that old house with your camera."

I growled under my breath. She could not talk me out of this. "Somebody has to. The deputies need a warrant, which they're not going to get, because Carson's father and the judge are old fishing buddies."

"I know. You should go."

That stopped me cold. "You're not going to scold me about minding my own business and letting the authorities do their jobs?"

"Sometimes the authorities need a little nudging. Hap's a good man and a fine sheriff in the normal run of things, but he gives too much weight to family connections."

"He won't consider Carson because he's one of the almighty Caines."

"The Caines are a fixture around here, like the courthouse or the old bank building. Carson has an important position in this county."

"Well, that's the motive, isn't it? Roger could have wrecked his marriage and destroyed his political career." I explained the new theory, keeping it short.

When I finished, she shook her head. "It's thin, but you know, the trickery sounds like Carson. The Caines show a bright face in public, but behind those iron gates, they've never been a happy family. Carson's grandfather was a mean old man. I didn't know him well, but I always had the feeling he ruled with a heavy hand. When the penalties are severe, children learn to be evasive and to blame others before blame can fall on them."

"Nick said meth can make people do all kinds of crazy stuff. Maybe that explains some of the parts that don't make sense, like the bracelet."

"Maybe so," Marion said. "Maybe they had their own logic at the time. But to my mind, the archer charm clinches it. Carson was born on Thanksgiving Day, you know."

"Are you sure?"

"Oh, yes. It's part of his campaign. Didn't you look at his website?"

I slapped myself on the forehead. I'd stopped too soon: one Google shy of the truth.

Marion rolled her eyes. "Well, there's still time to set things right." She glanced up at the clock. "Barely. Do you need me to watch your studio while you're gone?"

She floored me again. That made twice in five minutes. I laughed and gave her a peck on the cheek. "Marion, you are my absolute very most favorite second cousin twice removed."

She pushed me away, but with a big smile on her face. "Once, Penny. Once removed."

I told her about the evidence in the photographs on my computer, patted Jake, went out the back door, and revved up the Hulk.

The race was on.

Chapter 27

I stopped by the house to put my boots on and then swung past the bank for a final check. The Land Rover with the 3C logo was parked right next to the back door.

All clear.

I drove out to Ty's ranch, parked in front of the gate at the southeast pasture, and hiked across the grass. I climbed over the barbed wire fence at the post junction. It was easier without a bull snorting up my shorts.

I paused at the bend in the road, looking and listening. The car site appeared undisturbed, the yellow tape glistening with fresh dew. I smelled nothing but wet grass and cool rock, no lingering odor of exhaust or stirred-up dust from a passing truck. All I could hear was the faint click of insects and an occasional snatch of bird song. No engines, no voices. I was alone out here on this peaceful summer morning.

I walked around the bend and up the hill. The stone house looked peaceful too, with its door closed and the old truck rusting placidly under the trees. I took a deep breath and went inside. The door swung shut behind me.

"Penny, do come in."

I startled, caught in mid-stride. Carson knelt in front of the fireplace with a box of kitchen matches. He gave me that shiny politician's smile, then struck a match and tossed it on the stack of tinder. It burst into flames with a *whomp*. He must have made liberal use of the lighter fluid.

"You're at the bank." I said, stupidly. "I saw your car."

"We have more than one Rover, Penny. Skip's taking care of Hank. He's had plenty of practice bailing his brother out of jail. I figured I'd better get things cleaned up out here before Deputy Penateka gets his warrant. Judge Bogusch can't keep making excuses forever. And I had an inkling you'd dig up something, sooner or later."

I stood by the door and studied the room. The whole place wasn't much bigger than my living room. Light came from the fire and from two small windows high on the walls. A glass-fronted cabinet full of rifles stood against the right wall. Sacks of deer corn were stacked neatly in the corner.

A wide and well-worn sofa dominated the center of the room, overstuffed and covered with fading chintz. A cowboy coffee table stood between the sofa and two sturdy oak armchairs. A pink internet tablet sat on the table next to a small plastic tray with a razor blade, a tightly rolled dollar bill, and a pile of white powder. Next to that lay a small, black handgun.

Under the window on the left was what looked like a camp kitchen: a long wooden worktable with a portable stove and a wide metal washing pan. The top was littered with Sterno cans, Mason jars, cans of paint thinner and Drano, and a heap of colorful packages of cold medicine. On the floor stood rows of red and blue plastic gas cans and a couple of propane tanks.

That must be Hank's Kountry Kitchen, where he cooked up his methamphetamine for the unmotivated masses.

I fingered my lens cap and took a step forward. What would happen if I started snapping pictures? On the other hand, maybe I should come back later, with a few well-armed friends. I took a step back.

Carson watched my little dance routine with a wry smile. He picked up the handgun. "I'm sorry you're here, although I'm not all that surprised. But I like you. I had hoped we would become better friends after Ty went to prison."

"How did you get here?"

"You are quite the stickler for details, aren't you? Didn't you see the truck outside?"

I had seen, but had not observed. I should've put my hands on the hood to test for heat, like Ben had made me do.

Carson added some sticks to the fire and then sat in one of the armchairs. He used his left hand to swipe the tablet to wake it up, keeping the gun aimed in my direction with his right.

I glanced at the gun cabinet. The rifles were probably not loaded, but they could be swung like clubs. I shifted my weight on to my right foot. Could I edge a few feet toward the cabinet without alarming Carson?

Better yet would be to dash back out the door. Could I get clear before he shot me in the back? *Would* he shoot me in the back? Fear prickled up my spine and I shifted my weight back to neutral.

If I ran, even if I didn't get shot, I'd leave with nothing and he would get away with killing Roger and trying to frame Ty. Then he'd be out there every day, driving through town, smiling down from billboards on every county road.

How could I live with that?

Carson grinned at me. "It is a poser, isn't it? What's a girl to do in a situation like this? Why don't you sit down while you think about it?"

He gestured at the sofa with the gun. It didn't look very sanitary—I was sure it had been used for sweaty purposes without benefit of sheets—but I had bigger problems than germs at the moment.

I sat and pointed my chin at the tablet. "Is that Diana's?"

"Yes, it is."

"Is that how you got into her account?"

"Easy as pie. I didn't even have to log in. And did you know you can find step by step instructions for spoofing an email address? I had to do a little searching, but once you know how, it's nothing."

He seemed to be in a chatty mood. What the heck, we'd chat. Maybe I could get him to tell me exactly what happened. Maybe I could kick the coffee table hard enough to crack his shins, make him drop the gun, and buy myself time to get out the door. Once I got outside, he'd never catch me.

"Where is Diana, anyway?"

"I don't know," Carson said. "Not for certain. She said something about being sick of us men and needing some place quiet where she could get her head straight. I assume that means her rehab center." He wrinkled his nose at me. "It's more of a luxury spa with strict rules. They take your phone away when you check in."

"That explains why nobody's heard from her. I'm glad she's okay." I should have thought of that, or Ty should have. I'd bet Dare had called the place to check and had been too much of an uptight son of a beast to tell us. Or maybe he'd told Ty and told Ty not to tell me.

Suddenly, I felt very tired of this whole stupid mess.

Evidently it didn't show, because Carson rattled on. "You really are an amazing woman, Penny. If only you weren't so damned persistent. Ty might get off without your help, you know. He can afford a whole team of expert defense lawyers. Even if he's convicted, the penalty for manslaughter isn't that great. If he behaved himself like the model citizen he is, he'd get out in a few years."

"And come home to what? Everybody would believe he'd killed a man and tried to cover it up by blaming someone else. No one would trust him again."

"Maybe not." Carson smiled, not nicely. "He'd still be rich, don't forget. It might put an end to his fantasy spa project, though, and that is such a good idea. Someone else really ought to do it. I wonder who?" He grinned playfully, his eyes glittering from whatever he'd been snorting.

How had that angle escaped me? There wasn't room for two eco-spas in Long County. "That's why you tried to frame Ty. With him in prison, you'd have a free hand to manipulate Diana. You might even be able to trick her into selling you her half of the ranch."

"Bright girl! Now explain the part about making it look like Ty was trying to frame me."

I didn't like this game, but talking was better than being shot. "I guess because that way if anything turned up that implicated you, it would look like part of Ty's set up?"

"Very good! Although, mostly, it was for the fun. And because I don't like seeing a Hawkins get above his station." He tapped his chest. "Caines are the rich family in this county. Hawkins make good servants or mistresses, but we call the shots." He mugged a grin at the gun. "Pardon the pun!"

"Very funny. Except for the part where you killed a human being for a piece of real estate."

Anger flashed across Carson's face. "I did not kill Roger. It was an accident. A stupid argument, which he started, I'll have you know. I would have preferred not to have to do any of this. It's taken a lot of work."

The man actually felt sorry for himself, like the guy that kills his parents and then claims special consideration for being an orphan.

"It must have been a tough situation," I said, keeping my eyes on the gun. Was the safety on? How long did it take to release it, aim, and fire? Longer than it would take me to dive across the table, probably.

"Don't worry. I'm not going to shoot you. Bullets are so traceable. I'll think of something else, while I'm telling you my tragic tale. That's traditional at this point, I believe."

"You could let me go. By the time I got back to town, you'll have destroyed whatever evidence there is in here.

My credibility is nothing compared to yours. You could easily face me down."

He shook his head. "I'm afraid we've gone beyond that. Your credibility is better than you think. And now, thanks to you, they've got Hank. He was here that night, you see. He helped me with the clean-up. That will be quite the bargaining chip, when his drug case comes to trial." He rubbed his chin with the barrel of the gun. "What I really need is to get rid of both of you in one neat stroke."

That did not sound good at all. Although, if he wasn't going to shoot me, sooner or later he'd have to put the gun down and then I might have a chance to do something. I planted my feet firmly on the floor, ready to jump if an opportunity arose. "I know part of the story, I think. It hardly qualifies as tragic."

"High drama, I assure you. Well, I was high, anyway." He giggled. He was definitely high now. I recognized the symptoms from Nick's bad old days: the grandiose gestures, the glittering eyes, the rapid speech.

"Did Diana come up here after her argument with Ty? She must have still been angry, huh? Looking for a way to blow off steam?"

"Oh, she was boiling mad, the little vixen. Gorgeous. She marched in here and declared that she was tired of men jerking her around and treating her like an accessory."

"Accessory to what?"

Carson nodded. "That's what I said. You have to think like Diana. She meant 'accessory' like a scarf or a hat."

"Or a charm bracelet."

He gave me a sly look. "That confused everyone, didn't it? I mean, who would do such a thing?"

"Why did you?"

"It seemed so funny at the time. Diana threw it at me during the general blow-up. She almost hit me with it, the little minx!" He painted a pious expression on his face. "There's a warning in that for you. Drugs and alcohol exacerbate even minor disputes. Tempers run higher when you're high." He giggled again. That sound sent shivers up my spine.

I stuck to it, though. Asking questions was all I had. "Did Diana call Roger? Had they been meeting here?"

"Heavens, no! Do you think I'd give that sleaze ball a place to screw *my* mistress? No, no, and no. Besides, she was playing with the old Dodger to get Ty's goat. I'm the only one she really loves, you know. She dates her darling deputy and even I can see that he's good for her. She may even marry him, one of these days. But she and I go way back—all the way to her seventeenth birthday. I was her first. And I'm still the only one who can scratch all the itches in just the right way."

Brag, brag. If I weren't so scared, I'd be bored. "Then how did Roger get into it? Did he come up to buy drugs?"

Carson snapped his fingers at me. "Close, very close. He came to trade, or rather, share. He had a nice bottle of bourbon. He came up shortly after his much observed argument with Ty, also mad as a hatter and looking for relief." Carson paused and nodded, shaking his finger at nothing. "You know, ultimately, Ty is responsible for this whole situation. If he weren't so irritating, so pompous and self-righteous, I wouldn't have had to deal with two enraged individuals that night. Diana wouldn't have pressured me, Roger wouldn't have insulted her, and none of this would have happened."

"What did happen? You still haven't gotten to the main part."

"And whose fault is that? You keep digressing. All right, let's see. Diana came storming in here with fire in her eyes, threatening to tell my wife everything. She wanted me to get a divorce and marry her, if you can believe it. Sheerest fantasy."

"Why didn't you marry her in the first place, if she was the love of your life?"

"One doesn't marry a Hawkins, my dear." He made a sour face, like spitting out a bitter seed. "They're barely a step up from trailer trash, or they were until Ty turned himself into a millionaire. Such a hard-working boy. No doubt that's why you love him."

"That's not why I love him." I leaned forward and put my hands on the coffee table, pushing it slightly to test its weight.

"Hands in the lap, please. And stop interrupting. I'm a very good storyteller when I'm not interrupted every few sentences. Unfortunately, my wife is the one with the money. All I own is this ranch, which is worth nothing unless I sell it, which of course I would never do. And Queen Anorexia threatened to take half of it if we ever got within spitting distance of a divorce. Besides, I liked things the way they were."

"So you said no. Sounds simple enough. Then why kill Roger?"

"I told you, I didn't kill him. The stupid man felt the need to insert himself in our little domestic quarrel. Apparently, he had not realized that we meant more to one another than potential development partners. He had the *gargantuan* ego to imagine that Diana actually gave a crap about him. He thought he was winning her over." Carson gaped at me to underscore the enormity of Roger's self-delusion.

"So, she threw the bracelet at you, you tried to hit her and got him instead?"

"Absolutely not! I would never strike Diana. I love her. No, she threw the bracelet, nearly striking me in the face, I might add, and delivered her rant. Then she strutted out with her head held high, slamming the door behind her. I remember a deep silence following that thunderstorm. Then Roger, the vulgar brute, made a remark so crude about my Lady Di, that something went *snap* and I hauled off and hit him. I suppose it was the meth on top of the anger I'd absorbed from Diana." He smiled and drew in a breath. "It felt good. *Really* good. So I waited for him to get to his feet and did it again, twice. The second time his head cracked back against the mantle there." He pointed with the gun. "Right there in the middle. There are probably still traces of blood. Yet another thing for me to deal with this morning."

Yes, unwanted stains were the worst of it. Revulsion must have showed on my face.

"You disapprove," Carson said. "I told you I didn't mean to kill him. I just wanted to teach him a lesson in humility. My grandfather used to beat the holy crap out of me and I survived. It made me the man I am today."

"An egotistical murderer?"

"Manslaughter, please." He barked a laugh. "Oh! You mean you!"

Come to think of it, *yeah*. "You won't get away with it, you know. I told the whole story to Marion. She knows I'm here, right now. And I can prove Ty's innocent, really prove it, in court. I've got photographs proving the Escalade was moved during the time he was in jail."

Carson winced. "That wasn't terribly well thought out. I should have put it there in the first place, but there was so much to do that night, and we were so stoned." He shook his head at the memory. "My first thought was to implicate Diana, pay her back for throwing that bracelet at me, if the body was ever found, which I honestly didn't think it would be. Ty and his plans, always tripping me up! When he got arrested, it seemed like a gift. So I decided to try to build a case against him by staging the car scene."

"How did you get the arrowhead?"

"Oh, for pity's sake! You're an artist, have you so little imagination? From Ty's desk, of course. Hank slipped through the dog door and let me in. We were careful not to rearrange anything, and of course we wore gloves. We had all the time in the world. They have no staff. Ty was in jail and Diana in rehab, true to Hawkins family tradition."

Both conditions had been his fault, but of course he would never admit that. "It doesn't really matter. I can prove Ty didn't move the car, which lets him out for the rest of it. He'll be free in less than an hour."

"I wouldn't be so sure, my dear. Once those photographs get into the sheriff's offices, they're as good as mine. I've got Hap Hopper in my back pocket."

"Is he armed?" I inquired. "Because I doubt he would put up with this."

"Cheeky wench." He looked at me with a touch of admiration. "Why aren't you quaking with fear?"

"I quake on the inside. Keeps from wrinkling my clothes."

"As if you cared. You usually look like you stumbled out of a bread line. Where do you get that stuff, Goodwill?"

I resented that. You could get lots of good stuff at the G-Store, if you were a savvy shopper like me.

He swiped the tablet to wake it up and clucked his tongue. "Much as I'm enjoying this fireside chat, we do have a time factor to consider. They'll be getting out of court soon and I've still got things to do."

He double-tapped something. "The Internet really is the most amazing resource for the criminally minded. I also found instructions for preventing a propane tank from exploding. All I have to do is work backward and *voila!* When Hank comes back to play with his chemistry set, everything will go boom."

Boom? Was he seriously planning to blow up the whole house? "Assuming he gets out and assuming he's stupid enough to come fool with this stuff again."

"Oh, he'll get out. I authorized Skip to post however much they asked. I can't have Hank in jail, jonesing for nicotine and eager to talk. As for the stupidity, that should not be underestimated. He won't be able to resist making one more batch. Waste these ingredients?" He wagged his finger. "I think not. Ephedrine is not easy to come by in quantity these days."

He got up and walked over to the kitchen area, pacing back and forth, looking at me, scanning the room. "What I really want is for Hank to kill you, but I can't be certain he would. And you'd warn him about my sabotage gambit, wouldn't you?"

"No, sir, not me. Mum's the word." I mimed locking my lips. "You can leave me right here. I'll give that mantelpiece a good scrubbing for you."

"You're quite the wisenheimer, Penny. Has anyone ever told you that?"

"Pretty much everyone I know."

He regarded me with his hands on his hips. "I could knock you out, tie you up and gag you, and then stuff you under the sofa. You're fairly trim. Then Hank would never see you and you'd be blown up along with him."

"They'd know I'd been tied up first. There'd be traces and marks."

"They'd think Hank did it." He stared at me for another moment, then nodded, frowning. "It's good. I like it." He stepped around the table and put the gun to my head. "Stand up slowly and turn your back to me."

I obeyed. My options were better standing than sitting. He marched me around the couch to face the wall beside the fireplace.

"This will do," he said. "I suppose I can mess up the wound enough to obscure the shape of the gun butt." I assumed he was talking to himself, not asking me for advice.

I made a fist with my right hand, close to my chest, and folded my left hand over it. He didn't seem to notice. When I felt the barrel of the gun shift away from my head, I bent forward and shoved my right elbow into his solar plexus as hard as I could.

He grunted as the air rushed out of his lungs. The gun clattered to the floor. I stomped his instep with my right boot and turned on my left heel, pushing him away from me as I came around. He had partly doubled over, but managed to grab my braid and yank me sideways. I careened against the couch, nearly going over it.

I got my weight over my heels and braced my hands against the couch. I bent double and pushed off, aiming my head at his midsection, just as he was straightening himself up and drawing his fist back for a blow.

I caught him full on, right in the belly, one hundred and thirty-five pounds of solid Trigg. He reeled backward and his head hit the wall with a loud smack. His eyes popped open and then shut as he slid to the floor.

Holy Mother of God! Had I killed him? He lay still as a corpse.

I was shaking like a leaf, wrinkling my Goodwill outfit, but who could think about clothes at a time like this? I'd killed him, in exactly the same way he'd killed Roger. Now the boot was on the other foot, wasn't it, Penny old girl? Except I'd been defending myself, not teaching anyone any kind of a lesson.

Brain babbling nonsense. That's what quaking on the inside did to you.

But what if he wasn't really dead? In the movies, the bad guy always wakes up and grabs the heroine by the ankle. I shuffled toward the door, too scared and too shocked to pick my feet up from the floor.

I made it to the door and then remembered Diana's pink tablet. What if he woke up after I left and destroyed it? What if he succeeded in blowing up the house? He could still destroy the evidence that Roger had died there and not on Ty's ranch.

I kept my eyes on Carson's inert body as I tip-toed back to the coffee table and snatched up the tablet. I glanced at the kitchen area, thinking about taking a photo or two of Hank's meth lab.

A groan from the fireside made me jump, cracking my knee on an oak chair. The photos could wait. I needed to get the frack out of here. I dashed out the door into the yard and heard the growl of a big vehicle grinding up the road. If that was Hank, the Mighty Hunter, my ass was grass.

I ran for the woods. Better to risk hogs than felons. I heard a car door slam and a voice call, "Police! Stop right where you are!"

I almost fainted from relief. I turned so fast I skidded on the slippery oak leaves, wrenching my bruised knee. I hop-jogged back across the field in front of the house.

"Ms. Trigg?" Deputy Penateka stood beside his car. "What are you doing here?"

"He's in there. Carson. Be careful."

"Hold on, hold on." He took a step toward me, holding out a hand. "You're shaking all over. What've you got there?"

"Evidence." All of sudden I felt slow and stupid. Feet and brain stopped moving at the same time. "Car. In car."

"Yes, let's put you in the car." Penateka took my arm and led me back to his vehicle. He held on to me while he opened the passenger door.

"I'm okay." I looked back at the house. "Get Carson. He might be dead. But be careful. It could be a movie and he'll leap out and grab you."

"You're not making much sense, Ms. Trigg." He started to tuck me inside the car when a huge roll of thunder crashed and flames shot up out of the stone house.

"Holy shit!" Penateka shoved me into the car, slamming the door on me. He pulled his jacket off and used it to cover his face as he ran toward the house. Carson stumbled through the door in a cloud of toxic smoke. He fell to his knees in the yard, coughing.

Penateka cuffed his hands behind his back before Carson even realized he was there. Then he got him to his feet and half-dragged him back to the car. He opened the back door and shoved him in, none too gently. Carson sprawled awkwardly across the seat, breathing in raspy gulps.

"What the hell did you do?" Penateka pulled the radio mike out of its holder.

Carson wheezed, "Ask Girlock."

I pointed a stern finger at Penateka. "That nickname stops here."

His lips twitched, but he stayed mum.

I said, "He rigged Hank's meth lab to blow up and must've triggered it by accident. Or maybe he figured he could blow up the evidence and still get out in time."

Penateka's eyebrows lifted and I told him the story, keeping it short. Then he called out every emergency responder in the county: the sheriff's department, the highway patrol, the hospital, and the fire department. He packed Carson off to jail with the first deputy who showed up and bundled me into the ambulance.

Go figure.

Chapter 28

They released Ty Wednesday morning after his preliminary hearing. They sent Carson to the hospital ward at the Travis County Jail, since Long County didn't have a secure medical facility. Hank got out on bail and had a whole two hours of liberty before he got picked up for speeding north of San Antonio. They found meth in both his car and his bloodstream and popped him right into the Bexar County Jail.

Poetic justice, if ever there was such a thing.

Perline and Cracker were throwing a birthday party for me at the cafe that night, but Ty wanted a little quiet time at home, so I drove him out to his house. Somehow we got into a discussion about who got to keep the dog.

Ty wouldn't even admit we had anything to discuss. "He's my dog, Penny. I want him back."

"But I've had him for almost two weeks. We've really bonded."

"Ten days. Trust me, I know to the minute."

I pouted. "I deserve some reward for all I've been through."

He grinned at me, that lopsided grin that got me into this mess in the first place. "You'll get your reward, don't worry." He drew me into his arms for a long kiss.

That was pretty good, as rewards go, but I'm a Greedy Gus about some things. "Carson really scared me. He intended to kill me."

Ty kissed my forehead. "I know, baby. I'm so sorry."

"He pulled my hair, hard. And I wrenched my knee."

He stroked my hair, with the sweetest soft touch. "We'll have to spoil you for a while."

I liked the sound of that. "On top of everything else, he insulted my wardrobe."

Ty held me at arm's length, giving me a look of partisan outrage. "That brute! I'll boil him in vinegar! I'll personally plug in the electric chair. I love the way you dress. It says, 'low maintenance and easy to please.'"

I frowned. Could be time for a fashion upgrade.

Ty sensed his mistake. "Sporty and ready for action? Arty and independent?"

The guy had not made it into upper management on looks alone. "I'll settle for arty and independent. But you totally owe me a dog."

"The dog is mine."

He walked me to the door. I granted him one small kiss on the chin. "Do you want me to come pick you up for the party?"

"I'll pick you up. I'm thinking your place, for after." He waggled his eyebrows at me lecherously and my heart started doing a happy two-step.

I hummed *Chattanooga Choo-Choo* in the car on the way home, dancing in my seat until a passing car honked at me and I realized I was weaving recklessly across the center line. I sobered up for the remainder of the trip.

My house was too quiet with no dog in it, but at least I had time to clean the place and get ready for the party. I put on the most high maintenance outfit I could think of, a gauzy purple peasant dress with a load of costume jewelry from my aunt's stash. I even put on some pink lipstick, also from Aunt Sophia's vanity table. It was very sticky. It promptly got on my teeth, my towel, and my tea glass and required touching up within minutes.

That was maintenance. Wasn't that maintenance?

Ty whistled when I opened the door. Jake barked. I twirled to show off. We were all very pleased with ourselves. We left Jake in the yard with a soup bone to chew on. I pointed out how content he had become with

Flash Memory

my back yard. Ty snorted. "He's got a thousand acres at my place. Not to mention that *he's my dog.*"

People had crowded into the brightly lit cafe. It looked like half the town had turned out. They cheered and clapped when Ty and I walked in. Even the fish hanging from the ceiling looked jollier than usual. We were celebrating Ty's freedom as well as my advancing age. A banner on one wall read "Welcome Home, Tyler." On the other wall, there was another banner that read "Happy 30th Birthday, Penny."

Standing under the banner, looking like a million freshly rehabilitated bucks, was none other than the missing Diana, with Dare at her side. "*Dahlings!*" She held out both toned and tanned arms.

We let her hug us and she let us scold her, admitting her wrongs with sincere repentance. In fairness, her only crime had been not calling her brother for one measly week. She'd had no idea what was happening back home. Besides, it was impossible to stay mad at her.

She winked at me, then stood back a bit to tap her empty water glass with her spoon. "People! People!"

She waited until everyone stopped yakking and turned to listen. "We're here to honor one of Lost Hat's newest citizens, Penelope Sophia Trigg. She's one of the most wonderful people I've ever met. Aren't we lucky she decided to come live with us?"

Applause broke out, punctuated with cheers and whistles. I was overwhelmed. I had to duck my head like a bashful baby to hide the tears wetting my eyes. I hadn't had a real birthday party for eons and I'd never gotten a round of applause like this. I jabbed an elbow in Ty's side and he came to my rescue.

He held up his hands for silence. "Thank you, thank you. Thanks to Perline and Cracker for this great party and thanks to all of you for coming. I can't tell you how good it is to be free again and to have such good friends to come home to. But mostly, I want to thank Penny for everything she's done for me. Without her ingenuity, perseverance, and faith, beyond all the bounds of reason, I would still be in jail and Carson Caine might be standing here tonight."

There were boos and hisses mixed with cheers, as different people responded to different parts of that message.

Ty held up his hands again. "I'd like to propose a toast, ladies and gentlemen. To Lost Hat's own Girlock Holmes!"

More cheers, mixed with laughter. I closed my eyes and bit my lip.

They say small towns have long memories. If I could keep my head down for the next sixty years, I might just about outlive that nickname.

Thank you for reading my book. I hope you enjoyed it!

Word of mouth is important for all authors, but especially us indies. If you enjoyed this book, please consider leaving a review at the site where you bought it and sharing it with your camarades on your social networks. Even a few words is a big help.

To find out about upcoming releases, as well as special promotions and offers, please subscribe to my mailing list at www.annacastle.com.

About the Author

Anna Castle holds an eclectic set of degrees: BA in the Classics, MS in Computer Science, and a Ph.D. in Linguistics. She has had a correspondingly eclectic series of careers: waitressing, software engineering, grammar-writing, a short stint as an associate professor, and managing a digital archive. Historical fiction combines her lifelong love of stories and learning. She physically resides in Austin, Texas, but mentally counts herself a queen of infinite space.

Where to find me:
Website & newsletter signup: www.annacastle.com
Email: castle@annacastle.com
Blog: www.annacastle.com/blog/
Facebook: https://www.facebook.com/anna.castle.104
Twitter: @annacastl

Books by Anna Castle

Keep up with all my books and short stories through my newsletter. Sign up at www.annacastle.com

The Lost Hat, Texas Series

Book 1, Black & White & Dead All Over. 2015

What happens when the Internet service provider in a small town spies on his clients' cyber-lives and blackmails them for gifts and services?

Murder; that's what happens.

Penelope Trigg moves to Lost Hat, Texas to open a photography studio and find herself as an artist. Things are going great. She's got a few clients, some friends, even a hot new high-tech boyfriend. But when Penny submits some nude figure studies of him to a contest, she gets hit with a blackmail letter in her inbox. "Do what I want or your lover's nudie pix get splattered across the Internet." The timing couldn't be worse, so Penny is forced to submit to the blackmailer's demands. Then people start dying and all the clues point to her. She has to rattle every skeleton in every closet in Lost Hat to keep herself out of jail and find the real killer.

Book 2, Flash Memory. 2016

Nature photographer Penelope Trigg has landed the job of her dreams: documenting the transformation of over-grazed rangeland into an eco-dude ranch and spa, owned by her boyfriend Tyler Hawkins. Then a body is found on the ranch and Ty is arrested. The victim was fooling around with Ty's baby sister Diana, but so was the senior deputy sheriff.

Determined to prove Ty's innocence, Penny stirs up Diana's old flames, trying to shed enough light on the mystery to develop an alternative suspect. She mainly learns how to lose friends and annoy people, until she realizes someone has been manipulating the evidence. But is Ty the framer or the framee? Penny uses her eye for detail and her camera's memory to put the picture together and reveal the killer.

The Francis Bacon Series

Book 1, Murder by Misrule. 2014

Francis Bacon is charged with investigating the murder of a fellow barrister at Gray's Inn. He recruits his unwanted protégé Thomas Clarady to do the tiresome legwork. The son of a privateer, Clarady will do anything to climb the Elizabethan social ladder. Bacon's powerful uncle Lord Burghley suspects Catholic conspirators of the crime, but other motives quickly emerge. Rival barristers contend for the murdered man's legal honors and wealthy clients. Highly-placed courtiers are implicated as the investigation reaches from Whitehall to the London streets. Bacon does the thinking; Clarady does the fencing. Everyone has something up his pinked and padded sleeve. Even the brilliant Francis Bacon is at a loss — and in danger — until he sees through the disguises of the season of Misrule.

Book 2, Death by Disputation. 2014

Thomas Clarady is recruited to spy on the increasingly rebellious Puritans at Cambridge University. Francis Bacon is his spymaster; his tutor in both tradecraft and religious politics. Their commission gets off to a deadly start when Tom finds his chief informant hanging from the roof beams. Now he must catch a murderer as well as a seditioner. His first suspect is volatile poet Christopher Marlowe, who keeps turning up in the wrong places.

Dogged by unreliable assistants, chased by three lusty women, and harangued daily by the exacting Bacon, Tom risks his very soul to catch the villains and win his reward.

Book 3, The Widow's Guild . 2015

In the summer of 1588, Europe waits with bated breath for King Philip of Spain to launch his mighty armada against England. Everyone except Lady Alice Trumpington, whose father wants her wed to the highest bidder. She doesn't want to be a wife, she wants to be widow; a rich one, and the sooner, the better. So she marries an elderly viscount, gives him a sleeping draught, and spends her wedding night with Thomas Clarady, her best friend and Francis Bacon's assistant. The next morning, they find the viscount murdered in his bed and they're both locked into the Tower.

Lady Alice appeals to the Andromache Society, the widows' guild led by Francis Bacon's formidable aunt, Lady Russell. They charge Bacon with getting the new widow out of prison and identifying the real murderer. He soon learns the viscount wasn't an isolated case. Someone is murdering Catholics in London and taking advantage of armada fever to mask the crimes. The killer seems to have privy information — from someone close to the Privy Council?

The investigation takes Francis from the mansions along the Strand to the rack room under the Tower. Pulled and pecked by a coven of demanding widows, Francis struggles to maintain his reason and his courage to see through the fog of war and catch the killer.

Made in the USA
Charleston, SC
25 March 2016